A Fatal Fondness

by Richard Audry

The Fourth Mary MacDougall Mystery

Conger Road Press
Minneapolis

A Fatal Fondness
By Richard Audry

Copyright © 2019 D. R. Martin

Published by Conger Road Press
Minneapolis, Minnesota

ISBN: 978-0-9850196-9-3

Cover design © 2019 Steve Thomas
Cover art: "On the Porch" by William Chadwick

For more information, visit www.facebook.com/richardaudryauthor/
or drmartinbooks.com

Contact the author at drmartin120@gmail.com.

Chapter I

"And have you heard? A body's been found. Out in one of the inlets on St. Louis Bay. Some poor soul drowned apparently."

Mary MacDougall leaned sideways toward Mrs. Ivey, the better to hear her whispered gossip. Thank heavens the dinner party seating wasn't entirely boy-girl-boy-girl. Otherwise Mary might have missed this juicy tidbit. Foul play perhaps? Or simply an accident? Any unexplained death in Duluth was a matter of interest to her.

She was about to ask the lawyer's wife to elaborate, when all of a sudden, out of nowhere, a Parker House roll plopped into her lap, bouncing and then rolling onto the floor beneath the table. Mary twisted around and blinked in surprise at the serving maid—a dark-haired woman of about thirty. The maid was holding a basket of rolls in one hand and tongs in the other, and she didn't look the least bit contrite.

"I'm glad it wasn't the corn pudding you were serving," Mary said with a smile.

The woman offered a regretful look so bogus as to be comical. "Oh, *do* pardon me, miss. The darned thing slipped. Let me get it." She leaned down between chairs, bumping Mary with her shoulder as she descended, and snatched up the errant roll, jamming it into her apron pocket.

"Here's another one." This time, she managed to successfully target Mary's plate. Scurrying away, she collected a disgusted glare from Mrs. Davidson, the evening's hostess.

"I think that woman might want to investigate another line of work," said the handsome young fellow to Mary's left. "Domestic service doesn't quite suit her." He seemed amused.

Mary nodded her agreement and turned back to Mrs. Ivey, eager to continue their *sotto voce* discussion of the body in the bay. But Mrs. Ivey happened to be leveling her own glare at her husband, who was seated across the table. The bald, portly lawyer appeared to be enjoying a lively conversation with the much younger and quite comely niece of Mrs. Davidson. To judge from the look on his wife's face, he was savoring the young woman's repartee rather more than was good for him.

"So you were saying someone drowned in the bay?" Mary asked, trying to reclaim Mrs. Ivey's attention.

The woman looked back at her, transforming her pinched lips into a smile. "My husband heard something about it down at the courthouse." And then she launched into an account of the special tulip bulbs she had just received from Holland.

When Mrs. Ivey's horticultural soliloquy trailed off, Mary turned again to the smiling young gentleman seated to her left. "So, Aksel, how are things going in the building trade?"

Aksel was an old friend of her brother Jim, the "son" in Adamsen & Son Construction Company. He was a bit shy, but with his bright blue eyes and infectious smile, your average young lady wouldn't have found him at all unappealing. In fact, back during Mary's early teen years, she had suffered from a crush on Aksel—a secret she shared with only her nearest, dearest friend.

Aksel beamed at her, looking quite pleased to answer her query. "We're working on three projects. A school, a small office building in West Duluth, and a church up on Woodland Avenue. I'm the site manager for the new Swedenborgian church and I even helped the architect with the design."

"Isn't that grand! Your father must be so proud of you."

"He seems to be. And how's Jim doing? I barely got to see him this summer."

"Headed back to law school last week." Mary took a small bite of the pork cassoulet. "Keeping his head down and determined to have a good year of study. As long as the young ladies don't distract him, he should do fine."

Aksel's cheeks went a little red and he drew a deep breath, as if he were about to take a plunge into icy water. "I was wondering about something."

"Uh-huh," Mary said, dabbing her mouth with her napkin. "What is it?"

"You know that Żeleński, the Polish pianist, is playing a recital at the Lyceum on the ninth."

"Yes, I've heard. He's supposed to be quite wonderful."

In fact, Mary already had her tickets and intended to ask a friend to go with her. Żeleński's program included Haydn, Chopin, Liszt, and Brahms. She couldn't wait to hear him play.

"Well, I know that you're quite the pianist yourself," Aksel said.

"Barely adequate, is how I'd describe my pianistic powers."

He took another deep breath. "Better than 'adequate,' I'd say."

It was rather obvious where he was going. But Mary wasn't quite sure how to help him get there. She gave him a moment to make the leap, but he seemed frozen.

"Umm, ahh," he said, "you know…"

Oh well, Mary thought, *time to throw him a lifeline*.

"Were you thinking of asking me to go with you?"

He looked uncertain, but hopeful. "Yes. That is, if you're interested. I've already bought the tickets."

It was *so* sweet, *so* funny. *She* was asking *herself* out on his behalf. Well, she wouldn't mind an evening with good old Aksel.

"And dinner first, of course," he said, suddenly taking the initiative. "I thought perhaps the Palm Room?"

"Oh, excellent. I love the Palm Room," Mary said, pondering over whom to offer *her* recital tickets to. "I'll put it on my calendar and we'll arrange details later."

"And I do hope you'll come sailing with my chums and me a week from tomorrow. It'll be so much fun. Bring a friend, if you like."

They continued chatting until the courses came to an end. Mary excused herself and made her way to the powder room off Mrs. Davidson's foyer.

The Davidsons had come to Duluth from Ashtabula, Ohio, seeking their fortune in the west. Not long after, the MacDougalls had arrived from Pittsburgh. Moving in the same business circles, Porter Davidson and John MacDougall became friends. The Davidsons lived about two blocks west of the MacDougalls, also on Superior Street. Their house was only eight years old. But then, practically everything in Duluth was new or newish, the city itself being just a few decades old.

Mrs. Davidson had created a beautiful home, full of oriental wallpapers and trimmed everywhere in the finest mahogany and rosewood. Like Mary, she loved Impressionist art and scattered it around the place. The powder room, for its part, was lined in a paper teeming with colorful water lilies. Mary didn't know of a nicer lavatory in the city.

She had barely stepped inside it when the door flew open behind her. She twirled around in surprise.

"It's Wilbur." The churlish maid who had dropped the roll in Mary's lap stood there, hands on hips. "Slippery little fellow, Wilbur."

"For heaven's sake, Jeanette, get in here and close the door. And who in the world is Wilbur?"

"Mrs. Davidson's grandson." Jeanette Harrison collapsed onto a stuffed chair.

Mary laughed. "Well, what do you know? I guess that lets the domestics off the hook."

The exhausted maid rubbed her neck. "Thank goodness this job is over. I've had a headache all evening. And my *feet…*"

That helped explain Jeanette's mood, but Mary offered no sympathy. "Aren't something like a dozen silver napkin rings missing? How'd he get away with it?"

"Didn't I say he was slippery? I've been here six days now and finally I got lucky. Saw him grab one from the drawer. I cornered him as he was sneaking out of the kitchen. The little imp's been pilfering the rings so he could make a tunnel in his backyard, to shoot his marbles through."

"Well done, Jeanette." Mary nodded approvingly. "The first official case of Moody Investigations, a success."

Jeanette seemed less than thrilled by Mary's pronouncement. "Yes, well, perhaps next time I could impersonate an heiress rather than a servant. Did I mention my feet are killing me?"

"You can soak your feet when we get home tonight. And it had to be you. Everyone here knows me. I couldn't very well hurl Parker House rolls at Aksel Adamsen. He'd recognize me just like that." She snapped her fingers. "Anyway, didn't you have fun being a secret operative?"

Jeanette snorted. "My idea of a good time is sitting behind a desk with a stack of shorthand notes to type up. As we agreed, *you* are the field agent, the secret operative. *I* am the office manager and secretary."

"Point taken. Have you told Mrs. Davidson yet?"

Mary's first cousin once-removed bowed her head in mocking obeisance. "I am merely a lowly employee. You are the head of the agency and to you belongs the glory."

Moody Investigations was only a month old. Mary's father had offered to let her set up shop in a three-storey office building he owned on West Second Street—as long as Jeanette Harrison served as her companion and assistant. It amused Mary to think that she was perhaps the only consulting detective in the state who required a chaperone.

As for the Davidson case and the appearance of Aksel Adamsen at this dinner, she had certain suspicions.

It smelled of John MacDougall's meddling. Perhaps he ran into Mrs. Davidson, who complained about her small problem. She may have speculated that one of her servants had sticky fingers. And Mary's father saw an opportunity to set his daughter onto a simple case unlikely to land her in jail again. Moreover, he probably asked if Mrs. Davidson was interested in a spot of surreptitious matchmaking. Of course, most women her age were. So Mary's father could kill two birds with one stone.

It was just his style to try to keep a tight rein on his head-strong daughter.

Just as it was Mary's style to find a way around it.

Chapter II

Jeanette Harrison arrived at 335 West Second Street well before opening time the following Tuesday. It was a glorious late-September morning, but there was a touch of chill in the air. She had to be there early for the delivery of a bookshelf from Garlock & Larson. Mrs. Larson hadn't exactly *given* them the desks, tables, file cabinet, chairs, and bookshelf. But they had all come on a one-dollar-a-year lease to Mary Mac-Dougall, who had, for practical purposes, saved Mrs. Larson's life that past summer, as well as a goodly chunk of her fortune.

The two-room suite that housed Moody Investigations was on the second floor on the west side, between a clock repair shop and a dentist. The clock repairer sold them a wall clock that had once hung in a cloakroom at a Duluth train station. It showed eight fifty-five when Jeanette heard the thumping and clumping of someone carrying something heavy up the stairs.

She went out into the hallway and told the two men to bring the bookcase in. It had eight shelves and was made of a lightly stained oak, much like the other Garlock & Olson furniture. All the pieces were plain in style but solidly made. After the men placed the bookcase exactly where Jeanette wanted it, she gave them a fifty-cent tip and off they went.

The day before, Monday, had been Moody Investigation's grand opening. Except that it hadn't been so "grand."

Mary had placed a small advertisement in the Sunday paper that touted their services:

Moody Investigations
Confidential & Discreet Inquiries
Now Accepting Clients
Women's Problems a Specialty
335 West Second Street No. 202

The two of them had arrived at the office at nine sharp Monday morning nervous with anticipation. They took up their stations at their desks—Mary in the inner office, Jeanette in the reception area—and waited. And waited. And waited.

They went to lunch at Gustafsson's Café, a short trudge east on Second Street. By mid-afternoon, Jeanette was so bored that she decided the time had come to master the new Carpenter electric teakettle Mary had bought down at the Panton & White Glass Block Store. The primary skill that the thing cultivated in its user was patience—as the kettle seemed to take forever to heat water.

And again, no one came. Not a single soul, all day. Not even a friend or acquaintance.

Of course, Mary's involvement in the enterprise was not supposed to be bandied about. If it was known that the daughter of one of the wealthiest men in Duluth was setting up shop as a detective, who knew what sort of riffraff might show up. That's why they called the business "Moody Investigations," from the maiden name of Mary's mother.

By the end of the afternoon Mary looked so glum that Jeanette almost felt sorry for her. The girl so desperately wanted, indeed *needed*, success as a consulting detective. She had dreamt about it for years, ever since she started reading mystery novels and accounts of true crime in newspapers and books. Jeanette wondered if she herself would have felt so de-

8

termined to pursue a profession, had she had a bank account as fulsome as Mary's. Still, both she and Mary had expected someone to walk through the door that first day, if only the landlord—Mary's father.

It had been Jeanette's idea to set up a little office for Mary, so that her cousin might realize that running a business was hard, dull work requiring tenacity. At first, John MacDougall thought the suggestion far too risky. What if his daughter took to it? But on further consideration, he decided it had merit.

"With any luck the business'll be so boring that Mary'll get discouraged and give it up," he had told Jeanette. "She might find the bulk of her work is chasing down lost dogs and cats. Then, maybe, a good man and a good marriage won't seem so dreary."

John MacDougall had brought Jeanette Harrison to Duluth just months ago to be Mary's companion. And Jeanette was *very* relieved to be there, given her terrible failure in St. Louis. Bringing Jeanette into the household wasn't only a bit of charity on the widower's part, but an effort by him to keep control of his strong-willed daughter—very much a stubborn chip off the old Scottish block. Managing his mining, timber, and other business interests meant that John MacDougall couldn't very well supervise Mary day and night. So he called upon a trusted relative who was a bit down on her luck.

In addition to watching over Mary the sleuth, Jeanette was also assigned to keep the young lady away from a certain artist friend, Mr. Edmond Roy. Apparently, though, he wouldn't be a problem. Mary had assured Jeanette that, after their mutual misadventure in Dillmont, Michigan, she and Mr. Roy had decided to part ways—though she still intended to help him now and then in his artistic career. Jeanette felt relieved to hear this sensible tone from her young cousin.

As a child wailed next door in the dentist's office, Jeanette began to put criminal reference books up on the newly delivered oak shelf. A volume called *The Book of Poisonous Flora* caught her eye. It contained detailed illustrations of nearly two hundred dangerous and deadly plants, with descriptions of the symptoms they produced and their mechanisms of morbidity or mortality. In the margins were notes Mary had scribbled. Jeanette hoped they weren't for recipes.

When she finished with the books, she looked at the railway clock, which was hanging next to a large Duluth street map in the reception area. It was already nine-thirty. Where *was* Mary? They had spotted a mistake in their business cards that required reprinting. Mary had offered to stop by the printer and take care of the matter. But the printer was only a few blocks away. She should have been at work by now.

Jeanette nearly jumped out of her shoes when a sharp rapping sounded on the entry door's glass.

"Are you open for business?" came a woman's voice from out in the hallway.

Hastily putting the poison plant book on the shelf, Jeanette scurried over to open the door and found two visitors standing there. Peering through lightly tinted spectacles was a short, stout woman of middle age. She had a round face with reddish-brown hair piled atop her head. Behind her was a thin, pale man in a black suit with black hair parted neatly down the middle. They both looked to be about fifty.

"Is this Moody Investigations?" the woman demanded.

Jeanette's heart raced. Perhaps real clients? She earnestly hoped the couple hadn't stopped to sell something or ask for a donation.

"Indeed it is," she said. "Please come in. Take the chairs in front of the desk there."

As they all sat, Jeanette spied a gold band on the woman's left ring finger. "Welcome, Mrs....?"

"Fesler," the visitor said. "Mrs. Alfred Fesler. And you are?"

"Mrs. Jeanette Harrison." She stood and offered her hand across the desk. "And this is Mr. Fesler?" she asked, nodding at the man.

He tittered. "Oh, no, no, no. I'm Mr. Quentin Pettyjohn, a good friend of Mrs. Fesler and a fellow victim. Just come along to give a hand."

Ah then, Jeanette thought, *victims of some offense.* These two were obviously in need of a detective.

"And how may we help you?" she asked.

"Isn't Mr. Moody here this morning?" Mrs. Fesler said, glancing toward Mary's inner office. "We would prefer to talk to him."

Jeanette had anticipated that the agency name might cause some confusion. And she had a ready, if disingenuous, response. "I'm sorry, but Mr. Moody is unavailable. Your case would be handled by our chief operative, Miss MacDougall."

"And you're just starting in business?" Mr. Pettyjohn appeared skeptical.

"We have several successful cases under our belts," Jeanette answered, "as private consultants. And we're confident that we'll give you satisfaction, whatever the matter may be."

Mrs. Fesler, for her part, didn't look very confident. "Well, it's not as though we have very many options, do we, Quentin?"

"Alas, that is so, Dorothy," he said. "Please take no offense, Mrs. Harrison, but as a man of business... I am the chief bookkeeper at the Imperial Flour Mill. Well, I came along with Mrs. Fesler to assure we're not buying a pig in a poke. I'm a very good judge of people and their reliability, if I do say so myself. Our general manager values my judgment so highly that I'm often asked to help in the hiring for any important posts at the mill."

"The police have brushed us off, you see," Mrs. Fesler complained. "And the other detective agencies tell us they don't take cases like ours, seeing as how they're not likely to end happily. One fellow whom I visited on my own just laughed at me."

Jeanette tsk-tsked. "That's terribly unprofessional. If a client comes along with perfectly good money, one certainly must take her concerns seriously."

Mrs. Fesler looked pleased with the response. "Quite right." She turned to her friend. "What do you think, Quentin? Should we share our story with Mrs. Harrison?"

He pursed his lips, narrowed his eyes, and nodded. "Yes, yes. I think so. I believe she'll give us a fair hearing."

Jeanette felt as if she had just passed an exam. She grabbed a tablet and pencil, writing down the names of her prospective clients. "Now," she finally said, "what kind of assistance do you two need?"

"It's not just me and Mr. Pettyjohn who need your help. We also represent two other parties who have had similar trouble. And I can assure you, it's of the utmost importance to all of us. You see, over the last few weeks, members of our families have gone missing."

Jeanette was shocked. Family members disappearing? Why wouldn't the police undertake such a case? It's a wonder the matter hadn't turned up in the newspapers.

All of sudden, tears welled up in Mrs. Fesler's eyes. She took off her spectacles and dabbed away the moisture with a linen hankie. Mr. Pettyjohn reached over and patted her free hand.

"It's our precious, precious babies that're gone," she blubbered. "Our dear, dear little kitty-cats."

Jeanette suddenly understood why Mrs. Fesler had been

laughed out of the other investigators' offices. This was exactly the kind of case that John MacDougall had hoped would discourage Mary's dreams of detective glory.

But Mrs. Fesler looked so distressed and Mr. Pettyjohn so grim that Jeanette didn't have the heart to make light of their problem. "Now, now, Mrs. Fesler, please tell me what happened. And we'll see what we can do about it."

"Let me lay out the circumstances, if I may," Mr. Pettyjohn said. "I think my friend needs a moment to collect herself."

He proceeded to explain that all the victims were members of a local cat fanciers' club. "We meet monthly, you know. Anyone is welcome to attend, though most of our members are serious ailurophiles. Some of our pets have even been entered in cat shows in Minneapolis and Chicago."

Jeanette confessed she had no idea that such events even existed. "And how many were taken?" she asked.

Mr. Pettyjohn held up the fingers of his right hand. "Four animals, each one from a different home."

"Now Mr. Pettyjohn's Bastet has a bit of the wanderer about her," Mrs. Fesler said, having recovered her composure. "But my Princess and the other two are homebodies. They know where their next meal's coming from. They wouldn't go far." She leaned toward Jeanette. "I think someone stole them. Cat-napped them. Whatever you care to call it."

"Why would anyone want to steal cats? Are they valuable?"

"A top show cat or stud might be worth a hundred dollars or more," Mr. Pettyjohn said.

Jeanette was impressed. "A tidy figure indeed."

"Our cats certainly wouldn't be that valuable. But emotionally, their value is far higher. As Mrs. Fesler so aptly pointed out, they are members of our families."

"And you've received no ransom notes?"

Mrs. Fesler shook her head. "And we're getting quite desperate, I must say." She clasped her hands beseechingly. "Will you take our case, Mrs. Harrison?"

Jeanette knew she ought to consult with Mary first. But the opportunity to send her off hunting for lost cats was too delicious to pass up. John MacDougall would be pleased, having his prophecy come true.

"Of course we will."

"And your rates would be?" Mr. Pettyjohn asked.

"Our fee is five dollars per day for as long as our inquiries go forward, plus expenses."

Mrs. Fesler's eyes widened. "Seems like rather a lot." But after a few seconds she set her chin firmly and gave a nod. "Well, this is for our babies, isn't it? If it's all right with Mr. Pettyjohn, it's all right with me."

Mr. Pettyjohn appeared to deliberate for a moment. "Yes, yes," he finally said. "Please proceed. And keep us informed of your progress."

Jeanette took their addresses and made an appointment for Mary to visit Mrs. Fesler at her home the next morning. She told Mr. Pettyjohn she would be in touch later to set a time for a visit to his house.

The two brand-new clients had been gone only moments when there came another tapping on the door—and a rather tepid, timid tapping, at that.

"Goodness," Jeanette muttered as she strode over to open it. "Business is positively booming."

But instead of another client, three boys of about twelve or thirteen slouched there out in the hallway, battered golf caps in hand. One, with tousled brown hair and pale blue eyes, had on a reefer jacket of muddy gray so well used that it ought to have been in a rag bin. His plaid knee pants didn't look much better.

The black-haired urchin, who looked Italian or Spanish or something else Mediterranean, wore a filthy brown overcoat that was sizes too big. He sported a shiner around his left eye. The third youngster was nondescript, but for his sleepy eyes and a dense, hectic head of flaxen hair. It looked like a small haystack, strands going every which way, with a stubborn cowlick sticking up in back.

Jeanette narrowed her eyes and glared down at them. "What is it? What do you want?"

"Is this here the detective agency that had an advertisement in the paper on Sunday?" the brown-haired boy asked. He reached into his pocket and pulled out a scrap of newsprint, which he glanced at. "Moody Investigations?" His hands were grubby and so was his face. He could have done with a hearty scrubbing.

"It is," Jeanette said warily.

"Could we talk to Mr. Moody?"

Jeanette sighed. "No, Mr. Moody isn't here. Miss MacDougall is our chief detective."

The three young faces looked dubious. "A woman?" said the flaxen-haired boy.

"Is she any good?" asked the dark-haired lad in the oversized coat.

Jeanette almost answered in the negative, the better to chase these ragamuffins away. But a little itch of curiosity tickled her. She wanted to know why this improbable trio would need a detective—though she doubted they could afford even a cursory inquiry.

"Yes, Miss MacDougall has handled several successful cases. Now what brings you three here?"

The brown-haired boy puffed himself up a bit and held out his hand. "I'm Jiggs Nyberg. This here's my chum Bert Zanetti." He nodded at the dark-haired boy. "And that there is

Gordo Sinclair."

Jeanette reluctantly shook the grubby hand. "And I'm Mrs. Harrison. Please come in."

"Don't mind if we do," Jiggs said, sauntering first through the door.

Cheeky young fellow, thought Jeanette, sitting behind her desk. She found her pad and pencil, and gestured for the boys to sit. Jiggs and Gordo took the chairs and Bert stood behind them. "So, tell me about your problem."

"We gotta friend name of Beansie MacKenzie. He's one of our gang. And he's the problem." Jiggs placed his elbows on his knees and leaned forward. "The four of us hang around together. Me and Bert and Gordo and Beansie."

"Where do you live?" Jeanette asked. "And why aren't you in school?"

"That's a whole lotta questions," Jiggs answered sharply, "that got nothin' to do with our problem."

"If you expect us to help you," Jeanette said firmly, "we need to know the facts of the matter, including your situations."

Jiggs frowned. "Let's just say none of us reside at nowhere like a fixed address. We move around a lot. Catch work where we can."

"What about your parents?"

"We got three parents to go 'round among us. But they're just usually drunk or mean or sick. Bert here ran into his pop the other day and got that black eye. Then the old bastard emptied the money outta his pocket. A whole dollar twenty-five! Me, I got no mom or pop anymore. Gordo's mother's too sick to be of any use."

In spite of Jiggs's unschooled language, Jeanette couldn't help but feel sorry for the lot of them. "Why aren't you in the Children's Home, then, being taken care of?"

Gordo laughed a bitter laugh. "Taken care of? Betcha you never spent no time in that place, didja, lady? They put me in there three times and I flew the coop three times." He looked to his compatriot. "Jiggs, let's get outta here. I think she's gonna turn us in."

They both hopped up.

"No, no," Jeanette assured them. "I won't do any such thing."

The boys looked unconvinced.

"I've been through hard times myself," she said, "not too long ago. I know what it feels like. Please, sit down. Tell me about Bennie."

"Beansie," Bert corrected.

"Beansie then," Jeanette said. "Tell me what the problem is."

"You promise?" Gordo said. "No snitchin'?"

Jeanette made an X on her chest with her index finger. "Promise. No snitchin'."

"All right then," Jiggs said, sitting down again. "I got only one valuable that's worth anything. A watch that belonged to my granddad. From Sweden. A Linderoth. A jeweler told me it was worth fifty bucks."

"A healthy sum," Jeanette observed. "For your lot, practically a fortune."

"No kidding," Jiggs agreed. "But it's worth a whole lot more to me. Because inside the cover is the only picture I got of my mom."

"Let me guess," said Jeanette. "Someone has taken it."

Jiggs nodded. "Yup. Went looking for it about a week ago and it wasn't in the spot where I kept it hid. I don't like carryin' it around, 'cause someone could lift it real easy. Or beat me up and take it. And a couple days before was the last time any of us seen Beansie."

17

"So you think Beansie took the watch," Jeanette said, "and lit out?"

"Put yer finger right on it."

From behind his two friends, Bert raised his hand timidly, like a pupil in class.

"Yes, Bert?" Jeanette said.

"Well, ma'am, Beansie'd been telling us he had a lady friend." The boy had a high, whispery voice. "We figger they run off together with the money from Jiggs's timepiece."

Jeanette could hardly imagine any woman running off with a twelve-year-old boy. But there was many a disreputable female who could be motivated by a fat roll of dollar bills.

"Nothin' else makes any sense," Jiggs said. "So we went around to some pawn shops, looking for the Linderoth, but they chased us out."

"And you want us to find Beansie and the watch," Jeanette said.

Jiggs huffed. "The watch anyway. Beansie can go hang." He narrowed his eyes. "How much'll it cost?"

Jeanette felt it verged on cruelty to lead the boys on. Even the cost of a novice detective like Mary would be well beyond their means. But it broke her heart to think that Jiggs had lost his mother's only photograph. And what harm would there be in making a few inquiries around town?

"Our normal rate," she said, "is five dollars a day."

The three boys couldn't have looked more shocked if she had pulled a gun on them.

"Five dollars?" Jiggs whispered. "*A day?*"

"Five dollars!" Gordo squeaked.

They looked at each other and shook their heads.

"Sorry we bothered you, lady," Jiggs sighed, standing up.

"Well, tell me how much you can afford," Jeanette offered.

Jiggs nodded at Gordo, and back at Bert. "Show her what we got."

Bert reached into a coat pocket and pulled out a bulging sock that clinked a bit as it moved. He dumped the coins on Jeanette's desk, along with a couple of one-dollar bills. She quickly counted it.

"Seven dollars and twenty-nine cents," she announced. "I'll make you a deal, gents. I'll hang onto this. If we find your watch, we keep it. If we don't, we'll give it back. How does that sound?"

Jiggs grinned. "That'll do nice. That'll do *real* nice."

"All right then," Jeanette said. "I'll speak with Miss MacDougall. How can I reach you?"

"I sweep up at O'Toole's Stable up the hill," Jiggs said. "They got a phone. Just leave me a message. Mr. O'Toole won't mind."

The boys left and Jeanette typed up what she might have called, in her prior career as a professional typist, work orders. One for Mrs. Fesler's and Mr. Pettyjohn's missing cats. Another for Jiggs Nyberg's apparently stolen Swedish watch. Each with all the information she had collected in her notes.

"If Mary MacDougall truly wants to be in business," she sniffed, "then she had better be more businesslike and show up at work." At that moment came another knocking at the door.

A third case in just one morning? Wouldn't that be something?

Jeanette swung open the door to discover a gentleman of military bearing in a brown suit, his fedora in his hands. He was a bit taller than she was, with brown hair and brown eyes verging on hazel. His face struck her as almost, but not quite, handsome. It was a pleasing face, though. It also seemed a little taken aback at the sight of her.

"Hello." She smiled at him. "How may I help you?"

19

Looking mildly displeased, he gave her a silent stare. "I was expecting someone else," he finally said.

A bit rude, Jeanette thought, but she knew better than to get off on the wrong foot with a potential client. "You're probably looking for Miss MacDougall then."

He sort of grunted and nodded.

"Alas, she's out," Jeanette said, trying to sound amiable. "I'm Mrs. Harrison. And you are?" She had no idea why the man seemed so put out.

"Well, well, well, look who's here."

Jeanette and the visitor turned to see Mary MacDougall marching briskly up the hallway—her handbag in one hand and a brown paper sack in the other.

"How in the world did you know that this is my agency?" she asked, coming up to them. She smiled at the man. "But then you are a detective, aren't you, Detective Sauer?"

Chapter III

"So your father actually helped you put this enterprise together?" Detective Sauer said. "I was under the distinct impression that your ambition to become a consulting detective didn't exactly suit his expectations."

Mary and the detective had gone into the inner office, but the door remained open, so Jeanette could hear every word from her desk in the outer office.

"It's true my father was less than enthusiastic," Mary replied, "after that messy business in Michigan."

"But in the end you did rather well, for a beginner," the detective said. "Wasn't the great John MacDougall even a little bit pleased?"

"It was his daughter and sister getting thrown in jail that he particularly objected to," Mary replied.

Jeanette stifled a chuckle. The quickest way to raise John's temperature was to mention the unfortunate events that had transpired in Dillmont and Sault Ste. Marie—though she suspected he had amused his fellow industrialists with the tale of his daughter's incarceration.

"If I'm so poisonous to your career, Detective Sauer," Mary asked, "why did you come to see me? And how did you know to come here? The agency's called Moody Investigations, not MacDougall Detective Service."

"Actually, I didn't come to see you. I'm not here to pay a

social call. One of the miscellaneous tasks I'm assigned is making a visit to any new detecting shop that opens up in Duluth. When I saw your advertisement in the Sunday paper, I put Moody Investigations on my list. I noticed the address, too. And then I recalled something I saw last week."

"What was that?"

"A wagon from Garlock & Larson unloading this very desk in front of this building," he said. "And you out on the sidewalk talking to the two furniture movers. So when the advertisement for Moody Investigations listed this address, and I recalled your connection with Mrs. Larson, I simply put two and two together."

He had simply put two and two together, Jeanette thought with admiration. Nothing remarkable, just common sense put to work.

"So what is it you need to tell me," Mary asked, "in your official capacity?"

"The gist of it is that you are politely directed to not interfere in police investigations. And should you uncover any criminal activity in the course of your work, you are to notify the department. May we count on you to agree with these requests?"

Excellent, thought Jeanette. *Well done, Detective Sauer.* Mary needed some boundaries for her sleuthing activities. She wouldn't dare to transgress the gentleman's dictates.

"I would hate to cause any grief for the police," Mary said in a tone that sounded a tad insincere. "And speaking of police investigations, what are you up to these days, Detective? Anything...*juicy*?"

"The usual things. String of burglaries in your neighborhood up Superior Street. Tracking down some drunken sailors who broke up a Bowery bar pretty bad. An armed robbery at a haberdasher's not far from here."

"So nothing very exciting."

Jeanette detected a note of disappointment in Mary's voice.

"Not that I can tell you about." The detective paused. "Though in a few weeks you may read of a case with international implications unfolding here in our fair city."

"Oh, do tell me about it," Mary cajoled. "I'll keep my lips sealed tight. I promise."

"Sorry. Strict orders. Under wraps."

"Oh, well," Mary answered with resignation. "I'll just have to wait for the newspaper headlines."

Highly unlikely, Jeanette thought. She knew her cousin too well. Mary would do her very best to pry the secret from Detective Sauer.

"Afraid so," the detective said. "Now I suppose I'd better get going and leave you to your work."

He came into the outer office, looking as if he had quite enjoyed teasing Mary. But when he saw Jeanette surveying him, his subtle grin abruptly vanished and his posture stiffened. He turned back to Moody Investigations' chief operative, who had followed him out.

"Good day, Miss MacDougall. And remember—keep clear of police business."

With a curt nod of the head to Jeanette, he made his exit and the outer office door swung shut.

"I don't think he likes me," Jeanette said.

"What?" Mary sounded distracted. "What *are* you talking about?"

"He barely even looked at me. And when he did, I could practically feel the frost in the air."

"Don't be ridiculous," Mary scoffed. "That's the way he treats everyone."

"No," Jeanette argued. "I sensed a distinct air of disapproval when I introduced myself." She paused for a long few seconds, suddenly quite worried. "Oh dear. I wonder if he knows about the trouble I got into down in St. Louis."

Mary rolled her eyes. "Oh, Jeanette, you're just imagining things. Besides, since when was being a dupe to confidence tricksters a crime?"

Jeanette cringed, but it was perfectly true. She *had been* a dupe. A mutton-headed, idiotic, half-witted dupe who had managed to lose everything—her business, her house, her friends.

"I'll bet he was just preoccupied with that special case he wouldn't tell me about." Mary focused on the ceiling, as if she might be able to grasp some clue up there that would reveal all.

"Well, speaking of cases," Jeanette said, "I'm pleased to inform you that Moody Investigations has just booked two more inquiries. I already have the work orders written up."

Mary blinked at her. "Two jobs? Really?"

"Really," Jeanette answered. "First, a Mrs. Fesler and Mr. Pettyjohn stopped by and all but begged me to take their case. It seems no one else would help them."

"So what is it? What do they need?"

"It's really quite consequential," Jeanette said solemnly. "I hope we're up to the task."

Mary scowled. "Are you going to tell me or not?"

"Well, it seems Mrs. Fesler's and Mr. Pettyjohn's cats have gone missing."

"Two lost cats?" Mary whined.

"Two lost cats. But there's more."

Mary made a dispirited wave of the hand.

"Two other cats have vanished. And all of the owners belong to the same cat fancy club. And we're to hunt for those cats, as well."

"Four felines gone afield," Mary sighed. "Frankly, finding two cats didn't sound all that appealing. But four?"

"Work is *work*, you know," Jeanette reminded her. "Even if it isn't appealing. If you seriously mean to make a go of this, Mary, you'll need to take everything that comes through that door. Even jobs that are unappealing."

"I know, I know, I know," Mary conceded. "You're quite right. I suppose I'd better make an appointment to talk with the clients. What did you say their names were?"

"Mrs. Fesler. And the appointment has already been made. I've booked you to see her at ten tomorrow morning. I left Mr. Pettyjohn's interview open."

"Very efficient of you. And I want you to come along with your stenographer's pad and pencil."

"But who's going to mind the office?" Jeanette objected.

"Don't worry. We don't have to man the battlements every hour of every day. Now tell me about the second case."

Jeanette thought it a bad idea to close the office during regular business hours, but Mary was the boss, she supposed.

"A young gentleman named Jiggs Nyberg owns a valuable timepiece made by a Swedish watchmaker called Linderoth," she continued. "A family heirloom, it seems. His most valuable possession. A friend of his, one Beansie MacKenzie, has, apparently, absconded with it and run off with his new lady friend. I took down all the relevant information."

"Now that's more like it," Mary said, rubbing her hands together. "Give me all the details."

"Well, I think you'll find it a provocative matter. The gentlemen appear to be about twelve or thirteen years old and live at no regular addresses."

Mary looked utterly dismayed. "Street boys," she groaned. "You hired us out to street boys?"

"They've made a deposit in the amount of seven dollars

and twenty-nine cents, Mary," Jeanette noted. "For them, a fortune. And it isn't merely a timepiece. The watch's cover holds young Mr. Nyberg's only photograph of his lamented mother. And if you refuse to look into the matter, I'll tell your father you turned down perfectly good business. Heaven knows, you don't need the money anyway."

Mary looked as if she were ready to blurt out a retort, but didn't. "The only photograph of his mother?" She pursed her lips and tapped her toe a few times. "All right, then, we'll see what we can do." She grabbed her coat and hat from the coat rack. "Now, I have to run out for a bit."

"Where are you going?" Jeanette asked. "You've only just arrived."

"To Herr Neumann's studio," Mary replied, opening the door. "Then a trip to Madame Zoya's, for a fitting."

"Does Herr Neumann have some work for us?"

"No."

"You're running a personal errand?"

"Yes. He's in the middle of a landscape that I might buy as a Christmas gift for Tena. I wanted to see how it's coming along."

So buying a Christmas gift for one's aunt is more urgent than tending to work? Jeanette thought. *And a trip to Madame Zoya's atelier?*

"A new dress is hardly an important business matter," she said pointedly.

"But I need it," Mary protested. "For the holidays."

"And you're taking that nice ham sandwich Mrs. Erdahl made for you?" Jeanette said, eyeing the brown paper sack that Mary had in hand.

"Thought I'd eat it along the way."

Jeanette clearly disapproved. "Well, it's your agency. But I'd counsel you to take a more professional outlook. One oughtn't be pursuing personal matters all willy-nilly during business hours."

"Willy-nilly?" Mary said teasingly. "Certainly not. But I do think one is allowed to run important errands, don't you agree?"

"Where's this studio?" Jeanette asked, refusing to be baited by her cousin.

"It's in that red-brick office building at First Street and Third Avenue East," Mary answered. "I might not make it back this afternoon, so you can lock up on your own." And out she went.

"*I do think one is allowed to run important errands, don't you agree?*" Jeanette parroted sarcastically to the now-closed door. At this rate, it wouldn't take the young lady very long to run her newly minted business right into the ground. Of course, that was the outcome John MacDougall was hoping for.

But Jeanette had mixed feelings about it. Being back in an office had lifted her spirits considerably. After her dear Daniel had died, building up her own typing bureau with her partner in St. Louis had been the best medicine possible. It kept her busy, paid the bills, and allowed her to feel that she was worth something. The sound of a clacking typewriter was music to her ears. Now, sitting at her brand new desk, she felt like the captain of her ship again. Never mind that Mary owned it.

As grateful as Jeanette was to John MacDougall—who had rescued her from a dire situation—the distant goal she had set her gaze upon was to be her own woman again. Working for neither him nor his daughter. Running her own business, in the manner that *she* chose. Not being vulnerable to the whims of this bright and likeable young lady who was, truth be told, capricious and unpredictable. Still, Jeanette hoped Moody Investigations would last at least a few months. *This office is very nice*, she thought, as she ran her fingers over the shiny new keys of the Remington typewriter.

The phone rang just then. She picked up the receiver, put it to her ear, and leaned down close to the transmitter.

"Yes, this is Moody Investigations," she enunciated in her telephone voice.

"You have a call from a Mrs. Beach," the operator said.

"Ah, yes, please put her through."

A few seconds later the MacDougalls' housekeeper came on. "Hullo, Mrs. Harrison?"

"Yes, right here. Hullo, Mrs. Beach."

"Could I speak to Mary, please?"

"I'm afraid she's gone out and won't be back today."

"Oh, dear. Her seamstress, Madame Zoya, informed me that she won't have Mary's new dress ready for the fitting this afternoon, as arranged."

"Oh, dear indeed. I'll see if I can catch her. She left just a few minutes ago."

Mrs. Beach thanked her and rang off.

The coat Jeanette put on was heavier than anything she might have worn back in St. Louis. Even in early autumn, the Duluth air had a chill to it, what with that huge, cold lake just a few hundred yards away. She was already steeling herself for winter's fierce gales and deep snow.

As she stepped out the door, Jeanette remembered something. She popped back inside, found a piece of stiff paper, and printed on it with her fountain pen: WE ARE OUT FOR A FEW MINUTES & WILL BE BACK SOON. She tucked it between the glass and wood in the door, clicked the lock shut, and marched off.

Herr Neumann's studio was several blocks east and one block down, and it took Jeanette seven or eight minutes to get there—even at a brisk pace. It was all the way up on the fifth floor, tucked away in the back. She was certainly getting her exercise. A young woman's voice answered her when she knocked on the door.

"Come in, we're open."

Jeanette turned the knob and walked in. She was hit with the strong aroma of turpentine and oil paints. The studio was a single large space beneath a row of skylights. Paintings lined the walls. Portraits, pastoral scenes, ocean views of turbulent waves, windjammers at full sail, still lifes, even a couple of nude studies. All of them handsomely done. Herr Neumann knew how to paint.

An auburn-haired young woman peered at Jeanette from behind one of the easels. She had on a light blue smock and held a well-worn brush loaded with yellowish paint.

"How may I help you?" She set the brush down on the lip of the easel and came around.

"I was looking for a friend of mine, whom I expected to find here."

"And who might that be?"

"Miss Mary MacDougall. She just left our office to come over here."

"I know Miss MacDougall, of course. She studied with my father and she's interested in his newest landscape. A gift for her aunt, I believe. But she hasn't been here today." The young painter held up her index finger. "Just a moment."

She went over to the desk in the corner and paged through a diary with a red binding. "She has an appointment to see my father at the Oddfellows Hall, right about now. He's doing a mural for them. By the way, I'm Marlene Neumann, the professor's daughter."

The woman pronounced her name in the proper Germanic manner: *Mar-lay-nah Noy-mahn.*

"So pleased to meet you. I'm Mrs. Harrison, Miss

MacDougall's cousin. The Oddfellows Hall, you say. And where might that be?"

What is *that girl up to now*? Jeanette thought, tramping down the narrow staircase a moment later.

The Oddfellows Hall—like Herr Neumann's studio—involved several flights of stairs. Jeanette had almost been tempted to let Mary go and waste her afternoon traipsing out to see Madame Zoya in the West End. But now Jeanette's curiosity was piqued and she wanted to get to the bottom of her cousin's peregrinations.

The hall was a large meeting room with rows and rows of folding chairs and a permanent platform up front. The space also might have served well for concerts and lectures.

On the wall above the platform, a broad canvas had been mounted in a frame of dark wood about twenty or so feet wide by eight or nine feet high. An older gentleman stood up on a ladder before it, daubing at a figure to the left side of the mural—actually two figures. The ruddy-faced, kindly looking man depicted on the canvas held a small, barefooted little boy in his arms. Elsewhere on the canvas yet more prosperous gentlemen were helping other people who were variously lame, halt, malnourished, or otherwise down on their luck. An appropriate scene for the Oddfellows, well known for its good works. But only about half of the design looked finished, with the rest sketched out in charcoal.

Jeanette walked down the aisle between the chairs and stopped at the stage.

"Herr Neumann?"

The man on the ladder twisted around and smiled down on her. "Ja, guten Morgen. Vhat can I do for you?"

Jeanette was rather impressed by the painter's mustache and beard, which reminded her of Napoleon the Third's facial decorations.

"I'm trying to track down Miss Mary MacDougall, my employer. And your daughter told me she might be here."

He backed down the ladder and walked over the drop cloth beneath the mural, toward Jeanette. "Ja, she vas here a little vile ago."

"Did she say where she was going?" Jeanette asked.

"I do not know, meine gute Frau, but he might."

Herr Neumann pointed back over Jeanette's right shoulder. She turned and saw a tall, darkly handsome man walking toward her. If he was a painter, he certainly kept himself quite tidy. He was in shirtsleeves and there wasn't a spot of pigment anywhere on his person. He must have been working behind the screen at the side of the hall—probably where they kept painting supplies and implements.

"This lady," Herr Neumann said, "iss looking for Miss MacDougall."

Jeanette's eyes fixed on the partially eaten, rye-bread sandwich the younger man gripped in his left hand. A ham sandwich, from the look of it. She had seen it being prepared that morning by the MacDougalls' cook, Mrs. Erdahl.

Mary MacDougall! thought Jeanette. *You little dickens!*

Before the approaching man could make so much as a peep, she offered her hand to him. "Mr. Edmond Roy, I presume."

Chapter IV

Mary's artistic matchmaking appeared to be going swimmingly.

Herr Neumann effusively praised Edmond's ability to mimic his style and brushwork, and found the talented young painter a highly capable assistant. Edmond, whose broken arm had healed nicely, appreciated having the work and, more important, no longer seemed peeved at Mary for helping to break his arm in the first place. Because of the injury, he had lost two good commissions. Giving him a chance to make up lost income seemed the least she could do.

And, of course, Mary enjoyed having Edmond close at hand—as confusing and ambiguous as their relationship might be. She needed, though, to take care that her father didn't discover her chicanery. That's why, since their adventures in Upper Michigan, she had communicated with Edmond in a rather circuitous way.

Mary knew that any letters sent by him from Ishpeming to her home on Superior Street would instantly catch the eye of the housekeeper, Emma Beach, or that of the new resident busybody, cousin Jeanette. And in short order John MacDougall would hear about it. So Mary imposed on a co-conspirator, her Aunt Christena, who had, until recently, remained in Ishpeming with her new gentleman friend. Mary sent Tena several notes to relay to Edmond. Edmond gave his replies to Tena, who enclosed them in letters that, to all appearances, seemed to come from Miss Christena MacDougall. Mary arranged Edmond's employment with Herr Neumann this way, having heard the master painter needed help with his mural.

After bringing Edmond lunch at the Oddfellows Hall, Mary had caught the streetcar on Superior and rode it out to Twenty-Eighth Avenue West, in the West End. From there she made the brief stroll to Madame Zoya's little atelier of couture.

Mary had never thought of herself as a clotheshorse, but she didn't mind looking somewhat stylish. And that's where the talented Russian came in. Mary could bring her a magazine illustration from *Les Modes* and she would whip up a reasonable facsimile in just a few weeks. Zoya Kuznetsov was, quite simply, a treasure.

Of course, Mary could easily have afforded to go to Paris or London for the season's wardrobe. But it seemed like a lot of unnecessary fuss and bother over buying a few dresses, with Madame Zoya so close at hand.

She went up the brick path, climbed the steps of the narrow, two-storey house, rapped the doorknocker, and waited. A moment later the door swung open and there stood the striking, statuesque seamstress—who looked the part of a grand duchess caught at her ease in a shirtwaist and skirt. Recognizing her visitor, the woman appeared dismayed.

"Oh no. *I am so sorry*, Miss MacDougall. You did not receive my message?"

"Message? What message?"

"I telephoned your house and told Mrs. Beach the dress was not yet ready for fitting. She assured me she would ring you at your office."

"Oh, dear," Mary sighed. "My timing was bad, apparently. I was out running errands and I must have just missed her telephone call."

"Well, come in, come in, please," Madame Zoya said. "Where are my manners? Perhaps a cup of tea?"

With no reason to stay, Mary figured she ought to get back to the reproving glare of Jeanette and redeem at least a bit of the workday. But the seamstress looked so distraught, Mary couldn't refuse her.

"Absolutely, a cup of tea sounds lovely."

Mary knew just where to go—the little corner nook with a tidy table covered by a lace cloth and two chairs upholstered in a pink candy stripe.

"First, the tea," Madame Zoya said. "Then I will tell you what happened." And she scurried off to her kitchen in the back.

The whole front of the house—parlor and dining room both—was given over to Madame Zoya's workshop. Dress forms populated the rooms, some holding half-finished gowns, none of them Mary's. Bolts of colorful, elegant fabrics, stacked neatly, covered tabletops, and cabinets full of thread and buttons and ribbon hugged the walls. Sketches of madame's own creations were pinned to bulletin boards. Two stalwart Singer sewing machines stood at either end of the worktable, their heads threaded and ready for business.

A few minutes later, Madame Zoya returned, carrying a tray with two cups and a pot of tea. "Now, I owe you an apology and an explanation."

Mary blew lightly on the dark-brown brew. She took a tiny sip. Still quite hot. "Please don't concern yourself," she said. "I hadn't planned on wearing it until Jenny Alworth's dance on Thanksgiving weekend."

The seamstress looked relieved. "Good. Then we will have plenty of time to finish it. You see, I had expected to have your gown back here by last Friday. But Mrs. Petrescu still has it."

"Your lacemaker?" Mary asked. "The Ostovian lady?"

"That is right. She told me that she had almost finished with the lace for your gown's bodice and sleeves and she would sew it on herself. I took the gown to her a week ago Monday and she promised to have it back by Friday. But, then…" She shook her head. "Such a sad thing."

"What happened?" Mary asked, suddenly intrigued.

"Are you at all familiar with the Ostovian community out here in the West End?"

Mary managed to quickly dredge up some facts she had read in the newspaper and remembered from her European history class. "Immigrants from the Principality of Ostovia. It's tucked in somewhere between Bulgaria and Romania. A population in the tens of thousands, I believe, predominantly Romanian-speaking. Didn't they start arriving here back in the early '90s?"

"Yes, you are right. A group of them, Romanian speakers, followed Father Petrescu here. He is Mrs. Petrescu's husband."

Mary was surprised. "A married priest?"

"That is correct. Men who have wives before they become orthodox priests are allowed to keep them, you know. Father Petrescu was a cobbler before he took holy orders. But he and his family found themselves persecuted by the Ostovian authorities. They escaped just hours before the secret police came for him. He had read about Duluth, in the heart of America. That it held unbounded promise for immigrants. And he just got it in his head that this city was the place for him and his flock."

"The streets paved with gold, and all that."

Madame Zoya nodded and chuckled.

"But why did the secret police come after him? What'd he do?"

"He offended the powers that be, somehow," the seamstress said. "Who knows why? Autocrats do not need reasons to persecute their people."

Mary caught an electric edge of anger in the woman's words. Madame Zoya had been her seamstress for several years, but she knew hardly anything of the woman's life before she arrived in Duluth.

"And I'd imagine some of his congregation followed him here," Mary said.

"Yes, quite a few. The Ostovians are a close-knit community. That is why, when one of them dies like this, they all suffer."

Mary knew it was none of her business, but she couldn't help herself. "An Ostovian passed away? How sad. Was it an illness?"

"No, worse than that. He died in that terrible cold water out there in the bay. With no one to hear him struggling. All alone."

Mary instantly recalled the drowning victim that Mrs. Ivey had mentioned at the dinner party just that last Saturday evening. The poor fellow must have been an Ostovian.

"Well, I'm so, so sorry," she said. "Please tell Mrs. Petrescu that she must take all the time she needs. There's absolutely no rush on the evening gown. I won't need it for many weeks to come."

Madame Zoya gave her a grateful smile. "Well, I am sure she will get back to it soon. But with the police bothering everyone, knocking on doors, asking questions…" Her face darkened. "The Ostovian people take little comfort from the presence of the police. They remember them too well from back in the old country."

For a moment, it seemed Madame Zoya was lost in her thoughts—perhaps revisiting her younger days back in St. Petersburg. But then her eyes focused again on Mary.

"Now, tell me, Miss MacDougall, why do you have an office?"

"I finally decided to start my own detective agency," Mary said proudly. "I even have an assistant."

Madame Zoya nodded approvingly. "It is good to earn your way, even if you do not need to. It is good to be independent." Then her expression turned serious. "But take care to not turn your back on love, if it should appear. It is the most important thing."

It was apt of Madame Zoya to remind Mary of love—particularly with Edmond close at hand. But on the streetcar ride back downtown, Mary could only think about the apparently unusual level of police interest in the Ostovians. Especially regarding something as relatively inconsequential as a drowning.

And why, after all, had news of the tragic event not appeared in any of the papers? Mary would have seen it. Could this have some connection with Detective Sauer's little tease? The case that has international implications? What a deliciously baffling question.

Chapter V

Mary returned to the office well after three and was surprised to find the place empty. Jeanette's terse note, left on Mary's desk, said that John MacDougall had called her home to consult on a matter of some urgency. What in the world could her father have to discuss that was *so* pressing it couldn't have waited until dinner?

Before leaving, Mary jotted a few notations in her personal diary, mostly about her conversation with Madame Zoya. Ever since that kidnapping in Minneapolis the year before, Mary had gotten into the habit of writing down interesting occurrences that came her way. A detective could never know when bits of random information might prove useful.

A little after four, she ascended the red sandstone steps that led up to the MacDougall residence. As she came into the vestibule, she noticed a few envelopes lying on the table, one of them of the characteristic cream-colored stationery that her Aunt Christena used. She ripped it open, pulled out the single sheet, and began to read. After scanning a few sentences, her eyes widened.

"Oh, my, my, *my*," she muttered. "Now Tena's gone and done it. Wonder if Father knows yet."

She took off her hat and coat and proceeded through the foyer, where she promptly ran into Emma Beach. Tall and gray-haired, the housekeeper had been, for all intents and purposes, Mary's second mother. After Alice MacDougall passed away, it was Emma who took Mary and her brother Jim under her wing. Caring for them day in, day out. Tending them through little injuries and illnesses. Administering the flat of her hand to their backsides, when needed. And she was their only "parent" over those long stretches when John MacDougall was away on business.

Emma gazed at Mary through the gold-rimmed spectacles she had just reluctantly purchased—a blow to her vanity. "I see you've read the communiqué from Pittsburgh."

"Does he...?"

"Oh, yes, indeed. *His* letter from Christena came in the morning post, as well. I didn't think his face could possibly get that red."

"But when all is said and done, it *is* wonderful news, don't you think?"

Emma gave her a conspiratorial smile. "Of course it is. It's not every day you find a good man. Especially at *her* age." She glanced back toward the library, then lowered her voice. "But your father, as you well know, thinks Mr. Forbes is hardly an appropriate match. That is to say, a photographer. *Of all things.*"

"But Paul's a fine fellow," Mary huffed. "He adores Tena..."

"I've no doubt he's a fine fellow," Emma interrupted. "And I'm sure he's a good match for her. Christena's no dewy-eyed fool. But practically speaking, from your father's point of view, no one's good enough for his little sister."

Mary groaned. "Therein lies the problem, doesn't it? Where is he? I should talk to him."

Emma shook her head. "No, not yet. He's in the library with Jeanette, gleaning a female perspective on how to disen-tangle the two lovebirds. And since he views *you* as the main author of this outrage, best to stay scarce until dinnertime."

John MacDougall, in his usual position at the head of the table, was occupied with his baked trout, carrots, and bread fresh from the oven. Emma had just refilled his cup of coffee. Mary sat to his right and Jeanette to his left. Nobody yet had said a word about the two cream-colored envelopes that had arrived from Pittsburgh. But it felt to Mary as if they were all waiting for the shoe to drop.

The millionaire finally put his fork down and wiped his mouth with the napkin. "Ran into Aksel Adamsen downtown this afternoon. Mentioned that you and he are going to some concert. Hopes you'll be able to go sailing, too." He nodded at Mary. "Fine young fella, Aksel. I approve."

"Aksel is rather nice," Mary agreed, but committed herself no further. She didn't want to encourage Father too much.

"And I received a letter from New Haven today."

"Really?" Mary said. "What'd Jim have to say?"

"The old boy who teaches contracts is evidently a lot more interesting than your brother would've thought possible. He said the torts professor, though, is well known about the college as the cure for insomnia."

"Well, at least big brother hasn't flunked out yet." Mary knew Jim had the intelligence to become an attorney, but she wondered if he had the focus and determination.

"Not yet. And he reports that the young lady he was stepping out with told him she was done with him."

"Oh, my!" Mary exclaimed in mock surprise. "Doesn't she know his father's a millionaire?"

"So is hers. Owns a shipping company." John MacDougall shot his daughter a wry look. "Jim also said he met Mabel

Wheeler at a lecture she gave."

"The crusading journalist?" Jeanette chimed in. "I read her book about voyaging up the Amazon. Quite the explorer, Mrs. Wheeler."

"I believe she very nearly ended up in a cannibal's pot," Mary remarked.

"And she's a good friend of President Roosevelt," said John MacDougall. "He's something of a naturalist, too. Jim took the liberty of inviting her to come stay with us sometime. She quite likes *The Song of Hiawatha*, so the idea of visiting Gitche Gummee appealed to her."

Longfellow's great lake was better known as Lake Superior. That very inland sea sloshed around just a few blocks down the hill from the MacDougall residence. It stretched three hundred fifty miles, off over the horizon to the east. Though beautiful in its calmer moods, it could turn into a monster come the storms of November.

"How splendid!" Mary said. "I'd love to meet her."

"We'll see what happens," her father said. "By the way, I talked to Bill about your scheme to make his life easier."

"About getting an Oldsmobile, you mean." Mary and her brother had both been lobbying their father for months to buy an automobile. They argued that it was naïve to think the new vehicles wouldn't soon replace the horse and carriage.

"Well, Bill claims his bursitis has let up and he sees no need for one of those 'filthy, noisy contraptions,' as he put it. He and the General are more than happy to haul us around town."

Sometimes it seemed that Bill Logan, the MacDougalls' factotum and jack-of-all-trades, was fonder of his Dutch carriage horse—officially known as General Grant—than his own wife, the redoubtable Gudrun.

"But Father," Mary whined, "even President Roosevelt

approves of automobiles. He had his first motor ride just a few days ago. So, isn't it about time we MacDougalls dipped our little toes into the 20th century?"

John MacDougall furrowed his substantial eyebrows. "Haven't we dipped them enough? Haven't we electricity, Mary? Haven't we a telephone and a gramophone? Haven't you a typewriter down at your office? I won't be called an old fogey for not wanting to spend good money on an automobile when we have the General and Bill and a canopy-top surrey that was new just last year."

Mary slumped back in her chair, knowing this particular battle was lost—at least for the time being. And something about the expression on Jeanette's face suggested she shouldn't cause her father any further agitation.

"And you ought to know," Mary's father said, fixing that penetrating stare on his daughter, "that I'm leaving on my East Coast trip tomorrow morning."

"But I thought you were going Friday."

"So did I. But the necessity of a stopover in Pittsburgh came up, *quite* unexpectedly."

On the one hand, Mary knew that with her father gone longer, she would be better able to sneak in more time with Edmond. But the situation was a tricky one at the moment. "Ah, Tena and Paul."

"Yes, Tena and Paul. I aim to talk some sense into my sister, and I pray I won't be too late. Hopefully, they haven't already gotten themselves hitched by some blasted justice of the peace." He glared at Mary, drumming his fingers on the tabletop. "I know I can't fault you for stopping there in Ishpeming and exposing her to that man…"

"You'd like him, Father," insisted Mary. "He's an interesting fellow. And he is absolutely taken with Tena."

Her father grunted. "Could it be he's more taken with her

money than her sparkling personality?"

That comment simply made Mary mad. "Tena is one of the most gregarious and endearing people I know. As far as I'm concerned, a man would be a fool not to fall in love with her. And why shouldn't she have a chance at that kind of happiness?"

"Because she chose to be an old maid," John MacDougall grumbled, his Scottish burr becoming more pronounced with his increased irritation. "Turned down several solid men of business when she was young. And now, at her age! Well, it's just unseemly that a single woman that old..."

"Yes, *nearly* forty-one," Mary said with exaggerated drama. "Positively *ancient*."

Jeanette stifled a laugh and John MacDougall glared at her. Still, he was having none of his daughter's sarcasm. "That a single woman her age should take up with some impoverished bohemian artist of the camera, believing that he was in love with *her* and not her bank account..."

"Father!" Mary snapped. "That's unfair. You've never even met the man. Paul isn't like that at all."

"Now, you two!" Jeanette exclaimed. "There's no point in arguing. John, you'll have your chance to talk Christena out of it. And perhaps brotherly wisdom will prevail. But, as I told you this afternoon, you'll have your hands full, convincing a woman in love. Trust me, I know how that works. There's no more stubborn creature on earth than a love-struck female."

The millionaire made a dramatic sigh. "I suppose so, Jeanette. But still, I'll have to speak my mind to her. Why the good Lord burdened me with such headstrong women, I'll never know."

Without even thinking, Mary stuck out her tongue.

"I rest my case," John MacDougall said with a raised eyebrow.

Mary sniffed and took a dainty bit of trout on the tip of her fork.

Jeanette put her napking on the table and sat back in her chair. "Did I mention, John, that I had the opportunity to stop by the Oddfellows Hall this afternoon?"

Miraculously, Mary managed to not choke on her trout. She regarded her cousin with wide eyes.

"Madame Zoya cancelled Mary's dress-fitting, you see, but Mary had already left the office, so I couldn't tell her. I was under the impression that she'd gone to Herr Neumann's studio. But the young lady there told me she must have gone to the Oddfellows Hall instead." Jeanette offered her young cousin an innocent little smile.

You torturer, Mary thought. "Yes, I wanted to speak to Herr Neumann about that landscape. Tena's Christmas present."

John MacDougall nodded. "Ah, yes, I read he's doing a grand new mural for the Oddfellows. Fine organization. Good works among the needy and crippled. Reminds me I ought to write them a check sometime before the holidays. Now, if you ladies will excuse me..."

As soon as her father left the dining room, Mary glared across the table at Jeanette.

"All right," she said, "out with it. I know you discovered my little secret. So why didn't you tell Father?"

"I should have," Jeanette said, crossing her arms. "I really should have. But it may surprise you to realize that I was nineteen once. And when you're nineteen, insanity sometimes prevails. Or do you have another explanation for lying about your contact with Mr. Roy? After all, you swore to me that your personal relationship with him had ended. Let me be frank, Mary. Are you two romantically involved?"

Mary knew she should pretend outrage at the accusation.

But Jeanette had her dead to rights, for now. Mary needed to somehow bluff her way out of this pickle. She leaned toward Jeanette, trying to summon up an earnest look.

"Oh, Jeanette, do you think there'll ever come a day when a young woman and a young man can become dear friends and nothing more?"

"Well, I, for one, have no objection to the notion of a platonic friendship. But tell me, Mary, how is it that Mr. Roy finds himself in Duluth at this moment?"

Mary sighed. "You know Edmond broke his arm. Because of me. And he lost two good commissions. And when Herr Neumann mentioned he might need help at the Oddfellows..."

"You thought of Mr. Roy."

"The least I could do. He's really, *really* very good with a brush."

Jeanette had a sip of her coffee. "How long has he been here?"

"Just a few weeks."

"How often have you seen him?"

"Hmm, maybe two or three times. We've had lunch. Gone on a walk or two."

"And nothing more? You *know* what I mean."

"No, nothing more," Mary answered, a little sharply. "Heavens, Jeanette, I do have some self-control, you know." She bit her lower lip. "You won't tell Father, will you?"

Jeanette didn't answer for a number of long, nervous seconds. "Not immediately. Not until John returns from his trip, at the earliest. But I want to know each and every time you intend to see Mr. Roy. In fact, since you've made jokes about me being your chaperone, I may as well fulfill that duty and come along with you."

Mary knew better than to groan, though she wanted to. She was darned lucky that Jeanette hadn't thrown her into the soup.

"Fair enough," she conceded.

But Mary had no intention of letting Jeanette intrude into her relationship with Edmond. In fact, something he had mentioned that afternoon had given Mary a wonderful idea. But to put her plan in motion, she needed some help from her friend Lillian down at the university in Minneapolis. She would post a note and see if her friend would cooperate.

Chapter VI

They arrived at Mrs. Fesler's home, up off Woodland Avenue, just a bit before nine. It was a handsome house in the old Federal style, painted a slate blue, with a charming late-summer garden arrayed in front of it—lots of marigolds and mums. The Feslers, Mary gathered, clearly enjoyed some degree of prosperity.

Jeanette had argued again during breakfast that Mary didn't need her to come along on the hunt for lost cats. She could better serve the fledgling detective agency manning the office downtown. Office hours, she observed—not for the first time—required someone to actually *be* in the office, ready to help customers. But Mary countered that Jeanette would benefit from learning a bit about sleuthing by getting out and about in the greater world. Or so she said.

In fact, Mary figured that if Jeanette insisted on pursuing trivial cases—such as the four lost kitty-cats—she could darned well pitch in to solve them, leaving Mary free to pursue meatier matters. That is, if meatier matters should come their way.

A few raps of the brass knocker brought a quick response. Mrs. Fesler beamed as she opened the door.

"Mrs. Harrison, hello. Welcome. I'm so glad to see you. And this young lady, I assume, is Miss MacDougall, your chief operative?"

"It is indeed," Jeanette said. "Mary, this is Mrs. Alfred Fesler."

"Good to meet you." Mary shook the woman's hand. "Thank you so much for entrusting us with the matter of your missing feline."

"I'm just grateful I could find someone who would help," Mrs. Fesler said. "And don't forget, there are three other missing cats, as well. All of them belonging to members of the Duluth Cat Fanciers Club. Now do come in. I have a nice pot of tea ready and some biscuits."

Quick as a wink, she bent down and snatched up a black cat that was attempting to wriggle its way past her, into the great outdoors. "Oh, no, you don't." She held the green-eyed cat tight to her chest. "It's a game we play, Blackie and I. If *he* had disappeared, it wouldn't have surprised me. Quite the escape artist, Blackie."

The house was as nicely appointed inside as out, with lots of solid, comfortable furniture, and walls papered in tasteful floral patterns. It also had an ample supply of cats. Mary counted four, in addition to Blackie. They trotted up to the three women as soon as they saw them, purring and meowing.

While Mary liked cats—in fact, she'd had one when she was younger—this was just too many. Mrs. Fesler, it seemed, had a feline addiction.

"Now tell me, Mrs. Fesler, which cat went missing first?" she asked

"That would be my Princess."

Jeanette got out her notebook and began to scribble away.

"She's a black and ginger tortoiseshell. What you might call a tabby. Four years old. And very much unlike Blackie there…"

Mary could hardly fail to notice the ebony cat, who at that moment was vigorously rubbing himself up against her ankles.

"...Princess would never venture very far, left to her own devices. But my husband and I had gone to the theater one evening about three weeks ago, and when we came home, Princess was nowhere to be seen."

"Were there any signs someone had broken into the house?" Mary asked.

"No sign of a break-in, but the back door was unlocked. I'm afraid I'm rather notorious for forgetting to lock up. Now ladies, why don't you go out on the porch in back there, and I'll fetch the tea. It's such a pleasant morning to sit outside."

"I'll stay and help," Jeanette said. "Mary, you go sit."

Mrs. Fesler was exactly right. It was a very pleasant place to catch one's breath, underneath the porch roof. Mary could well imagine this backyard ablaze with fall colors in just a week or two. The colors had just started and it was already lovely.

Apart from being stuck hunting cats, Mary thought everything else was going quite well. The agency was up and running. Christena and Paul had decided to take a wonderful leap of faith. Jeanette was proving to be not so hard to handle as Mary had first thought. Edmond was close at hand. And Father was out of her hair for several weeks. All things being equal, not a bad situation.

"Here we go," Mrs. Fesler said, coming through the screen door. She set down a tray with three teacups and a teapot. Behind her came Jeanette with a plate of cookies.

When everyone was settled at the porch table, Mary began again to gather the facts, as Jeanette kept scribbling in her notebook. "Now, tell us a bit about the other three club members and their missing pets. Names, addresses, anything you can think of."

"Of course," Mrs. Fesler said. "Miss Fern Campbell is an elementary school teacher who lives down on East Fifth Street with two housemates."

"The address, please?" Mary asked.

The woman pulled a piece of paper out of her pocket, peering at it through her specs. "Eleven-forty-one."

"Does she have a phone?"

"Yes, she does," Mrs. Fesler said, providing it. "Her cat's named Romeo and he's a *very* handsome boy, a Russian Blue. She was out visiting friends on the evening of the…" She consulted her notes again. "…the twenty-fifth of September. She got back home quite late in the evening and found a window ajar, wide enough for a person to slip in through, or Romeo to slip out of. Fern swears neither she nor her housemates left it open."

Jeanette looked up from her notepad. "Was anything else missing from her house?"

"No. The only thing taken was Romeo. Now, Mrs. Vivian Sternberg comes to our meetings with her daughter, Virginia. Both of them great cat fanciers. Vivian is British originally, you know, and she calls their cat a moggie. Pixie's short-haired, white and cinnamon. Not really a tiger stripe, in my opinion. That puss is a sweet little girl and a homebody. Never would have left the backyard on her own."

As Jeanette wrote down the address and phone number, Mary tried to concentrate on what Mrs. Fesler was saying. But she couldn't help thinking how wonderful a nice jewel robbery or an unsolved embezzlement would be. And she was dying to know about the international case Detective Sauer had hinted at.

"And, of course, there's Mr. Quentin Pettyjohn," Mrs. Fesler continued, "whom you've met, Mrs. Harrison. He has just one cat, an Egyptian Mau called Bastet. An absolutely gorgeous little lady. Spotted, almost like a leopard. And I can tell you that poor Quentin was devastated when she disappeared."

"Bastet, Bastet." Mary furrowed her brow. The name sounded familiar. "An Egyptian god?"

"Close, but not quite," Mrs. Fesler said. "A goddess. The goddess of mystery. And of cats."

"And does Mrs. Pettyjohn participate in the club?" Mary asked.

Mrs. Fesler laughed. "The only Mrs. Pettyjohn is Quentin's mother, to whom he's devoted. Quentin is a confirmed old bachelor. No missus for him, now or ever, I should think."

"Now tell me about the Cat Fanciers Club," Mary said. "How it operates. Who belongs, beyond the people you've mentioned. How and when meetings are held. And so on and so forth."

❦ ❦ ❦

Mary and Jeanette caught the streetcar on Woodland Avenue and headed back downtown. But Mary surprised her cousin when she stood up to get off at Lake Avenue, three blocks before their regular stop.

"Where in the world are you going?" Jeanette asked.

"I'll join you in a bit," Mary said. "Just have to go see someone." She hopped down onto the curb and waved cheerfully at Jeanette, who peered back at her through the window, a look of distinct irritation on her face.

Salter's Saloon, as usual, was packed wall-to-wall with men taking their lunches—talking, joking, making a terrific din, filling the air with cigar and cigarette smoke. Two waitresses trotted from table to table, delivering loaded plates and glasses of beer.

Mary had taken a gamble coming here, and it paid off.

There, at a little table by the far end of the bar, sat Detective Sauer. Reading his paper and taking bites of a sandwich between sips of beer. A uniformed police officer sat across from him, also munching on a sandwich.

A fly in the ointment, thought Mary. It wouldn't do to have the fellow know she had come to talk to Detective Sauer. No one, least of all herself, would benefit from the detective getting the sack for consorting with her. Nothing for it but to try to blend in—no easy task for her in this establishment—and hope the other policeman wouldn't linger long. She sidled over to the opposite end of the bar, out of Detective Sauer's sight, to a vacant spot. The bartender approached her, drying a beer glass as he came.

"Hullo, miss. You sure you're in the right place?"

"Oh, I think so," Mary said with a smile. "I'm rather thirsty and I wondered if I could have a ginger ale." She leaned to the side, looking around the other bar denizens, and saw that the uniformed copper hadn't budged.

When the bartender brought the bottle and glass, she gave him a quarter and told him to keep the change, making a fast friend. She poured the fizzy drink, sipped slowly, and took occasional peeks at her quarry. Finally, after about ten minutes, the uniformed officer stood and made his way out of the bar. Happily, the detective stayed put. As Mary walked in his direction, a stout gentleman with a narrow mustache leered at her and invited her to join him at his table. She gave him a curt shake of the head and continued on.

The instant he saw her, Detective Sauer frowned. "Miss MacDougall. I can't say I'm happy to see you."

Not the greeting one would hope for, but not unexpected. Mary understood perfectly well that she had somewhat complicated the man's life.

"I feel terrible about bothering you," she said, taking the

other chair, "but we need to talk about the Ostovians."

Mary had always credited Detective Sauer for a degree of inscrutability, but this time his poker face failed him, however briefly. She saw a tiny flicker in his eyes. A very slight lifting of the eyelids, expressing surprise. Mary had struck a nerve.

"And why, exactly," he asked slowly, "would we need to address the Ostovians?"

"Well, you must surely know that the police have been making inquiries about a death in the Ostovian community. And I wondered if it had anything to do with that intriguing matter you mentioned yesterday. The case with international implications, I believe you called it."

"And how do you come by this information about the Ostovians?"

She smiled teasingly. "I have my sources, you know. But I'd really rather not say who."

"And I'd really rather not tell you anything about the matter. I shouldn't have brought it up in the first place."

"After all these months, you still don't trust me." She slumped back in her chair with a pout.

"Sharing the details of a sensitive police matter with a nosy teenager," the detective said, "would not auger well for my career in police work. I count myself lucky I managed to survive our last professional encounter."

Mary could hardly blame him for feeling that way—though being called a nosy teenager miffed her a bit. Why shouldn't the man value his livelihood more than the confidences of a neophyte sleuth? She sometimes had to remind herself that not everyone shared her enthusiasm for Mary MacDougall's aspirations.

"Well, it's just so odd. I was at a dinner party the other night and Mrs. Ivey..."

"The wife of the former city councilman?"

"Yes, that's her. She said that she'd heard about a body that washed up in St. Louis Bay. So I just naturally wondered if that might be the death your boys are looking into out in the Ostovian community. Perhaps it might even pertain to your international incident."

Detective Sauer took a deep breath. "Miss MacDougall, do you have any idea of how tiresome you can be?"

"My father made a similar observation recently, and not for the first time," Mary said. "We'll leave it there, then. Don't suppose you know anything about cats going missing?"

"Not exactly a police matter. But perfect for a lady sleuth. As to the Ostovian matter, trust me—keep your nose out of it." He took a slow sip from his glass of beer, almost empty now. "So, you not only have a well-equipped office, but a secretary, as well. Must be nice to afford an employee right off the bat."

Mary ignored the jab regarding her bank account. "Mrs. Harrison's my widowed cousin from St. Louis. She had a bit of bad luck down there and Father thought we could help her out. But, truth be told, the main condition that Father set down, with regard to Moody Investigations, is that Jeanette—Mrs. Harrison—keep an eye on me. No Mrs. Harrison, no detective agency. So, more like a prison guard than a secretary."

"Your father's a very sensible man," the detective said.

"And for some reason Jeanette thinks you don't like her."

The detective looked surprised. "Why in the world would she think that?"

"She says you're rather aloof. Unfriendly."

It was only rarely that Robert Sauer could be flummoxed, but this was one such occasion. "It's just that sometimes I can be a bit awkward," he muttered. "Umm, Mrs. Harrison—she's a widow? Surprising that a woman who looks like that wouldn't have remarried."

"Who looks like what?"

"Well, you know…"

Ah, Mary thought, *the master detective finds Jeanette attractive*. If she had known him better, she might have teased him, in a sisterly way. But that wouldn't do.

The detective straightened his shoulders and cleared his throat. "And by the way, the department's just hired another matron. So we're not caught without a female on duty, to handle girls and women taken into custody. Including the occasional obstreperous lady sleuth."

"Well, then, I'd better behave myself," Mary grinned, standing up. "And by the way, Detective, next May I'll finally turn twenty and you'll no longer be able to call me a teenager. You'll have to refer to me as that 'nosy woman' instead."

As she strode west on Second Street a few minutes later, Mary thought that Detective Sauer had made a good point. She *should* keep her distance. But what harm could there be in calling on Mrs. Petrescu, ostensibly to look at the lace she'd made for Mary's gown? And if something about police visiting the Ostovians should come up, why not ask about it?

Chapter VII

As Jeanette placed her dark straw hat on the rack back in the office, it occurred to her that she had, in a way, jumped into the fire by way of the frying pan. That is, after her disaster in St. Louis, she had hoped that Duluth would prove a respite from the storm and stress. Helping a wealthy young lady navigate the rocks and rapids of approaching adulthood—how hard could it be?

But she hadn't reckoned on how strong-willed and contrary Mary had become. It seemed inevitable that Jeanette would have to tell John MacDougall that there was nothing she could do with the girl. Mary was practically out of control.

After discovering that Mr. Roy was secretly ensconced in town, Jeanette had warned Mary about keeping company with him. Yet just twenty minutes ago, she had stepped off the streetcar three blocks too soon, telling Jeanette she was going to see "someone." Only a fool would think that "someone" wasn't Mr. Roy. And right now he and Mary were probably enjoying a little *tête-à-tête* conveniently out of everyone's eyesight.

But what could Jeanette do to stop what looked worryingly like an affair? For that matter, what could John MacDougall do with his obdurate daughter? Perhaps exile her to a convent? Jeanette, a Lutheran, wondered briefly if Presbyterians even had such a thing as a convent.

She plopped down in her secretary's chair with a groan and picked up the small stack of invoices that had to be paid. Since she had nothing else to do, she might as well disburse some money owed. She was writing a check to the stationers when a crisp knock sounded on the door's mottled glass.

"Come in," she said.

And who should enter but Mr. Edmond Roy himself, hat in hand. When he saw her, he gave her an apologetic smile. "Hello, Mrs. Harrison. I hope I'm not disturbing you."

So much for the theory of Mary bolting off for a secret rendezvous with the man. "No, not at all." Jeanette returned the smile. "I'm happy to have some company."

Edmond glanced into the unoccupied inner office. "I take it Miss MacDougall isn't here."

"You take it right. Off calling on somebody."

"Ah, a new client, perhaps?"

"No idea. Do you need to confer with her?"

"No, no. Just wanted to have a look at the office she's been boasting about. And quite fine it is. Looks efficient and up-to-date. She mentioned that your business experience has been invaluable in getting the agency up and running."

It pleased Jeanette to hear that Mary was praising her, though this was a small operation, compared to the secretarial bureau down in St. Louis. "I'd give you the grand tour," she said. "But it would take all of thirty seconds. So, do please have a seat and enjoy the ambience."

Edmond sat down across the desk from Jeanette. She had to admit he was pleasant to look at. His neatly trimmed beard and thick dark hair set off those deep brown eyes of his. Yet he didn't strike her as any kind of a dandy. In fact, she felt a comfortable easiness in his manner—as though he had nothing to hide from her.

"Mary tells me how grateful she is that you've come to

stay," he said. "She says if anyone can help make this impossible dream of hers come true, it's you."

"Yes, well, she's quite an unusual young lady, with quite an unusual dream."

Edmond looked amused. "I'd call that a distinct understatement. I've never run across any woman, young or old, quite like her."

Ordinarily, Jeanette wouldn't ask a relative stranger such a probing question. But, after all, she had been given the task of keeping Mary away from the man. And as long as he was sitting right in front of her, this seemed the opportune moment to broach the subject.

"May I ask you, Mr. Roy, what your intentions are towards Mary?"

It seemed the question didn't surprise him. The smile he gave her was almost bittersweet. "I hope, Mrs. Harrison, to be a good friend to her. Your cousin has been immensely helpful in my artistic endeavors. Barring the odd broken arm." He chuckled. "I know that she can open doors for me and introduce me to people I'd never meet otherwise." He fixed Jeanette with those piercing dark eyes. "I'm quite fond of her. But of course anything beyond a simple friendship would be ridiculous to consider, given our comparative positions in society. And I think, at the end of the day, Mary understands that."

Jeanette felt reassured by the man's common sense. "Wise words, Mr. Roy. One can always do with a good friend."

Edmond stood up and put his hat back on. "Well, I shouldn't take any more of your time. I enjoyed our chat. Please tell Mary I'm sorry I missed her."

So, Jeanette thought as soon as the door clicked shut behind him, perhaps not a gold digger after all, but a realist. John MacDougall should be reassured, knowing that. But Jeanette decided that, for now, she'd keep Mr. Roy's sojourn in Duluth a secret. Mary's father was at the moment on his way out east, hoping to discourage his sister from marrying some impoverished photographer, of all things. He didn't need to hear that Mary was keeping company with a man he considered an equally unsuitable match.

Just as the last check went into the last envelope, Jeanette heard a racket out in the hallway. The office door flew open and in tumbled those three street urchins, Jiggs, Bert, and Gordo, their shabby golf caps in hand.

"We was in the neighborhood," Jiggs said, "and figured we oughta see if you found out anything yet about my pocket watch and that skunk Beansie."

Jeanette gave them the severe schoolmarm stare that she well remembered from her own school days. She knew as well as anyone that demanding clients needed to be handled with patience and forbearance. But these young scalawags could also use a few lessons in good manners.

"Gentlemen, please come in and shut the door. And two of you, take a seat. I don't care which two."

Jiggs and Gordo—in their raggedy jackets and knee pants—did as instructed. Bert, again, lurked shyly behind them.

"Now," Jeanette said, "in answer to your question, we have started the process of formulating our inquiries into the incident, but have yet to begin interviewing subjects in the matter at hand."

Jiggs scratched his rat's-nest head of brown hair. "Umm, what's that mean?"

"Well, it means we're making plans, but haven't done anything yet."

"But you've had a *whole day* so far," he complained. "We gave you all the money we had. Seven dollars and change."

"Would you like your money back, then?" she asked with narrowed eyes, thinking it might be a relief to get shed of these pesky boys. "A full refund? Fine by me."

Jiggs scowled at her, mulling it over. "Naw, guess not. But how long'll it take, d'ya think?"

The door suddenly popped open and Mary rushed in. She looked surprised to see the three youngsters, but then she smiled. "So whom do we have here? Let me guess. The gentlemen hunting for the stolen pocket watch. And for their friend, a certain Beansie MacKenzie."

Jiggs appeared to be rendered speechless at the sight of Mary, who wasn't that many years older than him. He at least knew to stand when a lady entered the room, though Gordo needed a whack on the shoulder. But rather than introduce himself, Jiggs just stared at her—as if witnessing some vision of loveliness. Gordo seemed to be suffering the same effects. Bert looked down and scuffed the flooring with his shoe. Jeanette had to bite her tongue to not laugh.

"Quite right, Mary," Jeanette said. "They've come to check on the progress of their case. I've explained it's early days yet, but if they feel unhappy with our progress, we can gladly return their payment."

"No, no, no," Mary tutted, walking right up to the dumbstruck Jiggs, who stood a few inches shorter than her. "You have to give us a chance to make our inquiries in this intriguing matter." She offered him her hand. "I'm Miss Mary MacDougall. And you are?"

For a few seconds, it seemed as if Jiggs had forgotten his name. "Uh, Jiggs Nyberg," he finally mumbled. "And this here is Gordo Sinclair and Bert Zanetti."

Mary shook all three grubby hands. "Well, gentlemen," she said, "I plan to visit pawn shops tomorrow to ask after your Linderoth timepiece. I think it's likely your friend

Beansie turned it into folding money at one of them."

"Yeah, that's what we figgered," Gordo agreed. "Sure hope no one bought it yet."

"Well, if they have, we'll just have to track them down. And, more important, we'll track down the felonious Beansie. Give us a few days, and I hopefully will have news for you."

Jiggs looked to Gordo. The two of them exchanged a few whispered words.

"If you do find Beansie," Jiggs began, "I don't want him turned in to the coppers. We're all kinda like brothers. I just wanna get my timepiece back. That'll be enough."

Mary's face softened. "I understand it contains a photograph of your mother. I promise you we'll do our best to find it. And if we find Mr. MacKenzie, we'll put the fear of God in him—but won't turn him in to the law."

The boys looked relieved. "That'll do just fine," Jiggs said. "If you need me, you can get me at the stable. You can also get Gordo, Bert, and me at the soup kitchen down on Michigan Avenue. We have supper there most nights."

"Mrs. Purcell's place. I'm well acquainted with it."

"Chow's good and they're not chintzy with it," Gordo put in.

"Real good grub," Bert added.

"Just let Mrs. Purcell know if you need any of us," said Jiggs.

"Now, before you leave, I have just a few questions," Mary said.

"You betcha," Jiggs nodded. "Shoot."

"Where are some of the places Beansie might pick up a little work?"

"He sweeps up sometimes at the paint warehouse down on Lake Avenue, near the bridge," Gordo answered.

"And there's that German café down there where he

washes dishes," said Jiggs. "What's it called, Gord?"

"Umm, umm… Vogel's!"

"Beansie likes workin' in restaurants best of all," Jiggs continued, "'cause they usually give him free meals."

"Who're some of his other friends?"

Jiggs thought for a few seconds. "Frank Palmquist, George McLaughlin, Pete Monkonen."

"Now Beansie can't be his real name," Jeanette observed.

"No," said Jiggs, "but once you hear his real name, you'll know why he likes Beansie." He grinned.

"Go ahead," Mary said.

"It's Tavish Angus MacKenzie," Jiggs said. "I'd wanna be called Beansie, too."

"But why *Beansie*?" Jeanette asked.

"Simple," said Gordo. "He loves his beans."

"Can't get enough of 'em," Bert laughed.

Jiggs nodded in agreement. "Carries around a spoon and a can opener in his back pocket. When he has a spare nickel, he'll buy a can of pork and beans and eat 'em on the spot."

"Now this is very important," Mary said. "What does he look like? What does he wear?"

"Nothing special about his duds," Gordo said. "Old brown jacket, gray knee pants, dingy white shirt that could use a washing, cap like ours."

"Nice shoes, though," Jiggs noted. "He got himself new shiny brown shoes outta the Sears catalog last summer. Mrs. Purcell helped him order them."

"Cost a dollar fifteen," Bert added.

"What's his face like?" Mary continued. "His hair? Any particular features that stand out?"

Gordo scratched his head. "Just ordinary looking, ol' Beansie. No scars, no birthmarks, nothing like that. Blue eyes, I think. Brown hair."

Jiggs nodded. "Right, blue eyes and brown hair chopped short. Shorter than me and Gordo, but taller than Bert."

After Mary asked a few more questions, the boys sauntered out, looking as if they'd just had an audience with a Gibson girl. As the door shut, Jeanette shot Mary a look of amusement.

"I think the lads are smitten."

Mary fluttered her eyelashes. "Can I help it if I'm irresistible?"

"That reminds me," Jeanette teased, "you had another visitor."

"Oh? Who?"

"Mr. Edmond Roy."

Mary's eyebrows went up. "Edmond stopped by? What did he want?"

"Just to see your new and efficient modern office."

"Well, what did he say?" Mary sounded a bit annoyed at Jeanette's terse response.

"Nothing incriminating, if that's what you're fishing for. He did mention how grateful he was for the support you've given his artistic career."

Mary's expression seemed to gyrate between relief and disappointment. Jeanette wondered if she was relieved that Edmond had revealed no amorous intent, yet disappointed that he hadn't.

Though Jeanette enjoyed watching her cousin squirm, she decided the kindly thing to do was relieve her apprehension. "I've decided to keep your little secret for the time being. I won't say a word about it to your father. So long as you keep the man at arm's length, if you know what I mean."

"Understood, Jeanette. And thank you."

"Now, perhaps you can explain how you're going to canvas pawn shops tomorrow when you've committed yourself to interviewing more cat fanciers."

"It's very simple. While I'm out hunting for a Linderoth timepiece, you'll be working feline duty. *Me-ooow!*"

"But we've discussed this before," Jeanette said with irritation. "You're the sleuth, I'm the office manager. I'm no detective."

Mary grinned. "Well, until I can manage to be in two places at once, you'll just have to pretend to be one."

❦ ❦ ❦

Bright and early Thursday morning, Jeanette sallied forth from the MacDougall house on Superior Street, and hopped on the streetcar going downtown. At Seventh Avenue West she caught the incline up the hill, then the streetcar along Highland Avenue. She exited after a few blocks and walked the short distance to the residence of Mrs. Vivian Sternberg—stalwart of the Duluth Cat Fanciers Club. In her bag Jeanette carried her notebook, with the questions Mary wanted asked, along with a few of her own.

The Sternberg house was a tidy bungalow of cream-colored stucco, with dark maroon trim. The front door opened promptly after a few raps of the knocker and there stood the lady of the house—tall and thin, with a wiry jumble of bright red hair piled atop her head.

"Mrs. Sternberg?" Jeanette asked. "I'm Mrs. Harrison, from Moody Investigations."

The woman offered a smile that revealed a certain lack of dentistry, but ample good nature. "Welcome, welcome, come in. I can't tell you how relieved we are that you're on the case. Mrs. Fesler spoke very highly of you." She took Jeanette's arm and almost dragged her inside.

The interior was neat, if rather plain. Simple furnishings, a few family pictures on the walls, and a threadbare Persian carpet before the equally threadbare sofa. A lone tabby cat came languidly over, regarded Jeanette, and then walked away.

"That's our Little Nell," Mrs. Sternberg said, motioning that Jeanette should sit on the sofa.

"Named after the Dickens heroine?"

"A favorite of mine. And as you can well see, she's still pretty busted up about losing her best friend Pixie."

Actually, Jeanette couldn't see any particular distress in Little Nell. The cat seemed utterly cat-like—unconcerned and bored.

"Fact is," Mrs. Sternberg continued, "we're all pretty broken up over Pixie's vanishment."

The woman had a British working class accent and Jeanette wondered how she managed to end up in Duluth, Minnesota, married to someone called Sternberg.

"Well, that's why I came," Jeanette said. "We aim to find these missing felines and bring them home."

"Do you thig Pigsie's still alive?"

Jeanette turned to see a shorter version of Mrs. Sternberg padding toward them in stocking feet and a blue muslin nightgown—skinny, red-headed, all arms and legs. She snuffled and wiped her nose with a pink hankie.

"My daughter Virginia," Mrs. Sternberg said. "Home from school today. Has a nasty head cold."

Jeanette was relieved when the girl did not offer an undoubtedly germy hand. "Well, Virginia, we have no reason to think that Pixie's not among the living, do we? If she's run away, certainly someone would take her in."

"I should hope so," Mrs. Sternberg sniffed. "Sweetest little moggie that the good Lord ever did make."

"And if she was, well, cat-napped," Jeanette continued, pulling the notebook and pencil out, "why go to the bother, if not to keep her well cared for? Now tell me what happened."

By the time Jeanette went out the Sternbergs' front door, she had heard a tale much like Mrs. Fesler's. Of a beloved kitty which had been there one evening, but was gone the next morning.

It seemed that somewhere in Duluth there was a stealthy individual who took pleasure in stealing family pets. Literally a cat burglar. And how in the world could Jeanette and Mary stop him? Or her?

Chapter VIII

When Mary walked out of the house Thursday morning, she was slightly annoyed with her cousin. Over breakfast, Jeanette had continued to fuss about leaving the office unattended. She kept grousing right up to the moment when she set off for her appointment with Mrs. Sternberg of the cat club.

As Mary rode the streetcar downtown, she mulled over the delicate balance she needed to maintain with her cousin. Jeanette certainly had the advantage over Mary when it came to running a business. No doubt potential customers would, on occasion, come to the agency door and, finding no one home, take their problems to another detective.

But Mary had the advantage over Jeanette when it came to understanding the sleuthing trade. No one succeeded by sitting in the office. You nabbed a malefactor or recovered a stolen item by means of applying good old-fashioned shoe leather. And with two cases on their docket, Mary required Jeanette's shoes out pounding the pavement, as well as her own.

But that wasn't the only dilemma weighing on her mind. Truth be told, Mary was a bit uncomfortable with the fact that Edmond and Jeanette had apparently struck up an acquaintanceship. Jeanette's assurances to the contrary, Mary knew that anything Edmond said might make it back to the ears of John MacDougall. She needed, somehow, to nip that potential alliance in the bud—and keep the two of them apart.

By now the streetcar had deposited her in front of the first of the four pawnshops she intended to visit. Though it had dozens of pocket watches for sale, the owner had never seen a Linderoth timepiece like Jiggs Nyberg's. The second pawnbroker, however, knew the make, having worked for several years in a jewelry shop back in Stockholm. A Linderoth, he said, he would have kept for himself.

The third pawnbroker was located at Superior Street and Sixth Avenue West, near the Incline. And there Mary hit pay dirt—well, at least a few spoonsful. The clerk behind the counter, who was cleaning an old violin, recalled the Linderoth timepiece.

"The young rascal tried to convince me the watch was his to pawn," the man sniffed. "Didn't believe him for a second. It was stolen, sure as I stand here. We don't deal with thieves. I shooed him out."

Feeling excited at uncovering a clue, Mary asked, "What did the boy look like?"

The man thought about it. "Well, I dunno. Ill kempt, poorly spoken. About yea high." He held his hand out to indicate the boy's height, but moved it up and down enough so as to be practically useless. "Like so, I guess."

"So, nothing particular that you remember? No identifying marks?"

"Truth is," the man said, absent-mindedly strumming the violin like a guitar, "these homeless boys all look the same to me."

A streetcar ride west brought Mary to her fourth pawnshop of the day, on West Third Street not far from Madame Zoya's atelier. It was run by a white-haired old Italian, Signor Rossi. He went pale when Mary described the stolen watch.

"We bought it about two weeks ago. Signora Rossi visit our daughter in St. Paul. I was sick with ankle sprain at home.

Our grandson Gino, he run shop for two, three days alone. Gino is so proud. He tells me a boy bring in beautiful time-piece. *Dalla Svesia*, from Sweden. Did not want to pawn it. Wanted money now. Carlo gave him ten dollars and later in day sold it for thirty. So proud, our Gino, making such a profit. Twenty dollars!"

But then the old man's face darkened. "I love our grand-son, but I say to him, '*Stupido idiota*!' Is stolen, the watch. *Il povero ragazzo*, the poor boy, he cannot own such a thing."

Mary was almost vibrating with excitement. In a matter of two hours she had practically solved the case of the pilfered pocket watch. "Do you have any idea who bought it?" she asked.

"No. But maybe Gino know. Gino," he bellowed, "come here!"

A few seconds later a dark-haired, olive-skinned young man came out a door behind the pawnshop's counter, wiping his hands on a rag. "Yes, Nonno?"

"You remember the Swedish watch you sold two weeks ago?"

"Sure. Hard to forget a timepiece that nice." He grinned at his grandfather. "And you gave me quite a lecture for buying it."

Signor Rossi harrumphed. "*La signorina* want to know about man you sold it to."

Gino nodded to Mary and she quietly said hello.

"Well, miss, he was a middle-aged gent who's come to look at watches a few times. Tall, light-colored hair and beard, wears pinch-nose glasses. He told me he collects timepieces. He seemed excited to have it. I forget the name of the maker. Swedish. And a woman, to boot."

Mary didn't know why a woman couldn't make watches, but she didn't come to argue the point. "Her name is Linderoth. Mrs. Betty Linderoth. The watch was stolen from a client of mine. Do you know the man's name?"

The younger Signor Rossi looked crestfallen. "I had no reason to ask for it. He paid in cash."

Drat it, Mary thought. That one piece of information could have closed the case. "Can you recall what the boy looked like."

"Like any poor kid. Skinny, not well acquainted with soap and a washrag."

"Can you recall anything at all about him that was unusual? Any special details of his appearance."

Gino shook his head. "Sorry, miss."

"Well, if you should happen to remember anything, please get in touch, will you?" She took one of her business cards out of her bag and handed it to the young man.

As Mary stepped out from the cool mustiness of the pawn shop onto West Third Street, the sun beaming down from a blue sky up above, she knew, with a reasonable certainty, that Beansie MacKenzie was very likely still in Duluth. Ten dollars cash—while a fair sum—wasn't nearly enough to escape the city in the company of a fancy lady. That is, unless the lady was paying. He might have gone on alone, she supposed, but somehow she didn't think so. To cast aside one's familiar world for ten dollars made no sense.

Suddenly, she decided to postpone her return to the office. It was certainly warm, for a day in early October, and she wished she had her parasol, but it wouldn't prevent her from hiking west a few blocks to Mrs. Petrescu's workshop. Mary had a perfectly good excuse to drop in—wanting to see the lace for her dress. And if Mrs. Petrescu happened to bring up certain mysterious doings in that immigrant community relating to police visits, well what harm in that?

Mary recalled that when the Ostovians began arriving in Duluth back in the early nineties, they settled for the most part west of the Point of Rocks—the dark stone escarpment that divided the long, narrow city on a hill. Originally, they concentrated in and around Slabtown with other immigrant groups. But as they grew more prosperous, they spread out along West Third Street and Grand Avenue, in the West End and West Duluth. This was where they built their homes, set up their shops, and worked in factories. Father Petrescu's nearby Romanian Orthodox church had formerly been occupied by Baptists.

A few minutes later Mary arrived at Mrs. Petrescu's shop, which was tucked between a butcher shop and a small café. But it proved to be something more than just a purveyor of frilly female frippery. A large, somewhat faded sign of heavy cardboard, propped up in the window, announced:

PETRESCU

SHOEMAKING & REPAIR

FANCY LACE & EMBROIDERY

Mary squinted through the scuffed door glass, which made the shop's interior look murky. She turned the knob, but it was locked. She thumped on the door several times, then tried to get a better view through one of the big glass windows, leaning in and holding her hands up to the sides of her eyes.

Finally, a figure came striding from the back of the shop. The burly, muscular man wearing a workman's apron quickly unlocked the front door. He had a square, ruddy face, a thick but short-cropped black beard, and thinning hair on top. As he swung the front door open he said, in a thick accent, "I am sorry, miss. We are closed at present."

Mary made a little pout. "But I came all this way from East Superior Street to see the lace Mrs. Petrescu's made for the dress Madame Zoya is sewing for me," she fibbed. "I'm Miss Mary MacDougall." She offered her hand.

He looked down at it and displayed his rather grimy paw. "Best not to shake, I think. I am Adrian Dimitriu."

"Is Mrs. Petrescu available? I promise I won't keep her long."

The man reached under his apron and pulled out his pocket watch. "She is helping her husband, Father Petrescu, with a sick parishioner. Otherwise, the shop would be open. I am one of the shoemakers, you see. If you would like to try again, please go next door and tell Mrs. Luca you are waiting for Mrs. Petrescu. She will make you a nice cup of tea or cocoa and, if she is feeling generous, give you one of her famous raisin cookies. Then come back in half an hour."

Mary hadn't planned to spend this much time in the West End. But she was feeling a bit peckish. And she might never have a better chance to ask an Ostovian a few cagey questions.

"Thank you," she said. "I'll do that."

The café turned out to actually be a small bakery, too, with loaves of heavy dark bread stacked atop a glass display case full of cookies and cakes of various kinds. Several scrumptious delicacies turned out to be native to Ostovia, and rather than ask for a workaday raisin cookie—however "famous"—Mary picked a kind of sweet cheese pastry. The bakery sold sandwiches and soup, too, and she ordered a sandwich with ham paste.

When the woman behind the counter brought out the lunch, Mary observed that she walked with a pronounced limp. "Are you Mrs. Luca?"

Setting down the tray on the tiny table before her, the

woman gave her a wary look. "I am, miss, but I do not think we have met each other before. Or am I forgetting myself?"

Mary shook her head. "No, not at all. The shoemaker next door, Mr. Dimitriu, told me to ask for Mrs. Luca if I popped in. I'm waiting for Mrs. Petrescu to return. She's doing some lacework for a dress Madame Zoya's making me."

"Ah," the woman said, placing the two small plates in front of Mary, "Madame Zoya. A beautiful lady and such a seamstress. You are lucky to have her make your dress."

Mrs. Luca had a round, amply lined face with frizzy, graying hair pulled back tightly in a bun. Mary noticed that a library copy of *Little Women* was sitting next to the cash register.

"So," Mary said, "is that Alcott novel yours?"

Mrs. Luca's gray-blue eyes brightened. "I read English slowly, but I enjoy it so much. My French is much better. We Ostovians love to read, you know. Under Prince Anton, education and reading were encouraged and supported. He believed ignorance was dangerous to the well-being of any state, even one so small as Ostovia." She scowled. "The man who calls himself prince these days spreads ignorance like poison."

Mary's own education when it came to Ostovia was sadly lacking. "And he would be?"

"Vladislav the usurper," the woman hissed.

"Well, I must say, this sandwich is delicious," Mary said, steering the topic away from politics. "But I think a cup of tea would go nicely with it."

"Of course," the woman replied, "but may I suggest something else? I am well known in the neighborhood for my hot cocoa. The children love it and save their nickels to enjoy some. I use only Van Houten's finest powder."

Mary thought that sounded splendid, and so it was—rich, creamy, and so very chocolatey. She must bring Jeanette here some day. Her cousin had a passion for chocolate that bordered on addiction.

Mary wolfed down her sandwich, but savored the delectable pastry bite by bite. It was easy to understand why Ostovian bakers were so highly regarded. Sipping on the remains of her cocoa, she stared out the window onto the street, where dust rose up every time a carriage or wagon rolled by. Duluth could surely do with a bit of rain.

Glancing down at her Chatelaine watch, she realized she had been sitting in the little bistro almost half an hour. She bid Mrs. Luca *au revoir* and went next door. The shop was still closed, but Adrian Dimitriu emerged again and asked if she minded waiting there for a few more minutes.

Mary wandered around the front room, surveying the merchandise. On one side two headless forms showed off two party dresses—one with pretty blue lace around the collar and cuffs, the other with a beautiful lace cape. Other items were laid out on tables. Doilies and placemats, embroidered hankies and shirtwaists.

On the other side of the shop, a low rank of display shelves showed off a variety of men's shoes and boots. They were of a utilitarian style, in black and brown. Father Pretrescu clearly had learned his craft well, before he became a priest. It gave Mary an idea. Perhaps he could make her a pair of sturdy hiking boots, for tramping the trails up the North Shore at Deerwood, the MacDougalls' lake cottage. No one sold that kind of women's footgear in Duluth, as far as she knew—and she couldn't imagine why not.

Curious about the workshop in back, she quietly opened the door and stepped into a large, well-lit room that smelled of leather and wax and machine oil. Two young men, apprentices no doubt, were hunched over a long workbench. One hammered away while the other cut leather. Tools of the shoemaking trade—knives and awls, hammers and pincers—hung on well-organized pegboards. Dozens of lasts for men's shoes sat neatly arrayed on a shelf, according to size. A leather-stitching machine occupied a corner. Mr. Dimitriu was hunched over it, sewing a last to a sole.

As she turned to go back into the shop, Mary noticed an ornate little cabinet mounted on the wall to her right. Curious about it—some would say just plain nosy—she tiptoed over for a look, opened the two tiny doors, and felt something like a stab to the heart.

"Oh, dear," she muttered under her breath. "How sad."

Someone had taken a photograph of a dead boy in his coffin at the mortuary, skinny little hands crossed over his chest. He had light brown hair, badly combed, high cheekbones and a small, upturned nose. They had garbed him in a decently tailored suit and a fancy bowtie for his sojourn in eternity. His lips seemed slightly open, as if he wanted to say one last thing.

Mary closed the diminutive doors and tiptoed back into the showroom, pondering the simple shrine. She didn't have anything like that at home to honor her mother. But atop her dresser she had a favorite photo of Alice MacDougall—a snapshot from their Brownie, catching her laughing outside at some picnic. At one side of the framed photo rested a pink ribbon that Alice used to tie in Mary's hair and, on the other side of it, the last bottle of perfume her mother had used. The liquid had long since evaporated, but the aroma remained. Mary sniffed it once in a while, and was immediately transported back to the warmth of her mother's touch, the gentle magic of her voice, the complete happiness Mary felt when she was near.

Finally, Mrs. Petrescu appeared. She was a compact, sinewy woman with a narrow face, intense black eyes, and auburn hair piled atop her head. She wore a neatly made dress of dark wool plaid.

"Yes, may I help you?" she asked.

"I'm Miss Mary MacDougall. Please excuse me for dropping by unannounced. Madame Zoya told me you were delayed in finishing the lace for my Thanksgiving dress, but I wondered if I could see your progress so far?"

Mrs. Petrescu looked a bit flustered. "I must apologize for the delay, Miss MacDougall. I am usually quite timely in my work. But there were personal matters that I could not—"

"Not to worry," Mary interrupted. "Personal matters. Of course. No apology needed. We've plenty of time to get the thing done. The party's not until the end of November." She smiled at the woman. "I'd also like to talk about having you embroider some hankies for me. Your work is *lovely*."

Finally, Mrs. Petrescu's face relaxed. "Of course, I would be delighted to."

The lacemaker fetched Mary's gown and showed the almost-finished trim. It was even nicer than Mary had visualized—not fussy and fiddly, like so much lace, but elegant. Mary was profuse in her compliments and said she would stop by next week to drop off the linen handkerchiefs she wanted embroidered with her monogram.

Having dispensed with lace and hankies, Mary decided it was now or never to probe into the matter she was so curious about.

"I understand the police have been asking questions among the Ostovians," she said off-handedly.

Mrs. Petrescu gave her a blank look. "I am quite sure I do not know what you are talking about. We Ostovians are law-abiding folk. What would the police want from us?"

Well, it had been worth a try, Mary figured. But she understood that it would do no good to pry any further. If Mrs. Petrescu knew anything, she was clearly unwilling to talk.

Mary said goodbye and started for the door, but turned back. "Oh, one more thing. I took a peek in the workshop and I noticed a little shrine on the wall. The poor lad in the picture—who is he?"

The woman's face turned to stone. "I am sorry, miss, but I cannot..." Her expression softened a very little bit. "It is too painful. Please understand."

"Quite right," Mary apologized. "I'm sorry. None of my business."

Chapter IX

After riding the streetcar back downtown, Mary trudged up the hill to Second Street, then ascended to the second floor of the 335 West building. She pushed open the door of Moody Investigations and discovered Jeanette standing before the street map of Duluth. It laid out The Zenith City—as an early newspaperman had nicknamed it—all the way from West Duluth to Lakeside in the east. Arms crossed, head tilted, she was apparently pondering several colored pins that protruded from the map. When she heard Mary come in, she turned, shot a narrow-eyed gaze, and pointedly looked back at the big railway clock on the wall.

"One-thirty-seven," she said. "Goodness me, there must be *lots* of pawn shops to visit in Duluth, to require most of the day to do so. I, on the other hand, managed to talk with Mrs. Sternberg and her daughter, look around their neighborhood, and still be back here by eleven." Her eyebrows went up, as if to say: *How do you like that!*

"And exactly how many new clients have come through the door since your return?" Mary asked sweetly.

Jeanette huffed. "Well, none, but who's to say someone didn't come calling when I was gone. We'll never know, will we?" She tapped her foot impatiently. "So, how did you do?"

While Mary was sorely tempted to gloat a bit about her morning's success—and the triumph of shoe leather—teasing

Jeanette came with definite perils. It was probably best not to irritate her too much.

"Not badly, if I do say so. Not only did I find out where our culprit sold Jiggs's watch—a pawnbroker's out on West Third Street—I also have a description of the man who bought it. A collector of fine timepieces, it seems. In addition, I learned that Beansie only got ten dollars for the timepiece, which wouldn't have taken him very far. Chances are he's still in town somewhere." She tossed her bag onto Jeanette's desk and slumped into the client chair in front of it. "And since I was near the lacemaker's shop, I decided to stop in and check her progress on my Thanksgiving party dress. I discovered the nicest little bakery next door. I had lunch there. A ham paste sandwich and a delectable Ostovian pastry. And excellent cocoa. I'll take you there sometime."

Jeanette sat down behind her desk and gave Mary a grudging smile. "Well, I do love cocoa. And it does sound like you made progress. Much more than I did. All I really found out is that the Sternbergs' Pixie was the 'sweetest little moggie the good Lord ever made' and she just vanished into thin air one night. An account remarkably similar to what happened to Mrs. Fesler's Princess."

Mary nodded toward the colored pins. Three of them were scattered around Duluth's eastern half, and one up over the hill. "You're hoping to see a pattern of some kind."

"Correct."

"They look perfectly random, if you ask me."

"So it would seem," Jeanette sighed. "The thefts have nothing to do with geography, I'm afraid."

Mary stood and went over to examine the map closely. "I wouldn't get discouraged quite yet, Jeanette. You never know where we'll uncover something significant. Sometimes it's just a matter of luck. After you interview Mr. Pettyjohn and Miss

Campbell, we'll review your notes and come up with a plan to canvas their neighborhoods."

Jeanette crossed her arms again, clearly not on board. "My dear cousin, your father hired me to be your personal secretary and perform all duties therein required. Because John wants me to keep an eye on you as much as possible." She paused for a few meaningful seconds. "Perhaps I'm being tiresome, bringing this up again, but I did not sign on to be a junior investigator in the field. The application of shoe leather, as you call it, is not my job."

Mary, showing no reaction, settled back into the chair. Jeanette had a point. But if Moody Investigations had any chance of succeeding, simply having one active agent just wouldn't do. Some gentle persuasion was required.

"Honestly, Jeanette, I can't do this without you. I thought I could, but it's painfully obvious that a second pair of eyes and ears would make all the difference. You're smart, you're observant, you're a quick study, you understand human nature, and you're solid as the Rock of Gibraltar. I need you in the field as well as the office."

Jeanette seemed mollified and a little flattered. "Well, let's take it one day at a time. I will visit with Mr. Pettyjohn and Miss Campbell, and ask them about their blasted cats. But only if you come with me."

"Was your visit with Mrs. Sternberg that onerous?"

"Of course not. But it was, I think, a waste of time."

This wasn't exactly how Mary wanted to conduct the business—two operatives trudging around like Siamese twins—but perhaps Jeanette would come around to see how easy detecting could be with the right methodology. "All right then, we'll interview the remaining cat owners together."

"Good. I've made appointments with both of them for Saturday. I checked your calendar and confirmed that you have no other engagements."

Blast it! Mary thought. Now she'd need to get word to Edmond that she had to break their date—afternoon tea at a café east down Superior Street. If she tried to beg off visiting Mr. Pettyjohn and Miss Campbell, Jeanette would surely smell a rat.

"Excellent," she said, trying to sound like she meant it. "We'll sally forth together." She stood and headed into her own office, but turned around. "Now if you don't mind, I need to write a few letters. Would you please call the O'Toole Stables and ask them to send Jiggs around tomorrow morning?"

"That young fellow'll be over the moon that you have a lead on his timepiece. What's your plan, then?"

"Next week I'll be going to every jeweler I can think of, to ask after young Signor Rossi's mystery collector. Even if they don't know him, they might know other collectors who do. I think we can wrap this case up in a *timely* way." She gave Jeanette a big smile, but her cousin didn't appear to get the joke.

Mary plopped down behind her own desk and jotted a brief note to Edmond, with apologies, which she would have Jiggs deliver tomorrow. Then she scribbled out a long missive to her lifelong friend Lillian Burns. Daughter of the MacDougall family's doctor, Lillian was down in Minneapolis, attending the university with the goal of becoming a physician herself. Mary admired her grit and wanted to hear everything about her first weeks at school. At the end of her note she asked if she might come down for a visit on the weekend after next—which coincided with the school's homecoming celebrations. Mary explained that she would stay in her father's apartment in St. Paul. She folded the note, put it in the already addressed envelope, and posted it in the mailbox down on the corner.

When Mary and Jeanette arrived home a bit after five o'clock that afternoon, Emma Beach practically pounced on them.

"That nice Aksel Adamsen stopped by. You just missed him. He asked if you'd made up your mind about joining him on his father's sailboat Sunday afternoon. I suggested he invite you, too, Mrs. Harrison. He's very eager to meet you."

Mary and Jeanette exchanged smiles. Aksel had, in fact, met Jeanette, when she was playing the role of Mrs. Davidson's peevish serving maid.

"I would *love* to go sailing," Jeanette said. "Daniel and I had a little skiff that we took out almost every weekend in the summer. I miss it so much." Her look suddenly went very, very far away.

Jeanette's recollection caught Mary off guard. She sometimes forgot that her cousin had once had a great love. By rights, she ought to have a husband and, by now, two or three children—a life far better, no doubt, than serving at the pleasure of a millionaire and his whimsical daughter.

Mary loved sailing, too. She and Jim had spent years, unsuccessfully, trying to persuade their father to buy a little sloop or something of the sort. Without fail, he retorted that the only kind of boats he'd invest money in were iron ore and lumber steamers. What point, he huffed, is a boat that didn't make money?

"That does sound delightful," Mary said. "I'll give him a call after dinner."

"And there's this, as well," Emma said, handing Mary a little yellow telegram envelope.

Mary tore it open and quickly read the message inside. "From Tena, and I quote: 'Your father to arrive this weekend can see the storm clouds and hear the thunder hoping to honeymoon in Egypt. Love Tena.'"

"Your aunt is nothing if not plucky," Emma drolly observed as she left the two of them standing there.

After a light supper and some time perfecting her Haydn on the Chickering grand, Mary said goodnight. She was quite exhausted from all her tramping around. Shoe leather, indeed. Cozy in her room, she crawled into bed and started reading Fergus Hume's latest novel, *The Turnpike House*. A few minutes later, her eyes fluttered shut and she didn't even hear the book fall onto the floor.

She felt fully revived at breakfast the next morning, though Jeanette had already eaten and was back up in her room. As Mary spread butter on her toast, she glanced at the headlines in the copy of the *Duluth Herald* that Emma had left on the table. Normally, John MacDougall would be hogging the paper, but with him out east, Mary had the world's headlines all to herself.

As she munched away, she scanned the top of the front page. A bank robbed. The city council debates bonding for a new bridge. President Roosevelt considers action in the long-running United Mine Workers coal strike.

Brushing the crumbs off her fingers, she turned the front page over to look at the bottom half and saw a small headline over a brief item. She gasped, feeling a jolt of electricity run up her spine.

Body of Deposed Ostovian Prince Found in St. Louis Bay

Chapter X

Mary read the little article six times, afraid of missing some key point, then pushed the newspaper aside.

Now the puzzle pieces were starting to come together. Mrs. Ivey's story of a body washing ashore in St. Louis Bay. Detective Sauer's hint of an international incident. The distress in the Ostovian community. The interviews conducted by the police among those recent immigrants. The photograph of the dead boy in the Petrescus' shop.

Mary firmly believed she could be of some help, if only the police would let her get involved. She quickly scribbled a note to Detective Sauer before she left home.

Mary knew all too well she was *persona non grata* at Duluth police headquarters. So, as she dropped off her note, she hoped the scarf she was wearing and her pronouncedly slouching posture would mask her identity. No one, it seemed, paid her any attention—the desk sergeant didn't even look at her as he took the envelope.

When she finally arrived at the office, Jiggs Nyberg was leaning jauntily against the doorjamb.

"You told me to be here at nine sharp, and I been waiting for you. No one home, when I arrived."

As Mary unlocked the door, she wondered where Jeanette had gotten to. Jiggs swaggered in before her, taking off his cap as he did. Mary sat down behind Jeanette's desk and Jiggs took the seat opposite

"Well," she said, "I have good news and I have bad news."

"What's that mean?"

"The good news is that the thief sold your watch at a pawnshop in the West End."

Jiggs's face lit up. "Did you tell 'em Beansie stole it and that I'm the rightful owner?"

"Yes, I did, and they felt awful about that. Unfortunately, the watch was sold the day it was brought in, to a collector whose name they didn't know. I'm planning to visit every jewelry store in town to track him down."

Jiggs deflated. "The fellow'll say he bought the thing fair and square, and want his money back and..." He gave Mary a desperate look. "...*I can't afford to pay him.* And I suppose you'll want more money, too."

Mary felt a rush of pity for the motherless kid. "Don't you worry about it, Jiggs. I mean to persuade the gentleman to do the right thing, and get the watch back at *no* extra cost to you." She tilted her head. "As far as my expenses go, there may be a way for you to pay me in kind."

"Huh?" Jiggs scratched his head.

"I'm in need of a reliable runner, a messenger. You do errands for me when I need them, and I'll deduct your pay from my bill. After we're square, I'll pay you fifty cents per errand in the downtown area. More, if you have to go further."

Jiggs sat up straight, eyes bright and eager. "I can do that. I know this town like the back of my hand. I been *everywhere.*"

"We'll give it a try for a few weeks and see how it goes. Now here is your first job." She handed him an envelope.

He looked down at it. "Mr. Edmond Roy," he read. "Oddfellows Hall on Lake Avenue. Sure, I know the place. They had a free Thanksgiving dinner there last year—awful good grub. As much as you could eat. Turkey, ham, gravy, taters, cranberries, rutabagas, bread rolls…"

But Mary's thoughts were not on Thanksgiving feasts. She just hoped Edmond wouldn't be too disappointed that she was canceling their date on Saturday. With any luck, though, she would see him the next weekend, if Lillian Burns agreed to the plan Mary had suggested in her letter.

Jiggs stood and put his cap back on. "I'll get this delivered right away, miss." He ran out the door, practically knocking over Detective Sauer, who had just arrived.

"Watch it, boy," the policeman growled down the hallway at Jiggs's receding footsteps. He came in and glared at Mary.

"What are you doing letting a street ruffian like that in your office? Look away, and you'll have that fancy new type-writer walk right out the door."

Mary smiled. "Actually, Detective Sauer, he's one of our first clients. We're trying to recover a valuable timepiece for him that got stolen."

"A waste of time, if you ask me," the detective huffed. "Now you left a message saying you have something to tell me about this morning's newspaper headline. Perhaps some insights on the bridge bonding issue before the city council?"

"Very funny." Mary sat down again and gave him a Cheshire cat smile. "No, I meant another headline a bit lower on the page. The one about the Ostovian prince who drowned in St. Louis Bay. Prince Nicolae Floria."

The detective sat down and made a sound that was some-where between a groan and a sigh.

"What's that, Detective Sauer?" Mary cupped a hand to an ear.

He narrowed his eyes. "I distinctly told you not to go sticking your nose in where it doesn't belong. But why do I think you've already ignored my advice?"

Mary knew better than to deny it. She held out her hands,

palms up. "Here I am, ready to offer you the benefit of my network of contacts in the Ostovian community. The community in which you have been making serious inquiries." She failed to mention that her network of contacts was limited to a priest's wife, a shoemaker, and a baker.

The detective leaned back in his chair. "Thank you for your generous offer, but your assistance won't be required. You'll be pleased to know that the coroner and the chief of police consider it an open-and-shut case. No signs of foul play, no signs of a struggle, they tell us. A simple drowning. It's believed that he fell into the water from a boat that came up lake from Cleveland or Buffalo. The Ostovian mission in Washington and the State Department have accepted that conclusion."

"Who found the boy and how was he identified?" Mary asked.

"Doesn't hurt to tell you, I suppose. But don't blab it about."

Mary nodded.

"A worker at the big lumber mill spotted the body washed up on a sandy patch of shore. When the coroner was examining it, he felt a lump in the hem of the boy's jacket. Something sewn in. He cut open the seam."

Mary's eyes widened. "And what was it?"

"A heavy gold ring. A signet ring with rubies on the upper shanks and an eagle crest on the bezel, in relief."

"Oh my word! Not something an ordinary boy should have."

The detective nodded. "To say the least. We were stumped at first. But someone had the bright idea of taking it to Mr. Bernstein, the jeweler on Superior Street. He had a reference book and identified it as the signet ring of the Floria family. The dynasty that's ruled Ostovia for nearly two hundred years."

"A matter of international implications indeed! So you must have contacted the State Department immediately."

"Well, actually, no. We didn't want to take that action based solely on the ring. For all we knew, the victim might have stolen it from the real prince. That's when we contacted Father Petrescu, one of the leaders of the Ostovians in Duluth. He had been acquainted with Nicolae's father, Prince Anton, and knew what the boy looked like. He identified the drowned lad. We photographed his face in the morgue and wired it to the State Department, which confirmed our findings."

Mary could only shake her head in wonderment. "Well, this is certainly the most significant case I've ever been involved in."

The detective raised his eyebrows. "Pardon me, but this case is closed and you were *never* involved in it." He stood and put on his hat. "Now if you'll excuse me, I have to get back to some real police work."

As the detective reached for the door, it swung open and the knob rapped him sharply on the knuckles. Jeanette came in, but stopped in her tracks when she saw him. "Goodness," she said, "you gave me quite a start."

The detective stared at her a few seconds. "You ought to be more careful, ma'am, bursting into a room like that. You could knock someone off his pins." He turned back to Mary. "Remember, stay out of this Ostovian business."

Rubbing his knuckles he brushed brusquely past Jeanette and out the door, without another word.

Jeanette blinked at the closed door, then back at Mary. "I'll say it again. That man does *not* like me. I can't imagine what I might have done to offend him."

"Oh, you're just imagining things," Mary said, still occupying Jeanette's chair. She wasn't about to say why the detective came across a bit wary. Best to let things play out, *if* they played out. But she somehow doubted that Detective Sauer would overcome his innate reticence.

"And why did he say 'stay out of this Ostovian business'?"

Mary sighed. "I guess I just got overly curious about the prince's death."

"That poor boy. What a horrible thing." Then Jeanette cocked her head. "What do you mean, you got overly curious? For heaven's sake, Mary, you weren't trying to involve yourself in the case, were you?"

Mary rolled her eyes. "Don't be silly. What could I contribute to an international matter like that? By the way, where were you?"

"Well, I just popped next door to the clock repair shop, to ask Mr. Callahan if he knew any watch collectors. He doesn't, but it turns out he grew up in St. Louis. So we had a good talk about things back home. I do so enjoy getting to know my business neighbors."

Mary stood. "Speaking of timepieces, I need to visit Mr. Bernstein, the jeweler. I'm going to see if he knows of any watch collectors in town. Now that you're back, you can take care of office matters."

Jeanette stepped around the desk and plopped down in her chair. "Well, that's just the problem. There aren't any office matters to handle. I've done everything that needs doing. No bills to pay. No shelves to dust. Nothing." She sighed. "I know we've only been operating for just a few days, but unless our business triples, I'll be reduced to sitting here reading the dictionary. Unless…"

Mary blinked at her. "Yes?"

"Well, I have a notion. I could go around to the other businesses in the building, and nearby, and see if they need any typing or stenography. Just what I used to do when I had my own firm."

Mary had never considered starting a subsidiary of Moody Investigations, but she instantly recognized it for a good idea. Not that she needed the income. It was just that anything that kept Jeanette busy and happy had to be a welcome development.

"A capital idea, Jeanette. If you can fill in the gaps in your schedule and bring in some extra income, go to it, cousin."

🌾 🌾 🌾

Shmuel Bernstein tugged at his graying beard, then tapped the brim of his black fedora, regarding Mary intensely. All around were display cases filled with rings and necklaces and tiaras and timepieces, and on the shelves handsome mantle and table clocks. Just to her left, being helped by one of his assistants, a young couple was selecting their wedding bands, making constant goo-goo eyes at one another.

"A collector of pocket watches," he said slowly, pondering Mary's question. "Tall, with a light colored beard. Wears pinch-nose glasses. Let me think. We sell a lot of watches to a lot of people, some of them old and very special watches. Let me think."

He was still thinking when his assistant—a much younger bearded man, also in a black fedora—sidled up and whispered in his ear. Mr. Bernstein's face brightened.

"Ah, yes, Hirschel is right. Mr. Osgood. A shipping agent who's bought several fine timepieces from us. A Breguet and a Patek Phillipe. A Blancpain." He turned to his assistant. "Do we have his address?"

His lovey-dovey young customers still deep in discussion, the assistant ran off and returned a moment later with a scrap of paper, which he handed to Mary. "Thaddeus Osgood," it read, "229 West Superior Street, Number 414." The Duluth National Bank Building.

"Thank you, Mr. Bernstein. Much appreciated. And there was one other thing I wanted to ask you about."

"Yes, Miss MacDougall?"

"I understand that recently a very special piece of jewelry was brought to you for identification. A signet ring with rubies."

The jeweler's relaxed demeanor vanished and he leaned toward her over the glass-topped counter. "How do you know about that? It's supposed to be quite, quite secret."

Mary was tempted to blame the proverbial little bird, but didn't. "Well, I heard a rumor and I was wondering how difficult it would be to make an exact replica of the ring. A close enough copy to fool someone as expert as yourself."

Mr. Bernstein looked amused. "It would be possible, but highly improbable. I would stake my professional reputation on what I told the police. The ring was made in the early eighteenth century, and, from its wear, looks it. It's unquestionably the historic seal of the Prince of Ostovia." The jeweler crossed his arms. "But how the prince and his ring ended up in Duluth, I cannot even imagine."

Chapter XI

At ten-thirty Saturday morning, Mary and Jeanette stood on the broad front porch of a two-storey brick house on Wallace Avenue. The door opened even before they knocked, revealing a slender man in a black suit with black hair parted neatly in the middle. It showed no signs of gray, though Jeanette estimated Quentin Pettyjohn to be fifty or so. She suspected he relied on Dr. Rose's hair dye, or something like it, to keep his mane so dark.

Blinking out into the light, he said, "Mrs. Harrison! So good to see you again. And this must be Miss MacDougall. Welcome, welcome. Please come in. I am *delighted* to help you in any way that I can. Our cat club's been knocked for a loop, I can tell you. I miss my dear Bastet something fierce. My only cat, you know."

A few minutes later, the two were settled on Mr. Pettyjohn's sitting room sofa, each cradling a cup of tea. The walls around them were decorated with framed papyrus artwork in the manner of ancient Egyptian painting, with their hieroglyphics and stylized human figures.

"I think I understand why you named your cat Bastet," Mary said. "She was the Egyptian goddess of cats."

"And still is," Mr. Pettyjohn replied. "Yes, I must confess, since a boy, I've been fascinated by all things Egyptian. The history of the pharaohs and their gods. Their military conquests and social innovations. The most wonderful art and architecture in the world, if you ask me. I have a collection of nearly three hundred stereopticon slides of Egypt. My library…" He pointed to a packed bookshelf that nearly filled one of the walls. "…is full of volumes on Egyptian subjects. So, when I had the opportunity five years ago to obtain a real Egyptian Mau—well, I had to have her."

"My aunt tells me she may be taking her honeymoon in Egypt," Mary noted. "That is, unless my father persuades her to throw over her fiancé." She winked at Jeanette.

Mr. Pettyjohn nearly levitated from his chair. "I am *green* with envy, Miss MacDougall. I've never been there myself, though I hope to go some day. After Mother's finally gone on to a higher plane."

As if on cue, from another plane somewhere in the house, there came a resonant *tap-tap-tapping* on hardwood and a querulous, ancient voice called out, "Quentin, Quentin?"

He made a quick, deep sigh and rose to his feet. "Mother," he bellowed, striding out of the sitting room, "we have guests. Would you like to meet them?"

He returned in a moment with a white-haired woman all in black, holding a cane in one hand. Her face lit up when she saw Mary and Jeanette sitting on the blue-upholstered sofa. "Oh my," she said, a little giddily. "Company!"

Introductions were made. Mr. Pettyjohn installed the old lady in the rocking chair, and sat in the armchair next to her.

"Mr. Pettyjohn and I enjoy callers so much," she said in a high, creaky voice, "especially young people. Such a shame that my husband is off at work. He would have loved to meet you."

Quentin looked at his two guests and shook his head, mouthing the word *no*. "Mother's a bit forgetful," he whispered, reaching over to pat her hand. "Father passed a good ten years ago."

Over the course of the next twenty minutes, Mary posed a number of questions about Bastet's disappearance, which had occurred in much the same circumstances as the others. Cat mysteriously vanishes in the night—nowhere to be found. Jeanette did her best to chip in with a couple of trivial queries, but clearly she had a lot to learn about the art of interviewing subjects.

Quentin agreed with Mrs. Fesler that Bastet was a bit of a wanderer, but he was quite certain she had been safely ensconced in the house that evening. In the end, his answers shed no more light on the affair than Mrs. Fesler's and Mrs. Sternberg's. The missing cats, in all probability, could be scattered to the winds, or worse.

Taking their leave of the Pettyjohns, Mary and Jeanette went outside, where Bill had been waiting for them in the MacDougall carriage.

"I like the man," Jeanette said as they drove away. "A bit eccentric, perhaps, but very hospitable. And so solicitous of his mother."

After a leisurely lunch back home, they climbed into the carriage and set out again. Their destination this time was a shabby clapboard house in the 1400 block of East Fifth Street, where Miss Fern Campbell lived with her housemates.

The schoolteacher met them at the door holding a feather duster. "Oh, I do apologize, but this is my weekend to clean house and I just lost track of time." She ushered them in, laying down the duster and removing her apron. "Three of us share the rent, you see, all of us teachers. And we take turns cleaning."

"Sounds like a most equitable arrangement," Mary observed, as they went into the parlor.

"Yes, well, I'm afraid some of us aren't quite as diligent

with the broom as we should be. But you didn't come here to talk about housework. May I get you some tea or coffee?"

"No, thank you," Jeanette answered. "We've just had lunch. We simply want to ask a few questions about your poor cat, then we'll be out of your hair. First, just tell us the basic facts of what happened."

"Romeo isn't inclined to run away, like Mr. Pettyjohn's Bastet," Miss Campbell began. "Sometimes I just put him in the front yard, which, as you have seen, is fenced. He can loll in the sun, chase a mouse, do whatever he wants. He's never once bolted. The evening of the twenty-fifth, I was out for my meeting, and no one else was at home. It was about eleven when I got back, only to discover that Romeo was gone. I found a window ajar, wide enough for a person to slip in through, or Romeo to slip out of. Eliza and Millie both swear they didn't leave it open."

At that point, the back door slammed and a loud "Hullo!" echoed through the house.

"Oh, that's Eliza," Miss Campbell laughed. "Eliza Kozlow. One of the housemates. She's been out scouring the woods for specimens." Turning her head, she yelled, "We're in here, Eliza."

A moment later, a rosy-cheeked, strawberry blonde strode into the room in stocking feet, holding a jar full of squirming insects. "Oh, I didn't know you had company," she apologized, upon spying Mary and Jeanette. Her gray wool skirt was dampened about the hem.

"Please join us," Miss Campbell said. "And would you mind putting your creepy-crawlies somewhere?"

"Five different species of beetles," the excited educator boasted as she set the jar down on a side table.

"We've good reason to call Eliza 'the Professor,'" Miss Campbell joked. "Her pupils love her nature lessons—bugs, rocks, twigs, and all."

"I'm more of a geologist than an entomologist," Miss Kozlow explained. "I positively adore minerals."

"Quite the rock collection she has."

"Where do you two teach?" Jeanette asked.

"We're both at Lester Park Elementary," Miss Campbell said. "I've taught there five years, but Eliza just started last winter when poor Miss Hokansson took ill."

"I spent my first two years at a country school on the Iron Range," Miss Kozlow recounted. "I can tell you, compared to that one-room shack, Lester Park's a palace. I had nine students in six grades, not enough books and supplies, and a semi-tame crow that often attended lessons. I do believe he was smarter than most of the children." She laughed.

Jeanette made a face. "A crow? Aren't they dirty and disease-ridden?"

"No, no, not at all. They preen themselves a lot and they're quite clever. I called him Ebony. Though he might have been a she. Hard to tell with crows. Extremely bright. An exceptional representative of *Corvus brachyrhynchos*. When the weather was warm enough, I opened a window and let him perch on the sill. He particularly enjoyed it when I played the piano and the youngsters sang. We fed him little bits and pieces."

"In addition to being a scientist, Eliza's a terrific sight reader on the piano," Miss Campbell said. "She can play just about anything you put in front of her."

Mary suddenly perked up, almost bouncing on her feet. "So, you're a pianist, Miss Kozlow."

"I have some ability, I suppose."

"Favorite composers for the keyboard?"

"I particularly fancy Bach, Chopin, Brahms."

"Well, this may be your lucky day. I have a pair of tickets to the Żeleński recital at the Lyceum this coming Thursday. It turns out I don't need them. And on the program are Brahms's First Sonata and some Chopin Nocturnes. If you two would be interested…"

The two teachers looked at each other in amazement.

"Would we ever!" Miss Kozlow exclaimed.

"This is *wonderful*," Miss Campbell said. "How can we ever thank you?"

Leaving the two excited teachers to plan for their evening at the concert hall, Mary and Jeanette once more joined Bill in the carriage and made for the big stone house on Superior Street.

"I really don't see how we have any chance of recovering those cats after so much time has passed," Jeanette said. "Do you think it's too late to place queries in the papers? And offer rewards?"

"Not a bad idea," Mary replied. "But I'm more convinced than ever that we'll find our answers in the application of good old shoe leather. And by that I mean surveying neighborhoods and talking to anyone who'll answer our questions."

❦ ❦ ❦

When she laid eyes on the sailboat, Jeanette's breath caught.

Aksel Adamsen's father kept his ketch moored not far from the shipping canal between Lake Superior and St. Louis Bay. It was a handsome mahogany-hulled vessel far grander than anything she had ever sailed on. If she should ever happen to get rich—an unlikely occurrence—something like this would be high on her shopping list.

As she stepped onto the gangplank, Aksel Adamsen gave her a very odd look. "Umm," he said with furrowed brow, "aren't you Mrs. Davidson's serving maid?"

Jeanette laughed. "Briefly. I was working undercover for Mary."

"I needed a secret agent to gather intelligence," Mary said, coming up behind her. "We had to be extra sneaky to catch the culprit. Aksel, this is my cousin, Jeanette Harrison."

That sunny Sunday afternoon the lake was in a temperate mood, with waves at no more than a foot. They went up the shore about twenty miles, then swung south and around, farther into the vastness of the inland sea—the craggy, piney shore still visible, but distant.

After Aksel piloted the ketch out the shipping canal onto Lake Superior, he left the sailing to his three friends. Then he joined Jeanette and Mary back by the steersman, sipping lemonade and eating chicken sandwiches. The wind blew a little cool, but shawls were available.

Jeanette was positively in heaven. It was the most wonderful time she had had since well before those confidence tricksters swindled her back in St. Louis. For a few hours she forgot about all her problems, past and present. And she particularly enjoyed watching Mary and Aksel exchange playful banter. They'd known each other since childhood and Mary had a certain interest in him—or so it seemed to Jeanette.

Aksel—an intelligent, nice-looking fellow with a good career ahead of him—clearly would make a far better match for the girl than the talented but impecunious Mr. Roy. Jeanette understood how the handsome, carefree artist would appeal to Mary's girlish romanticism. He gave her a glimpse of a seductive life she had never experienced. But Aksel promised stability and a happy, contented domesticity.

If Jeanette had to choose between the two of them, she knew which one she would pick.

Chapter XII

The next morning, Mary could tell that Jeanette was still savoring the afterglow of their Sunday afternoon voyage.

She had been smiling nonstop since breakfast and had a pronounced spring in her step when they set out to catch the streetcar downtown. And now, sitting at her desk in the outer office, she was humming "In the Good Old Summertime," a popular ditty that seemed rather silly and treacly. For her part, Mary was still tickled at her little scheme involving the two teachers and the piano recital. It might prove a very good use for two unneeded concert tickets.

The humming stopped in mid-chorus. Mary looked up from her magazine to see Jeanette standing at her door. "I've been thinking that we need some sort of system for keeping track of our case notes," she observed.

Mary raised her eyebrows. "For all two cases?"

"Three, if you count the napkin ring caper. And you won't be laughing if we have fifty cases and you can't find the one you need."

Mary shrugged. "I suppose so."

"So here's what I suggest. I'll type our handwritten notes on my poor, underused Remington, and date them and file them. I'll start with the Fesler, Sternberg, Pettyjohn, and Campbell notes. Also, I'll make a master directory of cases, and cross-reference them by client name and date. How does that sound?"

Very businesslike, thought Mary, and not a bad idea, considering how readily she tended to mislay things. "Excellent, Jeanette. Please do forge ahead."

"And right now," Jeanette continued, "I intend to run over to the newspaper and place notices about the lost cats. Then to the printer for a flyer offering my typing and stenography services. I figure I'll start handing them out here in the building and in the offices across the street."

Mary smiled at Jeanette's newfound zeal. "Would you mind taking a little dictation before you go? I need to get my letter in the mail to Mr. Osgood."

"Of course, of course," Jeanette said, looking delighted to have such a busy morning stretching out in front of her. She scurried out for her notebook and pencil, then sat in the chair in front of Mary.

"Umm," Mary began, "Dear Mr. Osgood. I was given your name by Mr. Bernstein of Bernstein Jewelry, who confirmed that you are a noted collector of timepieces. Our detective agency, Moody Investigations, is looking into the matter of a stolen Linderoth pocket watch. I have reason to believe that you might have recently purchased said timepiece, in perfectly good faith, at Rossi Pawn in the West End. I represent its lawful owner and, if you do so possess the watch, would like to meet with you to discuss terms for returning it to him. Please contact me by letter or telephone so that we may arrange a meeting. Thank you for your consideration. Sincerely yours, Miss Mary MacDougall." She paused for a breath. "How does that sound, Jeanette?"

"Very diplomatic. You make a point of not accusing him of any impropriety."

"Well, I'm sure the man is totally innocent. No reason to put him on the spot."

"The printer's right around the corner from the Duluth National Bank. I'll type this up right away and drop it off at Mr. Osgood's office."

Twenty minutes later, letter tucked into her bag, Jeanette said goodbye and marched briskly out into the hallway, resuming her rendition of "In the Good Old Summertime"—which Mary was glad to hear the last of. It wasn't long before someone rapped on the door and came in.

Mary stepped out of her office to greet the visitor—a petite woman of about forty. Her thick brown hair was held up by ivory combs beneath a sort of stylish derby hat. She clutched a black leather bag in front of her. She had attractive amber eyes and a comely heart-shaped face.

"Do I have the pleasure of addressing Miss Moody?" she asked.

"No," Mary answered. "I'm Miss Mary MacDougall and I work here. How may I help you? Mrs....?"

"Timmons, Mrs. Loretta Timmons. I saw your advertisement."

"Come in, please, and sit." Mary gestured toward the inner office. "Now what can I do for you?" she asked, as soon as the woman was settled.

"It's about my daughter, Lorna."

"She's run away, or is in some kind of trouble?"

"No, she's fine and still at home. She's not in any trouble—yet. And that's how I hope things remain. But I'm afraid there may be some opportunity for misadventure and I'd like you to help find out about the man who'd be the cause of it."

"How old is Lorna?"

"Seventeen. My only child. And I'm a widow. Fortunately, my husband left us with some resources—enough to keep a roof over our heads and food in the pot, but not much more."

The daughter was only two years younger than Mary, but she wasn't about to confess the similarity in age. "Tell me about her potential for trouble and about this man."

"It's straightforward enough," Mrs. Timmons said. "My daughter's a singer. A soprano, and a good one, too. That's not just motherly pride. She's taken most of the soprano solos at church since she was fourteen. She's been in several operas staged at the Lyceum. Even had a nice role in *The Mikado* last year. Peep-bo. She sang four German songs at the Ladies Guild concert last spring."

That jogged Mary's memory. "I went to that recital. Schubert, was it?"

Mrs. Timmons nodded. "Suffice it to say, she has the potential of a professional career. And she's fanatically devoted to pursuing it. She dreams of some day singing at the Metropolitan Opera."

"Ambitious, as well as talented."

"And I support her to the best of my ability. But as for the necessary next step—sending her to study in New York City— well, I simply cannot afford it. That is where Mr. Ranko Kovac comes in. He's a manager and a former opera singer himself. He has offered to put together a half scholarship for Lorna, so to speak, with funds from wealthy music lovers whom he knows. We have to make up the rest. She would spend part of her time matriculating at the Madison Academy of Music, and part of her time studying with a highly experienced singing coach. She would have chances throughout the season to perform before influential people, and perhaps appear in operatic choruses."

"Sounds like a rare opportunity. But because you're here, you clearly have misgivings. You think, perhaps, that Mr. Kovac may not be entirely on the up-and-up?"

The woman wrinkled her brow. "I have no way of knowing. He came to town, heard Lorna sing, and here we are. He gave references, but no one local. He's quite charming, actually, and persuasive, and I think my girl has a bit of a crush on him. Miss MacDougall, I need to know if he's an honest, upright advocate for young singers before I entrust my daughter to him. You understand my apprehension, I'm sure."

Mary nodded. Older men taking advantage of younger women was always a concern. And white slavers were known to operate in great cities, particularly New York and San Francisco.

"I'm certainly not letting her waltz off to New York City until I have proof of his character. But if I forbid her to go, without *very* good reason, she'll make my life a pure misery."

Mary understood perfectly how a daughter could torment a parent. It wasn't too long along she was doing just that to her father. Come to think of it, she was still doing it.

"Is Mr. Kovac here in Duluth?"

"No, he's in Chicago at the moment."

"How long do you have before you need to give him an answer?"

"Only a few days, I'm afraid. He says he has another young soprano he's considering, down in Minneapolis. If we don't accept, he'll offer the contract to her next week."

"Not a lot of time. I can't promise results, New York City being quite a ways beyond Duluth street car lines. But there's one thing I can do in short order." Mary opened a desk drawer, and took out her notebook and pencil. "Now, tell me everything you know about this Mr. Kovac."

As soon as Mrs. Timmons left, Mary pulled out a sheet of blank paper and began to write a brief note to her friend Josie, whom she had met late last year. Josephine Borrell, as she was known professionally, was a prominent mezzo-soprano, a Welshwoman who lived in Manhattan and toured the world.

She owed Mary a favor.

When she finished her little missive, Mary left a message on Jeanette's desk, telling her that she needed to run her new hankies to the embroiderer for monograms and would return by mid-afternoon. She also wrote that a new case had walked in the door. Then, grabbing the gray striped cardboard box she'd brought to the office that morning, she set off.

First stop, the Western Union office. The clerk took her handwritten note and wrote it down in block letters, passing it on to the telegrapher on duty. Next stop was the restaurant in the Panton & White Glass Block Store, for a quick bite. Finally, she hopped on the westbound streetcar and soon found herself back at the Petrescus' shop in the West End.

Mary really didn't really need any frippery embroidered on her handkerchiefs. But it gave her a solid pretext to visit the Petrescus' shop and ask a few subtle questions about poor Prince Nicolae. Despite Detective Sauer's admonitions to keep away from the Ostovian case, she might be able to turn up a useful clue or two for him.

This time the shop was open, but Mrs. Petrescu was busy helping another lady. Rather than cool her heels in the shop, Mary went next door.

Mrs. Luca was behind the counter and greeted her warmly. "Ah, Miss MacDougall. I told Mrs. Petrescu about this charming young lady who came into the bakery a few days ago, and she said, 'That must be Miss MacDougall.' I have to tell you, I finished *Little Women*." She put her hand over her heart. "When Beth passed away, I cried. The death of young people, it is so terribly sad. But I am happy that Jo married the professor. I think they will have a good life together."

Mary smiled at the woman's enthusiasm, remembering her own reaction to the March family saga. She was much younger then, and wondered if the book would elicit the same emotions at the ripe old age of nineteen.

"I'm so glad you enjoyed it," she said. "Now I wonder if you have any of those sweet cheese pastries today. I'd like one of them to take with me, and something with chocolate, for my cousin."

Mrs. Luca pulled a dark chocolate tart out of the case and cut a generous slice. She reached below the counter for a small box and put the two treats into it with tissue. "I think your cousin will like my tart. It is very popular."

"I'm not surprised. You're an excellent baker. But it must be arduous, getting up in the middle of the night and baking for hours. Do you work alone?"

"No, Teodor Bogdan helps me in the early morning. His nephew Radu is apprenticing next door with Father Petrescu."

"I was so saddened to read about the death of Prince Nicolae," Mary said, as she dug into her purse for some coins. "I imagine it caused a lot of distress among Duluth's Ostovians."

The baker closed up the box and put it on the glass case. "More than you can ever know. As if all our hearts had been cut out."

Mary handed her two quarters. "Do you have any idea how he ended up in Duluth? Such an odd place to go to ground."

The woman gave a bitter laugh. "Perhaps he thought no one would look for him in a spot so out-of-the-way. But with assassins after him, he would not have been safe anywhere."

"Poor, poor lad. So young and so innocent."

Mary's sympathetic comment seemed to catch Mrs. Luca off guard. She was quiet for a moment and when she spoke, her voice trembled.

"You and I could not possibly imagine what it must be like looking over your shoulder in every waking instant, wondering if the bullet or the blade or the poison was coming in the next moment. That is the life Nicolae lived these past two years, since his uncle deposed him. A thirteen-year-old boy, fleeing across continents and oceans, only to die so far from home."

"Do you think he drowned accidentally or was murdered?" Mary knew she was being insensitive in the face of the woman's grief, but she couldn't help herself.

"What does it matter?" Mrs. Luca seemed to be fighting back tears. "He is dead and Ostovia has no more future, no more hope."

"But if he was murdered, surely you'd want the culprit brought to justice."

Mrs. Luca looked her square in the eye. "We Ostovians know who is responsible. Nicolae's Uncle Vladislav."

"But where's the proof? Where's the evidence?"

"Miss MacDougall, if you will permit me, may I tell you some history of my homeland?"

"Of course," Mary nodded.

"The people of Ostovia were ill-treated by the ruling family, the Florias, for generations, until Prince Anton succeeded his father. No one expected what he became. Especially the banks and the nobles—most of all his younger brother, Vladislav.

"Anton not only helped the poor, but the working people, as well. He opened schools and insisted every Ostovian learn how to read. He saw to it that the sick and the elderly were tended to. And he taught his son Nicolae to do the same. Anton was a strong, vibrant man, who hiked and climbed mountains. Why would he die of gastritis, of all things? Because Vladislav poisoned him! And Nicolae would have been next."

The woman's accusation sounded almost paranoid. But from her wide reading, Mary knew that black, bloody intrigue was as common as dirt in the depths of eastern Europe.

Her brain swimming with conspiracy notions, she headed

back to Mrs. Petrescu—who had finally dispensed with her other customer.

"Hello, Miss MacDougall," she said with a distracted tone. "But I am afraid you have wasted your trip. I finished your party dress and Madame Zoya has it for you, for the final fitting. She should contact you very soon."

"Fine news indeed," Mary said. "But that's not why I came." She held out the gray-striped cardboard box. "This is why. A dozen linen hankies that I want embroidered with my monogram."

"It would be much cheaper to go to an embroidery shop with a machine, you know."

"Oh, I don't mind paying for your custom work. Some people say they can't tell the difference, but I can."

Mrs. Petrescu gave her an approving nod. "So few people appreciate handwork these days, with all the devices that make things automatically. When I grew up, every girl learned how to use needles and thread." She went over to a small desk in the corner and took an order book from one of the drawers.

"Even wealthy girls," Mary said. "My father once dined at Andrew Carnegie's house in New York City. Mr. Carnegie had all his important guests sign their names on the tablecloth. And Mrs. Carnegie herself would embroider the signatures on permanently."

Mrs. Petrescu actually showed a tiny smile—unusual for her, given her sober demeanor. She opened the order book and began to write. "One dozen linen handkerchiefs with monograms. Your initials, please, Miss MacDougall?"

"M. A. M. Mary Alice MacDougall."

"So the monogram will be M M A. Wait just a moment while I get my samples."

Mary selected a flowing cursive script that was quite elegant and blue silk thread. After Mrs. Petrescu wrote down the details, she stood there, clearly expecting Mary to say goodbye. But Mary had other intentions.

"I've been wondering, Mrs. Petrescu, about that photo you have in your shoe workshop," she said with a certain tentative delicacy. "The dead boy in his casket."

The expression on Mrs. Petrescu's face hardened. "You should not have gone back there. It is not permitted."

"Is it Prince Nicolae?" Mary persisted.

Mrs. Petrescu crossed her arms and stood stubbornly silent.

"If it isn't the prince, who is it?"

"I cannot say."

"If you can't say, then it couldn't be your own child or some other relation, could it? So, who else could it be but Nicolae?"

The woman sighed deeply and made a dispirited nod.

"How did you come by the photo?"

Mrs. Petrescu looked around, as if making sure no one could eavesdrop. "After the police found the signet ring belonging to the Prince of Ostovia in the dead boy's coat, they came to my husband to identify him. He had known Prince Anton, Nicolae's father. Marius had been a priest at the Cathedral of St. Stephen and sometimes encountered Anton, and became friendly with him. Four or five years ago, after Anton became prince, it was safe for Marius to visit Ostovia, and he met Nicolae. A bright, wonderful boy. I beg you, do not tell anyone, but my husband saw several photos lying near the casket and took one."

"Mrs. Luca believes he was murdered. What do you think?"

Mrs. Petrescu flinched, as if she'd been stabbed. "The police act as if it was murder. They knock on doors and stop people on the street. It makes me so angry. People back in

Ostovia loved Anton. People here loved him. And we had great hopes for Nicolae."

How interesting, Mary thought. Detective Sauer had assured her that it was considered an open-and-shut case. The boy had accidentally drowned. Why, then, had his men treated the Ostovians with such apparent suspicion?

"If the police think someone killed Prince Nicolae, they should look to his Uncle Vladislav." The woman's voice was quaking with anger.

"Might I," Mary finally asked, "look at the picture again?"

Mrs. Petrescu gave a very weary shrug. "Yes, I suppose so. What harm is there, now that he is dead? Go look. I can't bear to see him anymore."

Mary went into the workshop and opened the little shrine. On the other side of the room, she noticed the two young men at the workbench, nudging each other and whispering when they saw her. Did they care about what happened in the old country as much as the Petrescus and Mrs. Luca?

Seeing that pale, young face for the second time, Mary didn't feel quite so desolated. What tweaked her heartstrings, though, was the thought of him being so far from home and so alone.

As she turned to leave, one of the boys came over. "Excuse me, but are you Miss MacDougall?"

"Yes, I am. And you are...?

"I am Dorin Petrescu. And that's Radu Bogdan." He nodded at the other boy, who glanced shyly over his shoulder, and went back to work.

"How did you know who I was?"

"My mother told me she was making lace for the daughter of the wealthiest man in Duluth."

Mary laughed. "Not the wealthiest, but pretty well off."

The boy straightened his spine, as if he were about to address some important personage. "I want to say how much I admire your father. I have read about him in the newspaper. Some day I hope to become a successful businessman, too."

Mary beamed back at him. He certainly had the confidence and charm to do just that. "My father started as an immigrant with just a few coins in his pocket. He'd tell you that if you work hard and treat people well, no one can stop you."

Waiting for the streetcar out on West Third Street a few moments later, Mary ruminated about what Mrs. Petrescu had revealed. She decided that Detective Sauer was not going to get away with trying to snow her. If the case of Prince Nicolae was open-and-shut, why had the police been interviewing members of the Ostovian community?

There was far too much going on here to suggest anything but foul play.

Chapter XIII

"Call for Miss Mary MacDougall," the operator said.

"Miss MacDougall is not in the office," Jeanette enunciated into the receiver on the candlestick telephone, "but I can take the call."

A second or two later a man muttered, "Hullo? Miss MacDougall?"

"No, I'm afraid she's out. I'm Mrs. Harrison, her associate, and I'd be glad to assist you."

A huffing noise came over the line. "Well, all right. This is Thaddeus Osgood and I received a note from Miss MacDougall about a pocket watch I recently purchased." The man had a resonant voice with a distinct New England twang.

"Yes, the Linderoth timepiece that we believe belongs to our client."

For a few long seconds there was a silence. "I am, of course, greatly distressed to learn that the watch may have been stolen. I can assure you I have never knowingly obtained any item that bore the taint of criminality. So, naturally, I would welcome a visit by Miss MacDougall or your good self to discuss how we might resolve this matter."

Jeanette consulted the calendar on her desk. "May Miss MacDougall drop by your office about ten Wednesday morning?"

"That would suit me fine."

As soon as Jeanette hung up the earpiece, she went to Mary's desk and jotted Mr. Osgood onto her calendar for ten o'clock Wednesday morning, at his office in the Duluth National Bank Building. Then she set to work typing up the case notes she and Mary had so far created—good, brainless toil for the hours stretching out before her. As she did so, she was interrupted by the afternoon mail—statements from a stationer and the printing shop. She went back to the scintillating affair of the nicked napkin rings, nearly finishing her account, when a telegraph messenger rushed in with a little yellow envelope for Mary. She took it, gave the boy a dime, and sent him on his way.

Apart from the Western Union banner across the top of the envelope, all it stated was Mary's name and address. Jeanette was briefly tempted to fire up the teapot in order to steam the thing open. But the proprietor of Moody Investigations could well stroll in at any moment and catch her red-handed. Jeanette wondered, for an instant, if it had come from John MacDougall, with news about his wayward sister. But no, he would have wired Mary at home.

It turned out a good thing that Jeanette didn't attempt an illicit steaming, as Mary came through the door just a few minutes later, bearing her bag and a small white box.

"Several items to report," Jeanette said.

Mary put down bag and box, then hung up her coat and hat. "Do tell."

"Mr. Thaddeus Osgood called. Your meeting with him is set for Wednesday morning at ten at his office."

"Excellent," Mary said. "I think I'll bring Jiggs with me. And the other items?"

From behind her desk, Jeanette held up the yellow Western Union envelope. Mary took it, ripped it open, extracted the wire, and quickly scanned it.

"More good news," she exclaimed, smiling broadly. "My friend Lillian has invited me down to Minneapolis this weekend for the university homecoming game. They're playing Beloit. And there'll be a party afterwards at one of the fraternities. Doesn't that sound like fun? And just think—you'll be shed of me for three days. You can do *whatever* you like."

The sweet smile that Jeanette returned disguised a good deal of skepticism. She didn't like the idea of letting her charge run off to the big city unescorted. Was this a genuine, spur-of-the-moment adventure? Or something contrived for some unknown purpose? With Mary, you never could tell. There was only one thing to do.

"Nonsense," Jeanette laughed. "I enjoy your company. I'll come with. Never seen anything of Minneapolis but the train station and I'd like to explore. If there's an extra ticket, I'd love to take in the game. Daniel and I used to go see the Washington University Bears play. We had so much fun at the games."

From her surprised expression, Mary hadn't been expecting that. But she quickly recovered. "Are you quite sure? You'll probably be bored. Wasn't that travel lecture this weekend?"

"Yes, 'Six Weeks on the Yangtze.'" Jeanette shrugged. "I'll read the book instead. I assume you're staying in your father's apartment in St. Paul."

Mary nodded.

"I'll go back to the apartment after the game, and you young people can have your fun. I'll take in the sights, have a walk on the famous Summit Avenue. Don't worry about me."

"Well, if you really want to come…"

"Oh, I do."

"Then I'll get train tickets for the both of us."

"Superb. Now in your note you said we'd picked up another case. Tell me about it."

Mary described her chat with Mrs. Timmons about the musical manager who required a spot of scrutiny. She explained she had sent a telegram to her friend in Manhattan, Josie Borrell. The mezzo-soprano might know something about this fellow. Jeanette took a few notes and created a new file for the case. She placed the folder in the file cabinet and turned back to Mary.

"And how was your visit with the Ostovian embroiderer?"

"She gave me a very good price for my dozen hankies. The script I selected is quite elegant. I couldn't resist asking her about the poor prince. The Ostovians, of course, are quite upset."

Jeanette nodded. "Well, naturally. But is there any reason to think it's something other than a terrible accident?"

"Not according to Detective Sauer," Mary said with a tone of skepticism. "But Mrs. Luca, the baker, seems convinced he was assassinated by his evil uncle."

Jeanette raised her eyebrows. "Well, if the police say it's not murder, I suspect that's the end of the matter. Now, while you were gone, I did these." She held up the street maps she had sketched. One each for the neighborhoods of Mrs. Fesler, Mr. Pettyjohn, Miss Campbell, and Mrs. Sternberg.

"Ah." Mary nodded approvingly. "Our search plans for the lost cats."

Jeanette suddenly eyed the white box Mary had brought. "What's in there?"

"Afternoon treats from Mrs. Luca. Including a generous slice of chocolate tart for my right-hand woman."

All thoughts of cats and Ostovians fled Jeanette's head. Chocolate was a pleasure she never denied herself.

"Well then, young lady, let's fire up that electric teapot."

They tramped up and down the streets near Mrs. Fesler's house Tuesday morning— Jeanette on one side, Mary on the other. They knocked on dozens of doors. Sometimes no one answered. Sometimes the person inside took a look at them, and slammed the door without a word. Occasionally someone would snap, "No saleswomen." Sometimes the occupant commiserated over Mrs. Fesler's lost Princess, but knew nothing that could help. A few people recalled seeing the ginger tortoiseshell tabby when Mrs. Fesler had been outside in her yard. But that was months ago.

By mid-morning Jeanette's feet were aching and she was cursing herself for bringing along Mary's heavy German field glasses—in case she spied some feline from afar. The binoculars were bouncing uncomfortably on her chest and giving her a neck ache. When they were done with Mrs. Fesler's search grid—a complete failure—Mary offered to take the optics, but Jeanette stubbornly insisted they were her burden to bear.

As they headed for Mr. Pettyjohn's neighborhood, Mary looked at Jeanette and smiled. "Have you ever read *Don Quixote*?"

Jeanette was briefly flummoxed by her question, then understood. "You refer to tilting with windmills, I presume."

"Precisely. We're trying to accomplish something that's highly improbable. Finding four cats, several weeks lost, in a city of nearly one hundred thousand souls. I am the deluded Don and you are my loyal Sancho Panza."

Jeanette couldn't help laughing. "At least I'm not riding a donkey."

"Nor I the swaybacked Rocinante," Mary returned with a grin.

They trudged down Woodland Avenue for a number of blocks, and by and by came to Wallace Avenue, which they door-knocked their way up and down. Just beyond the Pettyjohn house, they turned a corner and went down to the next street over. They proceeded back north on that street—Mary on the west side, Jeanette on the east.

"Jeanette!" Mary suddenly shouted from the other side of the street.

"What is it?" Jeanette hollered back.

"The field glasses, please."

Jeanette tramped across the packed dirt road. Lifting the strap from her neck, she handed the optics to Mary, who put them up to her eyes, adjusting the focus knob.

"What are you looking at?" Jeanette asked, squinting in the same general direction and seeing nothing.

"Mr. Pettyjohn's place. I can get a view of the back of it, between these two houses."

"So, do you spy anything?"

"Well, he has a stained glass panel in one upstairs window that, it seems, contains a stylized Egyptian image of a cat, sitting in profile. If there were a light behind it, I could see it better. And the window to the left..." Mary gasped. "Oh, my!"

"What? What is it?" Jeanette squinted even harder at the distant window, but it was no good. All she saw was a blur.

"Hey there, you two," said a man's raspy voice, "what's all this?"

The two women twirled to their right, blinking into the face of a policeman who had appeared out of nowhere. He was short and narrow, but looked hard as flint. He had his hands on his hips and he did not look the least bit amused to find them acting suspiciously on his beat.

"Missy, you ain't one of them peepin' Toms, are ya?" He wore a fierce frown.

Jeanette was struck dumb by the outrageous accusation, but quick-witted Mary put the glasses back up to her eyes and scanned some nearby treetops.

"*Corvus brachyrhynchos,*" she announced.

The police officer's eyes narrowed. "Did you just cuss me out?"

Mary lowered the binoculars and shot him a big, friendly smile. "Oh, heavens no, officer. I have nothing but respect for officers of the law. In fact, one of Duluth's finest is a friend of mine. I merely said *Corvus brachyrhynchos.*"

Then Jeanette remembered Miss Kozlow's tale of her semi-tame classroom pet, Ebony. "We're bird watchers," she quickly improvised.

"Right," Mary said. "Bird watchers. Just saw the most re-markable specimen on that roof over there. Gone now, but you should have seen it."

The officer clearly didn't realize she was referring to the common crow. His stubbly lower jaw shifted from side to side, as if he were masticating Mary's explanation like a piece of gristly chicken. He rubbed his chin a bit and said, "Well, okay then. Just don't be peekin' in people's windows when you're lookin' for birds." He nodded and ambled past them, down the street.

Jeanette turned to her cousin. "That was a close call. So what was it you saw over there?"

"Something much more interesting than a crow." Mary pointed to Mr. Pettyjohn's window. "I'm ninety-nine percent sure I saw an Egyptian Mau sitting on the sill." She turned to Jeanette. "I seem to recall Mr. Pettyjohn telling us that Bastet was a Mau—and his *only* cat."

Chapter XIV

On Wednesday morning a little before ten, the atrium of the Duluth National Bank was bustling with activity. There were lines three and four deep at the ornate brass teller cages, and every banker at a desk was consulting with men and women about their financial needs.

Mary hustled through to the elevator lobby off to the side. She arrived to find a portly bank guard wagging a sausage-like finger at poor Jiggs Nyberg.

"But I told you I got a meeting upstairs with a gent called Mr. Osgood," the boy pleaded. "He's got a valuable timepiece of mine."

"And I'm goin' fishin' next weekend with President Roosevelt," the guard snorted. "How could *you* have any business with Mr. Osgood? Let alone a valuable timepiece? Yer just a guttersnipe."

"But he does have an appointment with Mr. Osgood," Mary chimed in, walking up to them. "As do I."

The guard pivoted and peered at her with wide eyes. "Miss MacDougall?"

Mary had a savings account at the bank and she had made small talk with the man on several occasions as she waited in line. He wasn't a bad fellow, but she supposed that poor Jiggs seemed distinctly the wrong sort to him.

"I realize young Mr. Nyberg doesn't look like the typical

habitué of this institution," she said, smiling, "but I'll gladly vouch for him."

The guard seemed rather dubious, but made a single slow nod. "If you say so, Miss MacDougall. He gives you any trouble, just let me know." And he walked back into the main atrium at a slow, majestic pace—casting one withering glance back at Jiggs. The boy sniffed and followed Mary to the waiting elevator. "Fourth floor," she told the operator, and the cage ascended.

As they approached the door of Osgood Shipping, Inc., Mary could tell that Jiggs was nervous. She stopped and faced him. "You know, I can see Mr. Osgood on my own, if you like. You seem a bit uneasy."

He rubbed his neck as if his collar was chafing him. "Just scared this might not work out. You don't think he maybe threw Mama's picture away, do you?"

"I should hope not," Mary replied, having harbored that very same fear. "But we've no way of knowing until we talk to him. And I still think having you along might help to tweak his conscience. That is, if he has one." She patted Jiggs on the shoulder, then rapped three times on the mottled glass door.

"Come in, please," a woman's voice said.

They went into the office and Mary introduced herself, saying that Mr. Osgood was expecting her.

"But who is the boy?" the secretary asked.

"The owner of the item that's under discussion."

She and Jiggs sat and waited for a few minutes, before Mr. Osgood came out of his private office. He was just as Gino Rossi had described him. A lanky, middle-aged gentleman with blond hair and beard. Pince-nez spectacles perched at the tip of his thin, straight nose. After exchanging brief pleasantries with Mary, he turned to Jiggs.

"Is this the young fellow who claims ownership of the

Linderholm timepiece?"

Jiggs looked like he was about to reply with some words he might regret, but Mary shook her head at him: *Be polite*.

"Yes, it is. This is young Mr. Nyberg. A friend of his stole the watch and illicitly sold it to Signor Rossi."

"Some friend," the shipping agent grumbled. "Well, then, come in and we'll talk things over."

They sat down before Mr. Osgood's broad walnut desk. Ensconced in his rolling office chair, fingers tented beneath his chin, he furrowed his eyebrows. "Naturally, I would prefer if Master Nyberg could provide some special knowledge of the item, before we begin to discuss its potential return."

"Meaning some unique identifying mark?" Mary asked.

"Correct."

"That's easy," Jiggs said with a sniff. "Inside the cover's a photograph of my mother." He crossed his arms and stuck out his chin, as if he'd just won a bet.

"All right. And what else?"

For a second or two, Jiggs looked panicked. He thought hard, then his face lit up. "Emil Haglund," he blurted. "My granddad's name. It's engraved on the inside of the cover."

Mr. Osgood's expression softened and he nodded. "I'll return the photograph to you, of course. But let me make you an offer, my young friend. I've already paid thirty dollars for the timepiece. I'm prepared to pay you another thirty for it." He paused and peered intently at Jiggs. "Now just consider. Thirty dollars in your pocket. A *lot* of money. Plus the keepsake of your mother's image. A good deal, I think. What do you say?"

Jiggs looked to Mary, who said, "Your decision."

The boy frowned, then shook his head. "Naw, Mr. Osgood. The money'd be nice, but I want the watch back. Please. It was my granddad's, then my mom's, now it's mine.

It's all I have left of 'em."

"You hardly ever see a Linderoth here in the states," the man said wistfully. "Beautifully made and quite unusual. It was to be one of the showpieces of my collection." He leaned back in his chair. "I'm not sure I can let it go."

"You can't be serious, Mr. Osgood," Mary protested. "That's a rotten thing to do."

"Yes, indeed. A rotten thing to do. But the fact is that I'm out thirty dollars, and I detest wasting money. I didn't get to where I am today by wasting money." He regarded her evenly. "Nor, I'd imagine, did John MacDougall."

"What's John MacDougall got to do with it?" Jiggs asked, a bit confused.

"Oh, didn't you know?" Mr. Osgood said with a tiny smirk. "He's the young lady's father."

Jiggs stared at Mary with wide eyes. "Holy cats! Really?"

"Really," Mary confirmed, amused by his reaction.

Mr. Osgood peered at her. "I have a proposition for you. I will return the Linderoth, at a loss of thirty dollars, if you will do me one little favor. Arrange a meeting for me with your father. Half an hour of his time. That's all. I've tried for years to earn business from the MacDougall companies, without success. I feel if I could speak personally to the man himself, I might make some inroads."

Mary could well imagine her father grumbling something fierce about his daughter taking the liberty of scheduling a business meeting for him. But she was confident he would agree, at least this once, after she explained the situation.

"No guarantees can be made," she stressed firmly, "regarding the outcome."

"Of course not. I don't expect any. I just want to talk with him." He raised his eyebrows. "Do we have a deal?"

"We do." Mary stood and shook Mr. Osgood's hand across

the desk.

Jiggs hopped to his feet. "I'd be obliged if I could have my watch back now."

"Sorry, young man," Mr. Osgood said, "but I don't have it here. Come back this time tomorrow and you can pick it up, along with the photograph."

As they walked out onto the sidewalk in front of the bank building, Jiggs turned to Mary with a look of bafflement. "If you don't mind, Miss MacDougall, could I ask you something personal?"

Mary didn't know quite how to react. What if the little scamp tried to ask her on a date, for heaven's sake? She wouldn't put it past him. "Well, ask away."

"First, thanks for gettin' my watch back. But I don't understand. If you're John MacDougall's daughter, why'd'ya need a job? You could lay about, travel anywhere, eat fancy food all the time, order people around. Does your dad have money troubles, then? You need to chip in or something?"

Mary wanted to laugh, but it was a perfectly fair question. Why would someone with buckets of money decide to open a detective agency?

"Because, Jiggs, lying about and traveling anywhere is so, so, *so* boring. And I don't want to end up just another wife of another rich businessman. I want to do something interesting and make a difference. And what better way to do it than finding lost objects—like valuable Linderoth timepieces and pictures of someone's mother?"

Jiggs had no comeback for all that, but did have another question. "Speaking of finding lost objects, in case he's still around, could you keep an eye peeled for ol' Beansie? I could get together a few more dollars for you, if that's what it'll take."

People were flowing around them out on the sidewalk. A

few shot disapproving glances at this very odd couple blocking their way.

"I'd be happy to, Jiggs. I happen to believe he's almost certainly still in town. He only got ten dollars for the watch. Hardly enough to go touring with, let alone take care of a fancy lady."

"Just ten bucks? It's worth five, ten times that." Jiggs looked disgusted. "Well, anyhow, the thing is I'd like to see him, you know, so I can pop him one in the nose. Then we maybe could be friends again." He readjusted his shabby golf cap and gave her a sad smile. "Beansie's a funny kid, you know. Makes me laugh. I kinda miss him."

Mary figured she wouldn't feel like the job was finished until the suspect was apprehended. "Let's both keep our eyes peeled, Jiggs. We'll track down the scalawag one way or another."

Back at the office Mary dictated a brief letter to Jeanette, to be mailed to Mrs. Fesler. In it she described how certain information had come into her possession that might lead to a successful culmination of the case of the purloined pussycats. But further confirmation would be needed.

Then she put her coat back on and announced she was setting off for her final fitting with Madame Zoya.

"You're not going via the Oddfellows Hall, are you?" The suspicion in Jeanette's voice was transparent.

"Don't be ridiculous," Mary snapped. "I do declare, you have Edmond Roy on the brain!"

As Mary twirled around in front of Madame Zoya's full-length mirror, she couldn't help but think that the Thanksgiving party dress would be an absolute triumph. The pale amber color of the silk brocade nicely complemented her chestnut hair. And the antique-tinted lace, which topped the bodice and shoulders, perfectly framed the low, wide neckline. Mary imagined how her mother's favorite pearl-and-diamond necklace would look draped there.

If only Edmond could see me now, she thought.

She turned back to the dressmaker with a huge smile.

"What can I say? You're an artist *nonpareil.*"

Madame Zoya, standing with her arms crossed, gave a modest little smile and shrugged. "Mademoiselle is too kind. All I seek is to please you, and it gratifies me that I have. And let us not forget, much of the credit must go to Mrs. Petrescu, for her lace. She created those beautiful snowflakes for your gown last Christmas, too, you may recall."

Mary went back into the cramped changing room and put on her blue serge blouse suit—serious, businesslike, just the thing for a lady detective. When she emerged, she handed the gown back to Madame Zoya and arranged for its delivery.

"Madame Zoya," she said, as she pinned on her hat, "you are aware, of course, of the prince's body being found in the bay."

"Naturally. Here in the West End people have been talking about little else."

"What are the Ostovians saying?"

Madame Zoya's face went as dark as the bottom of a thundercloud. "Hardly anyone believes it was an accident. They know perfectly well that Prince Vladislav has had agents hunting for his nephew for nearly two years. They suspect he poisoned the boy's father, Prince Anton, though it has never been proven. Vladislav realizes that the boy could come back some day and depose him. One of my Ostovian friends heard rumors that Nicolae nearly took a bullet in New York City last year, and one of his protectors died. Well, now it seems

Vladislav's men finally caught up with him."

Mary was aghast at the thought. "Assassins on the loose in our city? Who would have thought it possible?"

Chapter XV

It took Mary hours to get to sleep Wednesday night, thinking that Ostovian agents might have stalked and drowned Prince Nicolae right there in Duluth. And when she woke up about seven the next morning, the thought popped right back into her head. That's when she decided that she needed to make another visit to the Petrescus' shop in the West End.

On the long streetcar ride, she pondered all the ramifications. What, if any, danger was there to other members of the Ostovian community? Based on what little Mary knew, Father Petrescu could well be in peril. He had been friendly with Nicolae's father, Prince Anton, which alone might make him a target. And Mary remembered Mrs. Luca, the baker, expressing admiration for Nicolae's father as well.

If, indeed, it was murder, what if someone had witnessed it? Workers or transients who frequented the nearby saloons late at night might have noticed something. Had the police even bothered to canvas more people than the area's Ostovian residents?

Mary was so in the thrall of her detective daydreaming that she very nearly missed her stop out on West Third Street. But she caught the mistake just in time to jump off about half a block from the Petrescus' shop. She consulted her pendant watch. Just a little before nine-fifteen. After a brewery wagon full of barrels trundled by, kicking up dust, she darted across the packed earth of Third Street and hiked down to the shop.

She went in. "Hello," she called. Mrs. Petrescu promptly came out of the open door to the workshop in back, wiping her hands on a blue-striped towel. "Oh, Miss MacDougall. I am afraid I have not even started on your handkerchiefs."

"I didn't think you had," Mary returned. "I stopped by about a couple of other things."

The woman indicated that Mary should have a chair. "Yes, how may I help you?"

"I had my final fitting with Madame Zoya yesterday and I wanted to tell you that your lacework looks splendid. It makes the dress so special. I think people are just going to say 'wow' when they see it."

"Wow?" The woman wrinkled her nose. "What is wow?"

"It means wonderful. Superb. Marvelous."

Mrs. Petrescu smiled. "Thank you so much. Very often I do not hear back from customers and I only know they are happy if they give me more work. So, this makes me feel..." She paused. "...*wow*!"

Mary laughed. "And I'm sure your husband is just as fine a craftsman. He's my second reason for coming today."

Mrs. Petrescu looked puzzled. "You want shoes for your father? Or a brother perhaps? My husband can certainly make him a very fine pair. But he would need to come in to be properly fitted."

"No, no," Mary said. "You see, we have a little cottage on the shore, just north of Two Harbors. And we usually stay there a few weeks in the summer. And I like to go tramping in the woods up behind it. Well, it's rough on ordinary shoes, let me tell you. Nothing I have can properly handle the rocks and roots and mud. So, I want a pair of boots like your husband makes. Like those." She pointed at a low shelf full of men's boots in black and brown. "A sturdy boot."

The woman frowned. "But my husband and Mr. Dimitriu do not make women's shoes. They have no experience in that kind of feminine styling."

"Oh, I don't give a fig about feminine styling," Mary sniffed. "Do they make boots for boys? For teenagers?"

Mrs. Petrescu nodded. "Of course."

"Then why can't they make a boot for me? My foot shouldn't be all that different from a teenager's."

The embroiderer looked dubious. "Let me get my husband." She vanished into the workshop and returned a moment later with him, giving Mary her first look at the cobbler-priest.

He was a handsome man of middle age, with craggy features and a dark, well-trimmed beard and mustache. His full head of salt-and-pepper hair was brushed back, and held firm by some kind of pomade. Around the collar of his black shirt he wore a chain that vanished beneath his smudged, soiled apron—probably holding an orthodox cross.

Mary offered her hand, but the man shook his head and held up his very dirty fingers.

"Father Petrescu, it's good to finally meet you."

"And I am pleased to meet *you*, Miss MacDougall. Here in our little business, we highly value customers like your good self. Now my wife tells me you are interested in a pair of boots in the style of our men's footgear. You like to walk the woods?"

"I do, indeed."

"As do I," the priest said. "And this beautiful place gives so much opportunity to do so, with forest all around us. You can find God out there, in every twig and leaf. A wise man once said, 'In the wildness is the preservation of the world.'"

"Good ol' Thoreau," Mary nodded. "Most apt, Father Petrescu."

"Well," the priest continued, "if you do not mind a lack of

style and fashion, I do not see why we cannot make you some sturdy boots." He turned to his wife. "My dear, ask Dorin to find the leather samples for our best quality boots. And bring blank paper and a pencil."

As they waited, Mary listened to the priest's account of a recent tramp down the banks of the St. Louis River. It was a hike she thought to take some day herself. And it was a hike that took the hiker not far from where the prince's body was found. Perhaps Mary should visit the spot in coming days.

Finally, not one, but two young men came out from the workshop. Dorin Petrescu carried a stack of leather squares, while his fellow apprentice Radu Bogdan followed with paper and pencil.

"Here you go, Papa," Dorin said, handing the leather pieces to his father. He grinned at Mary. "Good morning, Miss MacDougall, I hope you are well."

Father Petrescu frowned at the boys. "It takes two of you to bring me my samples and paper? Both of you, back to work. Those new lasts won't shape themselves."

The priest turned to Mary, shaking his head. "If you will permit me to say so, my son and Radu are at the age where any pretty girl who walks by is a distraction."

Mary smiled as the two young men returned to the workshop. Dorin and Radu were probably not much older than Jiggs and his chums. Yet these two had much brighter futures stretching before them. They were learning a craft that would always be needed. They belonged to a tight-knit community that would protect and support them. She wondered if they realized how lucky they were, in the grand scheme of things.

"Now if you please, miss," the priest said, kneeling in front of her chair, "take off both of your shoes."

Mary did as instructed. He traced outlines of her feet on a big sheet of blank newsprint and used a tape measure to note the dimensions for the custom lasts. He showed her the leather samples one by one, and she selected a heavyweight brown stock. The extra sturdy sole, he promised, would last for many a season of tramping the woods. Mary paid five dollars in advance and had him make her out a receipt. He said he would have the boots done in three to four weeks.

As she put on her black patent Oxfords, Mary figured now was as good a time as any to bring up the touchy topic of the prince.

"In your religious capacity, you must be helping your people cope with the death of Prince Nicolae," she said. "Such a terrible, terrible thing."

He nodded, gathering together his paperwork for Mary's boots. "The boy represented a kind of hope. His father had begun to bring Ostovia to modernity, to liberal ideas, and Nicolae, I am sure, would have continued in that direction."

"Your wife and Mrs. Luca made the same observation. And the present prince is not of the same mind?"

"Prince Vladislav wants a return to the old days of ignorance and greed, when life was hard and cruel for most Ostovians." The priest's face darkened. "Many believe he poisoned his brother, Prince Anton."

"I understand that there are rumors the young prince might have been murdered. By assassins." Mary held her breath, worrying about Father Pestrescu's reaction.

The priest's face reddened. "Why not kill the son, as well? Why be a regent when you can be a prince? Vladislav is a brute, a savage. The only reason the truth is not in the papers is because the American government does not wish to offend him and the bankers who own him. There are hundreds of millions of dollars and pounds and francs and rubles sitting in Ostovian banks. Some say as much as a billion dollars. And Vladislav guards them like the dog he is."

"But if it's murder, it has to be investigated and the culprits found," Mary insisted. "Bankers and billions be damned." At the spur of the moment, she decided to share a confidence with the man. "Father Petrescu, I haven't told your wife, but I'm a consulting detective. I happen to count one of our police detectives as a friend and colleague. And I would so like to get to the bottom of this matter. Perhaps you could help me."

If Mary had just claimed that she sprouted wings every morning and flew up into the clouds, the priest could not have looked more dumbstruck. Then he laughed and shook his head. "You American girls. You are having a bit of fun with me, are you not? A detective, indeed!"

Mary stiffened her back and narrowed her eyes. "No, I am *not* having a bit of fun with you, Father Petrescu. I am quite serious. I've solved several cases and even have an office downtown."

His face took on that look that John MacDougall often cast in her direction: Parental disapprobation. "But this is not a suitable activity for a young lady. Your business is finding a husband and obeying him and giving him many, many children. What else is there for women?"

So much more, Mary thought. *So much more.*

With a deflated goodbye, she walked out of the shop and popped into the bakery. She was hungry and wanted something to nibble on during the streetcar ride back downtown.

"Hello, Miss MacDougall," said Mrs. Luca, limping out from behind the counter. "I am so glad you stopped by. I wanted to tell you about a new discovery of mine. After I returned *Little Women* to the library, one of the ladies there recommended a volume by Miss Emily Dickinson. She takes my breath away. Poems so true and sharp that they almost break my heart."

"She was a dazzling talent, that's for sure," Mary said.

"Hard to believe no one had ever heard of her until just a decade ago. A bit obsessed with the grim reaper, though. But you're right—sharp as a razor's edge."

"I have several favorites so far. 'I'm Nobody! Who are you?' 'I Heard a Fly Buzz When I Died.' 'Because I could not stop for Death.'"

"Speaking of that dismal old fellow with the scythe, I want to apologize for upsetting you last time I visited. I shouldn't have brought up poor Prince Nicolae. Insensitive of me."

Mrs. Luca took Mary's hand in both of hers. "No, it is nothing to worry about. It is fair to wonder what we Ostovians think. We are guests in your city and you have a right to know. Now, how would you like a bite of something and a nice cup of hot cocoa? And you can help me with my reading list. I want to know some American novels I should read."

"I'd love to stay and chat," Mary said. "But I must be going. A little treat for the streetcar ride is all I need. I'll write up a list for you when I have a chance."

❦ ❦ ❦

"So," Mary said, trudging wearily into the office, "anything new?"

Jeanette looked up from her desk. "By our standards, it's been positively bustling."

"Do tell." Mary put her hat and coat on the rack.

"I received a telephone call from a Mrs. Hollister, who is the secretary of a women's organization called the Twentieth Century Club. Maybe you know of it."

"I do," Mary said. "A forward-thinking group of ladies."

"They gather twice a month for discussions of science and technology and literature, and they're creating a scholarship fund for young women."

"Well, who wouldn't approve of that?" Mary said, thinking peevishly of Father Petrescu's antediluvian attitudes.

"And they're about to start on a fund-raising campaign."

"Very nice. I should contribute. But what does that have to do with us? Is someone stealing their napkin rings?"

Jeanette sniffed at Mary's joke. She could be pretty humorless sometimes.

"In fact, they need one hundred typewritten letters by Monday, Tuesday at the latest. To send to potential donors around town. And they saw our typist advertisement in the paper." She shot Mary a regretful look. "And I'm afraid it means…"

"Yes?"

"I'm so sorry, but I won't be able to go to Minneapolis with you. I'll be typing all weekend long. And I had been *so* looking forward to it."

Mary made a pouty face. "Well, that's too bad. I'll miss you. But business is business, isn't it? We'll go together another time. Shop and eat and take in a show or two. So much to see in the Cities."

"And then these came in." Jeanette held up two yellow Western Union envelopes and waved them at Mary. "From your friend Miss Borrell, perhaps?"

Mary snatched them out of her hand, ripped the first open, and read it, then the other—a communiqué in two parts. She put the wires back on the desk. "Mrs. Timmons was smart to be suspicious."

"The fellow's a confidence trickster?"

"According to Josie, Ranko Kovac brings eager singers to New York City, but doesn't provide all he promises. All of them young women, and almost always lookers. After a short spell in a so-called music school, they're found jobs in theatrical choruses and go to parties where rich, married men express interest in their careers. You get the drift. None of them end up at the Metropolitan Opera, shall we say. Josie says a letter's in the mail, with more details."

Jeanette looked appalled. "They're grooming the girls to become *mistresses*?"

"Apparently. I can imagine it might be easy for some of these innocent girls to get seduced into a dissolute life."

Jeanette huffed. "Well, at least we can save Miss Timmons from that fate."

"Perhaps we can do more." She placed a finger on her chin. "Josie says that it's rumored Ranko Kovac may be a criminal using an alias. She suggests Detective Sauer look into the matter. So, how about we write a little message to our friend at police headquarters?"

❦ ❦ ❦

The lobby of the Lyceum Theater was chockablock with concertgoers during the intermission, in all their finery. People chatted and jabbered away beneath the luminous grand chandeliers. Mary had on a stylish maroon evening dress with black trim and Aksel Adamsen looked very sharp in a gray suit and fancy red silk tie. He clearly meant to make a good impression.

The lobby, like the auditorium, glittered with color and splendid detailing that verged on, but didn't quite achieve, baroque ornateness. Mary adored attending shows and concerts here, in the grandest interior in town. Just last holiday season, the Ladies Guild of Duluth—of which Mary was the youngest member—had staged its annual Christmas Gala Musicale on this stage. It was how Mary first made the acquaintance of Miss Josephine Borrell, the Musicale's star attraction.

"Traphagen and Fitzgerald are really fine architects," Aksel said, surveying the decorative filigree of the grand lobby. "A splendid space."

"And the acoustics are superb," Mary replied, scanning the crowd for someone she hoped to see. She focused back on her companion. "Didn't you just love the Haydn sonatas? And the Chopin nocturnes? Lovely. I can hardly wait for the Liszt and Brahms."

As Aksel murmured his agreement, Mary spotted the two people she hoped she would encounter. The next few minutes would tell if her little scheme might hit pay dirt.

"Miss Campbell!" she called, waving her hand. "Miss Kozlow!"

When the two schoolteachers caught sight of her, they waved back, and wended their way through the crowd toward the couple.

"Oh, isn't Maestro Żeleński just splendid?" Eliza Kozlow gushed. "If I could ever play a tenth as well, I'd die happy."

"At affairs like this," Fern Campbell confided, "I often find the people as interesting as the music. I'm always so impressed with the level of culture in Duluth. You'd have to go to New York or Chicago for an event of this quality."

"So pleased you're enjoying it," Mary said. "Now, let me introduce everyone." And she did just that.

"If I may ask, what do you ladies do?" Aksel said.

"We're both of us teachers at Lester Park Elementary," answered Miss Campbell. "And you?"

"I work with my father. He's a general contractor and we subcontract, as well. Not too long ago we finished our part of the new Normal School. And I'm the on-site supervisor for the new Swedenborgian church on Woodland Avenue."

Eliza Kozlow's eyes widened. "Ooh, the new Romanesque church? I've gone by there several times. The stonework is just superb. You must be so proud."

Askel puffed up a little, looking quite pleased with himself. "We're using bluestone from the Hunter's Hill quarry. And I don't think there's another structure in the country built in this style with stone like that."

"I'm wondering," Eliza said, "how exactly do they quarry the bluestone? I believe it's awfully hard rock. Almost seven on the Mohs hardness scale."

Miss Campbell laughed. "There goes the Professor again, with her slates and cherts and gneisses. She can be quite obsessive about her minerals. Once you get her started, she'll talk your ear off."

"Oh, I don't mind one bit," Aksel assured the amateur geologist. "In fact, I could take you over to the quarry this weekend, if you're available. We're free to roam the site and inspect the stone bound for my project."

"You'd do that?" Miss Kozlow's face was glowing. "How about Saturday morning? Afternoon's fine, as well."

"You could come, Mary," Aksel said. "And you, too, Miss Campbell."

Mary made a bogus frown. "I'd love to, I really would. But I'm booked for a visit to Minneapolis. My best friend Lillian Burns—you know her, don't you, Aksel?—she attends the university and she's invited me down for homecoming."

Miss Campbell grimaced, too. "Sorry, wish I could. Going home to visit my folks."

Aksel turned back to Eliza Kozlow. "Well, then, it'll just have to be the two of us. You know, our bluestone is some of the oldest rock on the planet."

"I know, I know," Miss Kozlow enthused. "It's *fascinating* stuff."

Mary glanced at the two of them. They'd make a fine couple. Which was precisely what she had in mind when she promised those tickets to the two teachers.

Chapter XVI

Jeanette briskly typed the words "Very sincerely yours," returned the carriage three times, and then tapped out "Mrs. Reginald Hollister." She pulled the Twentieth Century Club letterhead sheet from the Remington and, with practiced eye, scanned it for mistakes. Perfect. Like the other thirty-nine copies she had already stacked in the empty stationery box. Only one error so far, only one wasted sheet. She figured she would have no trouble finishing the letters and envelopes by the end of the business day on Monday—though it meant she was spending Saturday in the office, since Mrs. Hollister hadn't delivered the stationery until after lunch Friday.

Jeanette was quite disappointed about missing out on the weekend jaunt with Mary. She had been anticipating a stimulating weekend exploring the big city. Cities, actually, there being two—Minneapolis and St. Paul, divided by the mighty Mississippi. While Mary was having a good time visiting with her friend Lillian, Jeanette had planned to walk about and ride the streetcars. Taking in the sights and sounds. Talking to the natives.

But business always came first for Jeanette Harrison. And as she typed away, she found satisfaction in the fact that she would actually be earning her keep and making the agency some money.

Who, though, even knew how long Moody Investigations

would last? Mary had been flushed with excitement when she came home from her musical date with Aksel Adamsen. She had said the evening went even better than she thought it would. A great success. And this after the very pleasant afternoon of sailing with Aksel last Sunday. It seemed the young lady was finally coming to her senses, realizing that Mr. Adamsen—with his excellent prospects in business and a genial personality, to boot—was a fine match. John MacDougall would be so relieved to hear this news.

Still, Jeanette felt some sympathy for Edmond Roy, about to be left behind. He wasn't at all a bad sort. In fact, he seemed perfectly affable. But he was so very, very wrong for Mary. A strong-willed young heiress and a charming but penniless painter? No, it wouldn't do. Wouldn't do at all. A recipe for disaster.

Nonetheless, Mary's instincts about Mr. Roy's artistic ability were probably spot on. From what Jeanette had seen of his part of the Oddfellows mural, he was quite talented. It might be interesting, she thought, to have another look at it, and see how Mr. Roy and his employer were progressing. It had been almost two weeks since her first viewing.

Just then her stomach growled woefully. Yes, time for a bite. She fixed up a nice cup of tea and slowly munched on the chicken sandwich Mrs. Erdahl had made for her. Feeling satiated and a bit sleepy, she decided to kill two birds with one stone. An amble would refresh her, and she could stop in at the Oddfellows Hall to check on the mural.

The early October air felt a touch brisk. But the sun had come out and cheerful clouds scudded along up above. She went through the ornate double doors of the Oddfellows Hall and climbed the several flights to the capacious meeting room. The big artwork up on the wall behind the platform was progressing nicely. More of the sketching had been filled in—

more prosperous gentlemen and downtrodden poor folk in colorful oils. Herr Neumann was up on a scaffold, daubing at a hungry child's face.

"Excuse me," Jeanette said from the front edge of the platform.

The painter turned around, peered down at her with narrowed eyes, and took a few seconds to recognize her. "Ah, Miss MacDougall's secretary. *Guten Morgen.*"

"Afternoon, actually," Jeanette said.

"Vell, you often lose track of time up here." He stood there—brush in his right hand, palette in his left—making no attempt to dismount. "How may I help you?"

"I just wanted to stop by and see how you've progressed on the mural. You're doing splendidly, I must say."

Herr Neumann made a single, self-satisfied nod. "Danke. I like to think so. We are a little behind schedule, but not by much. We feel fortunate to have Edmond helping. Much talent, good man. He has a bright future, I think."

"He's not working today?"

"No, he is not here, I am afraid. He has taken a little trip down to Minneapolis to visit friends."

Somehow, instead of boiling over, Jeanette managed to maintain her smile, offer a polite *"Auf Wiedersehen,"* and march out of the Oddfellows Hall.

Back at the office, Jeanette made typographical errors three times running—wasting three sheets of letterhead. Unheard of, for her. She realized the need to simply sit for a stretch and calm down. It wouldn't do to run out of clean stationery before she completed all hundred letters. Only ten redundant sheets and envelopes had been provided.

Yes, take a few deep breaths and assess the situation.

It could merely be a coincidence. The heiress and the painter just happened to decamp for the Twin Cities on the same weekend, by chance. Edmond was off somewhere sipping coffee or absinthe or something else with bohemian acquaintances—painters, say, or poets—while Mary was enjoying the homecoming game with her friend Lillian. It might be that simple.

But somehow Jeanette doubted it.

More likely, Mary had tricked her and set a secret rendezvous with the tall, dark, and handsome artist. What else could it be? It wouldn't surprise Jeanette to learn that this typing project had somehow been arranged to keep her from accompanying her young cousin on the trip.

"Well," she muttered to the empty front office, "*this* is the final straw." When Mary returned on Sunday, Jeanette would read her the riot act. The church mouse cousin could tolerate many flaws in character, but not deception and deviousness on this scale. If Mary continued to play this game, Jeanette would have no choice but to tell John everything and resign.

"I'm perfectly capable of getting a secretarial job," she said with a self-affirming nod. "I don't *need* the MacDougalls to take care of me."

She resumed her typing. For a little while, she hit the keys rather too vigorously, as she continued to fume about the predicament Mary had apparently put her in. But moment by moment the anger bled out of her and, by the time the clock struck four, she had completed twenty more letters. The smart thing would be to come in for a few hours on Sunday, to assure meeting her deadline. There were envelopes to type, as well— a few more hours of work.

She was in the middle of the last letter of the day, when a rapping came on the hallway door. Who would be visiting so late on a Saturday afternoon? "Come in," she snapped, without looking up.

The door squeaked open and she saw who it was.

"Detective Sauer, hello."

"Mrs. Harrison." He stopped and stared, as if he was surprised to find her there. "I saw that one of your windows was open and thought I'd see if Miss MacDougall happened to be in."

Jeanette was not in the mood to put up with the detective's off-putting manner. She had lately had her fill of ungracious people.

"Well, sorry to disappoint you, but while I've been slaving away here, Mary is down in Minneapolis, cheering on the university football team." She harrumphed. "Though I wonder if she'll even remember who they played, let alone who won."

"It's the Gophers against Beloit," the detective informed her. "I have a dollar on the Gophers."

Jeanette scowled at him. "Well, *rah rah*. I do hope the Gophers come through for you. Now, did you want anything else? I've had a long day and I'm looking forward to a quiet evening with a good book."

"Well, actually," he said, a bit sheepishly, "I've only just read the note Miss MacDougall sent on Thursday, about the matter involving Mrs. Timmons and her daughter. I'd like to hear more about this Ranko Kovac character. But I won't bother you anymore. I'll try back on Monday."

Jeanette felt sorry for the man. He looked a bit frayed around the edges himself—dealing, as he had to, with people undoubtedly far more difficult than even Mary MacDougall.

"Please, Detective Sauer, sit down," she said "I have my notes on the case and I can tell you what I know."

As Jeanette finished a few minutes later with Mrs. Timmons's address, Detective Sauer jotted a last few words in his little notebook. "Worth looking into," he nodded, flipping it shut. "I'll get in touch with colleagues in Chicago, Cleveland, and Cincinnati and see if the moniker Ranko Kovac means anything to them."

"Mrs. Timmons will be so grateful, I'm sure. And there's nothing better for a new business like ours than happy clients."

"Have you picked up many other jobs?"

"Well, the case of the stolen pocket watch has been successfully resolved, but the matter of the missing felines remains open."

Jeanette noticed that the corners of the man's mouth actually turned slightly upwards for a brief instant after her little jest. Something she had rarely seen on his face—a smile.

"But I'm not certain how Moody Investigations will succeed so long as its owner is distracted by personal errands during office hours." She sniffed. "Lately Mary has spent more time rubbing shoulders with the Ostovians in the West End than with her only employee downtown."

Detective Sauer's expression darkened. "She's spending time with the Ostovians? I distinctly told her to stay out of that business." The detective remained tight-lipped for a few long seconds. "The coroner determined that the Ostovian prince died accidentally of drowning. And that should be the end of it. Your cousin really needs to mind her p's and q's."

"Absolutely. That girl has a terrific knack for doing things she's told not to."

"I agree. I don't deny that she has a natural aptitude for detective work. But I wonder if she realizes she isn't indestructible. Wrong place, wrong time, she could get into serious trouble." He stood up but didn't move, as if he had no idea how to conclude the conversation.

Jeanette decided to help him out. "Well, I think I'll be tucking my Remington in for a good night's sleep," she said, laying the cloth cover over it.

The detective watched her, then spoke hesitantly. "I was wondering, umm, ahh, Mrs. Harrison, if you might be interested in a bite to eat."

Jeanette felt a little flush in her cheeks. Perhaps he was realizing she wasn't so fearsome after all. "I could be persuaded, Detective Sauer. Mary tells me you're quite fond of a place called Salter's."

He frowned and shook his head. "Oh no, not Salter's. Passable sandwiches, cheap beer, but not for the ladies. How about Gustafsson's Café? Good home cooking. Even beer and wine, if you fancy a tipple."

A glass of wine sounded heavenly, Jeanette thought. And she wouldn't mind getting to know the enigmatic detective a bit better.

"Gustafsson's it is, Detective Sauer. Give me a minute and we'll be on our way."

Chapter XVII

As soon as Mary returned to her father's St. Paul *pied-à-terre* on St. Peter Street late Saturday afternoon, she spread out a heavy, green plaid blanket in front of the sofa. She threw a couple of plush pillows down on it. Then she went into the kitchen, to arrange the food she had picked up on her way back from her day in Minneapolis. There was a loaf of crusty bread, a waxed wedge of rich cheddar, a pound of smoked Virginia ham, a tin of liver pâté, two plump oranges, and a bottle of claret from her father's little rack—a Château Dauzac '94, one of his favorites. She set out the plates, knives, and goblets. She had all the fixings for a fine indoor picnic on a crisp October evening.

Satisfied with her preparations, she gave her face a good scrubbing, putting a little pink in the cheeks, and redid her hair combs. There were times she wished her chestnut mane would lie a bit straighter, but tonight it looked nicely contoured and, she hoped, attractive. Lastly, she changed out of her gray walking skirt and jacket, and into a cheerful blue-striped dress. She wanted to look her best for her evening guest.

The weekend had gone by in a flurry so far. Mary had arrived mid-afternoon Friday at St. Paul's Union Depot, walked up the hill to her father's apartment in the Collonade, and settled in for a breather. She dined at a little Italian café she was fond of, and spent the evening practicing Haydn on the upright—inspired by Maestro Żeleński. In the morning, after a cup of tea and bowl of oatmeal, she hiked up to University Avenue and caught the westbound streetcar to the University of Minnesota in Minneapolis.

Lillian Burns was waiting for her in the lobby of Sanford Hall, the women's dormitory. She took Mary up to her room on the third floor and introduced her to her roommate. Then Mary and Lillian went on a sightseeing ramble around the campus. It seemed that Lillian, far from being homesick, was reveling in her first classes and the cultural amenities of campus life.

Mary had toyed with the notion of attending college. Indeed, her father had offered to send her to any school she might choose. But she was too excited by the immediate prospect of a career in detective work to spend the next four years matriculating somewhere or other.

They returned to the dormitory for lunch in the dining room and then, with two of Lillian's new friends, headed over to Northrop Field. Mary was amused that the girls called each other by nicknames, with Lillian answering to "Burnsie."

The grandstand was packed and raucous. The quartet of females found themselves squeezed in among a gang of boys from Delta Tau Delta, who kept offering them sips of liquor from the little flasks they all had secreted in various pockets. Mary politely declined, but both of Lillian's dorm-mates partook and got a bit giggly. The game itself was a bore, the Beloit squad being rather overmatched. The final score was 29 to 0 in favor of the Gophers.

As the crowd was dispersing, one of the boys urged the girls to come to the party that evening at the Delta Tau Delta house. It was sure to be "a terrific affair."

"Sounds grand," Lillian countered, "but we're all going to the homecoming celebration at Gamma Phi Beta. They're looking for pledges, you know. And it'll give Mary a tiny taste of Greek life."

Lillian's friends both looked a little torn, Mary thought. They probably felt that there would be more unattached males at Delta Tau. But they fell in line with Lillian's preference.

"Thanks, gentlemen," one of them said, "but we must regretfully decline."

It was Mary who ended up disappointing her friend.

"Sorry, Lillian," she said. "I can't stay for the party. I happen to have a prior engagement, and I can't break it now."

Lillian narrowed her eyes—that look she had when she thought Mary was trying to put one over on her. "Really? Who do you know in Minneapolis well enough to spend a Saturday evening with?" Her eyes went wide. "Not *him*, surely?"

Lillian was Mary's closest confidante, and one of the few people she had trusted to tell all about Edmond and how she felt toward him. But she couldn't exactly reveal the truth about this evening. Not yet, anyway.

"For goodness sake, Lillian, Edmond has a huge project he's working on in Duluth. Quite a lucrative one, in fact. Do you really think he'd take the time to come all the way down here for a secret assignation?"

It wasn't quite a lie. And Lillian, fortunately, didn't press the matter. But her look remained skeptical.

It was seven o'clock now and Mary had everything ready for Edmond's imminent arrival. As she stared out one of the windows, overlooking the skyline of downtown St. Paul, she congratulated herself on how smoothly her plans had unfolded. When she had originally found out that Edmond would be visiting artist friends in Minneapolis that weekend, she quickly finagled an invitation from Lillian to come down for homecoming.

Jeanette almost threw a wrench in the works when she

invited *herself* down. Mary had to scramble for a way to block her. She knew that the Twentieth Century Club was planning a fundraising campaign for the autumn. Mrs. Hollister, whom she had known for years, happily accepted Mary's donation supporting a mailing, and agreed to hire Jeanette to type the letters. Mrs. Hollister had assured Mary that they weren't needed as soon as the following Monday. A week or two later would be fine. But Mary asked her to request that Jeanette meet a quicker deadline, and keep Mary's name out of it.

And Mary was still basking in the apparent success of her matchmaking at the concert hall. Of course, she liked Aksel. But she needed to get rid of him, as it were, and Eliza Kozlow had the look of someone who could handle the job. It was early days, though, and there could be many a slip between love at first sight and the altar.

By the time the sharp rapping came on the apartment door, Mary had spent a couple of hours alternating between annoyance and worry. Where was Edmond and why was he so tardy?

She rushed to the door.

There he stood—tall, dark, lean, and looming well over her. And so handsome that Mary's knees almost buckled. He had a single red rose in his left hand and offered it to her.

Immediately all was forgiven.

"So sorry I'm late, Mary," he said with an endearing, crooked smile, as she took the flower. "Had quite a time getting away from the party. And the streetcar connections took forever. Mind the thorns now."

There came a whiff of beer on his breath. Mary knew he'd spent the afternoon at a reunion of his old artistic acquaintances. Apparently it had been quite the convivial gathering.

"Think nothing of it," she said. "I'm just glad you're safe and sound and here." She took him by the hand and drew him into the apartment. "Come in. I have a terrific spread for us."

But when the door clicked shut, all thoughts of food and wine flew right out of her head, as Edmond wrapped his arms around her, leaned down, and planted a long, slow kiss on her lips. By the time he stopped, Mary felt positively lightheaded. She set down the rose, which she had been carefully holding in her left hand.

"Did you have much to eat at the party?" she said, leading him into the parlor.

"Well, no, as a matter of fact." Edmond took off his jacket and fedora and threw them on a chair. "I didn't want to spoil my appetite for our little picnic repast." He sat on the sofa, elbows resting on his knees, chin resting on his hands. "I figured I'd only had a couple of beers, but now that I think about it, someone was always refilling my glass."

It might not be wise to open that bottle of claret, Mary thought, heading for the kitchen. She returned with the Virginia ham and cheddar on one plate, and the bread on another. She went back for the necessary utensils and the liver pâté. When she returned, Edmond had slid off the sofa onto the green plaid blanket. He was uncorking the Château Dauzac. Oh well, she thought, taking the bottle and pouring a couple of inches into each goblet.

Edmond swirled the purple liquid, sniffed it, and took a sip. "Oh my. What a treat! That's lovely, just lovely. *Much* nicer than the swill I usually drink. You sure do know how to treat a slightly inebriated dauber."

"Not too inebriated, I hope," Mary said, only half-jesting.

Edmond looked a bit apologetic. "The thing is, I visited with so many people that I wasn't paying attention to how much I was drinking. You should have been there, Mary. There was talk of forming an artists' guild. You know, to support each other and teach folks how to make their own art."

As he talked, Mary put a slice of ham and chunk of cheese

on his plate, along with a hearty piece of bread.

"And my friend Randall just sold a big canvas to one of the Washburns. The most money he's ever made. Five hundred dollars. Do you believe it?" He stopped for a few bites. "Oh, and you'll never guess who was there. Eloise Memminger and Nan Burton. Remember them?"

Mary did indeed. Fellow students in the painting class that Edmond had taught at the Minneapolis School of Fine Arts. It was Mary's introduction to him, nearly a year and a half earlier. He had gotten tangled up in a criminal investigation. On her very first case, Mary had saved him from jail and became quite, quite fond of him.

As Edmond chattered away about the artists' gathering, Mary nibbled and drank. After a while, she took up the conversation, as Edmond ate. She told him all about her day at the university and how much fun it had been.

"Oh, and before I forget it," Edmond said, "I wanted to invite you to a little dinner party at Herr Neumann's next Friday evening. He's hosting a friend from Munich, a former student, and said I ought to invite you. Mrs. Harrison, too, if she'd like to tag along."

"Oh, I'd love to come," Mary said, picturing a table brimming with hearty German fare. "And I'll ask Jeanette if she's available."

As Edmond continued to jabber away, Mary smiled to herself. He seemed so excited, as though being around other artists had filled him with fresh energy. When he finally finished talking and eating, he took a few sips of wine and smiled mischievously at her.

"This is almost like Manet's 'Luncheon on the Grass.' Only there're just two of us, not four. And no one's naked." He made a wicked but silly grin. "Yet."

In spite of herself, Mary felt a blush in her cheeks. But she wasn't about to let his little tease pass without comment. "Yes. I've seen Monsieur Manet's painting. It seems that unclad young woman is very warm-blooded indeed, compared to the fully dressed men in their jackets and trousers."

Edmond laughed and slipped closer to her. She slid up next to him and he wrapped his arm around her shoulder. They sat for a few long seconds like that and then he cupped his hand under her chin and gently pulled her face toward his.

They kissed, a passionate smoldering kiss, Mary arching her back and pressing into him. He ran his hand over her waist and hip, where it lingered. Then he lightly caressed her bosom, producing in her something like a mild electric shock.

As he twisted his body toward her, Edmond somehow kicked over one of the goblets sitting near him. It rolled off the blanket and onto the tile of the hearth, dripping its remaining liquid.

"Blast it!" he cursed.

She pulled away from him. "Not to worry, it's all right. Let me take the dishes back to the kitchen. It'll be just a few seconds."

She gave him a peck on the cheek and gathered up goblets and plates, as many as she could carry. She stacked them in the sink and went back for the rest, bringing a towel and damp rag.

Edmond was lying on his back on the blanket, his hands resting on his stomach.

"I'll just wipe this up and be right back," she said, smiling over at him.

But as she did, Mary noticed that his eyes were shut, his mouth slightly open, his breathing slow and regular. He was dead asleep.

"Edmond," she said, nudging him gently on the shoulder. "Edmond? Wake up." She didn't want to speak too loudly. She nudged him again.

But it was to no avail. He snorted and rolled onto his side. The beer and the wine had done their job too well.

She placed a pillow under his head and covered him with another blanket. Sitting for a while on the sofa, she watched him intently, hoping he might revive. It struck her how innocent people look when they sleep—almost childlike.

She sighed. *What are you playing at, Mary MacDougall,* she thought. *You're toying with the man, leading him on. Making him think who knows what. That you want to spend your life with him? Have his children? Grow old together?*

She finally rose and went to bed, certain the night would hold little slumber for her.

Mary was sitting at the kitchen table the next morning, nibbling on a piece of toast and reading the Sunday newspaper, when she heard Edmond stirring in the parlor. A few minutes later he appeared in the doorway. Though he had obviously attempted to freshen up—his hair combed, his tie straightened—his face looked a bit ashen.

"My head hurts something fierce." He stood there awkwardly, his coat and hat in his hand. "I made a terrible mess of the evening, didn't I?"

Mary couldn't help but smile at his forlorn expression. "Doesn't surprise me, you having a headache. And I'd imagine you're feeling a bit stiff, sleeping on the floor like that. A piece of buttered toast and a cup of strong coffee would do you some good. Sit down and let me fix them up."

Edmond did as instructed, laying his coat and hat on another chair. "I should have had *more* to eat and *less* to drink at Randall's party."

Mary set a cup of coffee down in front of him. "It's okay,

Edmond. We'll just have to try again some other day."

"But that's the problem, isn't it, Mary?" he said as she tended to the toast. "I thought when I came to Duluth, we'd be able to spend more time together, just the two of us. But it hasn't worked out, has it? You always seem so busy."

Mary placed his toast on a plate, avoiding his intense stare, and put it in front of him, along with a butter dish. "It does seem that way, doesn't it? But with the agency starting up and all…"

"I meant to ask you something last night. Did you manage to find your watch thief?" he asked, scraping butter across the toast.

Mary plopped back down into her chair. "The culprit, a certain Beansie MacKenzie, is still at large, but the watch has been recovered. I have a good lead in the matter of the filched felines. We're looking into a confidence trickster, who may be setting up a young lady and her mother. And then there's the poor Ostovian prince."

Edmond stopped in mid-bite and looked at her with concern. "Good heavens, you're not involved in *that* business, are you? Neumann says he's heard rumors of Ostovian assassins in Duluth. I don't care how clever you are, Mary, you shouldn't let yourself get anywhere near people like that."

"Well, I'm only informally involved." Mary was glad that Detective Sauer wasn't within earshot as she delivered such a whopper. "I'm feeding the police any information I can glean from the Ostovian priest and his wife."

Edmond looked perplexed. "Why are you visiting an Ostovian priest?"

"It's nothing to do with religion," Mary laughed. "Father Pretrescu is making me a pair of hiking boots."

The man looked even more confused but just shrugged. "Well, why not? Say, I was wondering, do you have any jam?"

Mary went over to a cabinet and pulled out a pot of marmalade. She set it on the table next to Edmond's toast. Then he caught her totally by surprise, when he firmly took her wrist and pulled her down onto his lap.

She almost laughed at the awkwardness of it. "I see you're feeling better, Mr. Roy."

"I am, Miss MacDougall, thanks to your kind ministrations. Now, I want to tell you about a crazy idea I have."

"Yes, go on," Mary said, cuddling up against him. "I'm open to a certain amount of craziness."

"Yesterday afternoon," he began, "Randall told me about some people he knows who are starting up an artists' colony out in Old Monterey. He said I ought to spend a few months there come springtime. I'll have finished with the Oddfellows and I just heard there's a chance I can get back my old Minneapolis teaching job over the winter. I could build up some cash."

Suddenly alarm bells began going off in Mary's head. "Minneapolis sounds fine. But I can find more work for you in Duluth, Edmond, I'm sure of it. And why would you want to go all the way out to California?"

"For the fun of it," he said, putting his arms around her waist. "To see something I've never seen before. They say the coast is magnificent. And you *must* come along with me. It'd be grand! The two of us, on our own!"

"Me?" Mary gulped. "In California? What in the world would I do out there?"

Edmond's face was full of excitement. "You could practice your painting. We could hire a good piano for you. You could hike and ride and explore that glorious countryside. Leave cold Duluth behind for a time."

"Leave Duluth?" Mary repeated, shaken by the immensity of Edmond's scheme. "Leave the agency? Abandon my

153

career?"

"Forget about detecting for a while. But if you must, set up shop out there. I'll bet California could use a sharp lady sleuth."

"But what about my father? What about Jeanette?"

"I know you'd miss them. But *we* would be together, just the two of us. With no one demanding our time. No one telling us what to do. No one watching us. No fear of being caught out."

The idea of spending undistracted weeks with Edmond anywhere certainly had its appeal. But could Mary do something so radical? What kind of bridges would she have to burn to take such a leap? And indeed, what about her career, just now gaining traction?

"What do you say, Mary?"

His look was so earnest, so hopeful.

"I, I, I…" She stood, disengaging from him and taking a deep breath. "I think you need another piece of toast."

Chapter XVIII

Jeanette was scribbling away in her journal early Sunday evening, when she heard the front door slam. A young woman's voice called out, "Hullo, anyone home?"

"Only the hired help," came Emma Beach's voice, echoing through the big house on Superior Street. "That is, Mrs. Harrison and myself."

Seated at the desk in the library, Jeanette kept writing until, a moment later, Mary appeared in the door, looking rosy cheeked and invigorated. If she knew what Jeanette was about to say to her, she wouldn't have looked nearly so jolly.

"I'm back," Mary said, collapsing onto the dark leather settee next to one of the bookshelves.

"I can see that," Jeanette replied, putting down her fountain pen. "And how were things in the big city?"

"Oh, just splendid. Lillian and I had a grand time. We took a walking tour of the campus. You wouldn't believe how it sprawls out, on the bluff above the river. Just beautiful. And all the handsome buildings and masses of students." The words tumbled out of Mary in a torrent. "I met some of Lillian's new friends, and at the game we ended up sitting next to a mob of boys from Delta Tau Delta, who were quite insistent we come to *their* homecoming party. To tell you the truth, I wouldn't have trusted them as far as I could throw them. I mean, they kept offering us whiskey out of little flasks."

"My goodness! Scandalous behavior," Jeanette muttered, with Mary apparently not noticing the mockery in her tone.

"Well, we turned them down, of course. Lillian was determined we go to the shindig at the Gamma Phi Beta sorority, though I think her two friends seemed disappointed at missing out on meeting all those boys."

"And the sorority party? Was it fun?"

"Oh yes, very much so."

"Did you notice the two letters from Pittsburgh out on the side table?"

Mary's eyes widened. "From Pittsburgh? My gosh! What did they say?"

"For heaven's sake, they're addressed to you. I don't open other people's mail."

Mary ran out of the room, her shoes clattering down the hallway. She was back in a few winks, clutching two envelopes. Throwing herself back on the settee, she ripped open one of them and pulled out a single sheet of stationery.

"From Tena." She scanned the note, summing up the contents as she read along. "It went well, as well as can be expected. Father was wary at first, but after he talked with Paul a while, he came to understand that Paul is a proper businessman who just happens to be a photographer. It helped that Paul's brother manages a manufactory in Chicago and Father knows the firm. Apparently, he was persuaded that Paul wasn't out to rob Tena blind. The ceremony will take place in December sometime. Then it's off to Egypt for their honeymoon."

Jeanette couldn't help but feel a little envious of Tena. Since Daniel had passed, she had never had the good fortune to find the man who could replace him. She perhaps expected too much. But she wouldn't compromise. In any worthy match she expected kindness and humor and intelligence. Honesty and concern and basic decency. Daniel had all that and more.

"Now let's see what Father has to say for himself." Mary opened the second envelope, read the letter, and laughed. "Typical John MacDougall. A few curt sentences." She cleared her throat, and, with a bulldog expression, lowered her voice and applied a Scottish burr. "'Dear Mary. Your aunt is as stubborn as you are and she is not to be dissuaded. I have given her and her fiancé my blessing. Not that the lack of it would stop Tena. Paul seems a decent sort, as far as I can tell. All best, Father.'"

Jeanette smiled at Mary's impersonation of her father. Emma arrived with tea and a sandwich—the traveler having missed her supper. Mary updated the housekeeper on the news from Pittsburgh. After Emma left, Jeanette decided the time had come to talk turkey.

"Let me tell you about what I did," she began, "after you left. I worked most of Friday on the Twentieth Century Club's letter. And, of course, I worked on Saturday, as well. But when lunch rolled around, I felt the need for a little constitutional. One gets stiff sitting in front of a typewriter all day."

"Naturally," Mary said, taking a bite of her sardine sandwich.

"And what should I walk by, but the Oddfellows Hall."

Mary chewed for a few seconds and swallowed. "Oh, really?"

"Yes, and I went upstairs to the meeting room to see what kind of progress your friend Mr. Roy had made on the mural. And guess what I found?"

"What?" Mary's eyes were focused nervously on the sandwich, not on Jeannette.

"Mr. Roy was not there. But Herr Neumann was. He told me Mr. Roy had taken a few days off to visit friends in Minneapolis. *What* a coincidence—you and he being in the same city at the same time. I don't suppose you bumped into him down there, did you?"

Mary looked up at Jeanette for a few long seconds, straightening her spine. "I didn't bump into him in Minneapolis. I bumped into him in St. Paul. In our apartment at the Collonade, in fact. And to answer the question you most certainly want to ask, other than chatting and eating, *nothing* happened. The truth is, he'd been drinking all afternoon and fell asleep on the parlor floor." Mary jutted out her chin. "And I must say, as an adult with my own career and resources, I'm getting a little annoyed with constantly being treated like a child."

Jeanette was so astonished by Mary's candor that she didn't know how to react. She finally said, "And I am getting annoyed at constantly being lied to. Go ahead, make love to the man. I don't care anymore. Because you just won't listen to me one way or the other. You've made it entirely impossible for me to do the job your father hired me for."

Mary started to reply, but Jeanette cut her off with a brusque wave of the hand.

"Clearly I cannot keep you on the straight and narrow. Quite the failure as a chaperone, am I. So, as soon as your father returns from his trip, I intend to tender my resignation. I'm grateful for his kindness, of course, but it just hasn't worked out. If I can't find other employment in Duluth, I'll return to St. Louis."

Mary looked stricken. "Don't be silly, Jeanette. You can't quit. I need a reliable secretary. We don't need Father's money. I can pay you exactly the same." She paused. "And you won't have to be my blasted chaperone anymore. Father can hire his own detective if he wants to keep tabs on me."

After that last remark, Jeanette tried hard to maintain her serious demeanor. "I will agree to these new terms on one condition."

"And that would be?"

"You must tell your father what happened this weekend with Mr. Roy. *Everything*." Jeanette softened her voice. "John adores you. He doesn't deserve all this disrespect and dissembling. You *owe* him some honesty, at the very least."

"All right, I'll tell him." Mary sighed. "But I'm not sure what to say."

"Why don't you just tell him how you feel about Mr. Roy?"

Mary slumped down. "Easier said than done. I'm not even certain I know how I feel."

Chapter XIX

Still feeling chastened by her cousin's lecture and threat, Mary was up very early the next morning and out the door before Jeanette had even started eating breakfast. Sitting in her office, Mary mulled over the fix she found herself in. It was of her own making—she had let her infatuation with Edmond distract her from the work at hand. And she meant to redeem herself in Jeanette's eyes. It wouldn't do to let the woman quit. It wouldn't do at all.

But even as Mary tried to focus on the problem of Quentin Pettyjohn and what she saw in his window, her mind kept wandering back to the California adventure Edmond had proposed. Though she supposed she ought to be flattered that he wanted her there with him, she felt resentful that he didn't take her work seriously. If only he would let her manage his commissions. She knew she could find enough work in Duluth to keep him prosperous *and* close.

But what would she do, if she had to choose between her calling and Edmond? Shaking her head, she tried to put the matter out of her mind. Surely it wouldn't come to that.

Her ruminations were interrupted when she heard Jeanette finally come through the door. Mary yelled a cheerful "Hello" and asked her to come have a chat.

"Sit down, please," Mary said with a chivalrous gesture toward one of the client chairs. "I just want to review where we stand on our cases. First, did anything happen on Friday that I ought to know about."

"Yes, indeed," Jeanette replied. "Jiggs came in to show me his pocket watch, and quite handsome it was. He asked me to remind you that Mr. Osgood looked forward to having a few minutes with your father, as you agreed to."

Mary grimaced. She had almost forgotten that she promised the man access to John MacDougall in exchange for the return of Jiggs's treasured timepiece.

"And he told me he hopes that you can find Beansie, who still hasn't turned up. The boy seems awfully eager to let bygones be bygones and get his friend back."

Mary nodded. "I think I'll start the Beansie hunt this morning with a visit to Mrs. Purcell's soup kitchen. Did anything else happen while I was gone?"

"Well, as you know, I was here on Saturday as well as Friday. And that afternoon Detective Sauer stopped by. He said he hoped for answers today to the queries he sent to Chicago, Cleveland, and Cincinnati regarding the shady Mr. Ranko Kovac. He promised to stop by this afternoon with an update."

"Wonderful! Mrs. Timmons will be so pleased to know the police are on the case. If I do say so myself, the excellent rapport I've built with Detective Sauer will give us quite a leg-up in future investigations."

"Yes, indeed," Jeanette said. "In fact, Detective Sauer and I were discussing that very same topic over dinner at Gustafsson's Saturday evening. You know, talking about how often you two see eye-to-eye on criminal matters." She paused and offered a coy smile. "Now if you don't mind, I need to get my dear Remington going. I have a hundred envelopes to finish for Mrs. Hollister."

Jeanette went back to her desk, leaving Mary in a minor state of shock. Detective Sauer and Jeanette went to dinner together? Mary was amazed he had worked up the nerve to ask.

And they talked about her?

Good grief! What in the world had they said?

Mrs. Purcell's soup kitchen down in the Bowery on Michigan Street was squeezed in between a rundown transient hotel and a saloon. The good lady and her volunteers kept it running with contributions from all kinds of Duluthians—from those who could chip in a dollar or two to people like Mary, who had given hundreds. Mrs. Purcell's clients ran the gamut from street lads like Jiggs and Gordo to poor families to unemployed workmen to the destitute elderly.

Mary arrived at about a quarter to ten. One of the volunteers fetched Mrs. Purcell from the kitchen in back.

"Miss MacDougall," she said, wiping her hands on a towel, "so good to see you. Welcome. To what do I owe the pleasure?"

Mrs. Purcell was a short, wiry woman with hair pulled back in a no-nonsense bun. Despite her petite size, she was known to adeptly handle cantankerous drunks who tried to push their way in through the front door. She had a strict policy that her guests be sober to take a meal there—not for reasons of temperance, but to preempt obnoxious behavior.

"I came to ask you about one of your regulars," Mary said. "He's gone missing and his chums have hired me to find him."

Mrs. Purcell's face went solemn. "I assume you mean Tavish MacKenzie."

"Beansie."

"I always call him Tavish. You can't very well grow up properly and have everyone calling you Beansie. We've been quite worried about him, but the police, of course, won't be bothered with a mere missing orphan. Friday night was baked bean night and Tavish loves his beans. He never would have missed it."

"Do you have any knowledge of him engaging in thievery?"

Mrs. Purcell frowned. "Lord knows, poverty and hunger can drive anyone to extremes. But I don't know of anything like that." She shook her head. "Not Tavish. At least I hope not."

"There's one other thing. I know you have a Brownie camera and keep a scrapbook with pictures of the folks who come in. And I'm hoping you have Beansie in one of your snaps."

Mrs. Purcell thought it over. "Probably in several. Sit down and I'll check." She strode off through the kitchen area and disappeared into the office in back.

From a bench, Mary surveyed the place. Long tables ran parallel to each other for the length of the room. Mrs. Purcell could feed upwards of fifty at a time. And in back was the open kitchen where the bread was baked, the beef and chicken roasted, the soup simmered, and the coffee brewed. Two volunteers were busy over a stove and a preparation table. A third was loudly stacking plates and implements for the lunch hour. There was also a diminutive figure pushing a broom back there, by the kitchen. Mary squinted hard and made out Gordo Sinclair hard at work.

"Gordo," she shouted, waving her hand. He looked up and, recognizing her, grinned. He marched to the front, swinging the broom up on his shoulder.

"Miss MacDougall," he said, "howdy. Whatcha doin' here? You don't need a bowl of soup, do ya?" He ran his free hand through that haystack of blond hair. His cowlick once again refused to stay down.

Mary couldn't tell if he was joking or not. "Oh, no, I just came to get a photograph of Beansie. Mrs. Purcell has one in her scrapbook. Still no word from him?"

"Nope, sorry. Not a word. Like Bert said back at your office, it gotta be he took off with that lady friend of his and the cash from Jiggs's watch. They could be all the way to Chicago by now."

Mary informed him it was unlikely that Beansie and some female had run off together with only ten dollars in cash. "So, you volunteer here?"

"Only right to give back a little," Gordo said, "considering how much of Mrs. P.'s food I eat. I sweep Mondays and Wednesdays. Now, if you don't mind, miss, it's back to work."

Mrs. Purcell returned a moment later with a big black scrapbook. "I have three pictures of Tavish. Two of them are rather blurry, I'm afraid. He must have moved. The third is quite clear." She put the book on the table in front of Mary and flipped it open.

Mary squinted at the snapshot that Mrs. Purcell tapped with her index finger. Four young friends. Standing in front of the soup kitchen like the Four Musketeers, shooting silly expressions at the camera. Mary recognized Jiggs on the left, with his exaggerated grin.

"There's Alberto next to Jiggs," Mrs. Purcell noted, tapping her finger on the little Italian boy. "Then Gordon— looking all full of himself, as usual. And finally, here's Tavish on your right. A bit of an imp, Tavish, but we're all fond of him."

Mary focused on that last face for a few seconds. "Oh my goodness," she pronounced slowly, putting her hand to her cheek.

"Are you all right, my dear?" Mrs. Purcell asked. "You look like you've seen a ghost."

Mary blinked up at the woman. "May I please take this photograph for a little while? I need to show it to someone. *Urgently.*"

Chapter XX

The very brisk walk from Mrs. Purcell's soup kitchen in the Bowery up the hill to the public library on Second Street took Mary only about twelve minutes. Panting a bit, she went through the doors of the handsome brown stone building, newly opened just a few months before. Then it was a quick climb up to the reference room to find a volume she earnestly hoped they had in their collection.

Behind the counter a librarian, silver-rimmed spectacles perched on her nose, put down the document she was reading and regarded Mary. "Good morning, miss. How may I help you?"

"Do you happen to have a world almanac? Not a new one. Something two or three years old would be ideal."

"We have *The American Almanac Year Book Cyclopedia and Atlas* of 1900. Will that do?"

"Yes, just the thing," Mary nodded.

The librarian went to a broad shelf off to her right and plucked out a volume in dark blue, with gold lettering on the spine. She handed it to Mary, who thanked her.

Ensconced at a small table by a window that looked out on First Avenue West, Mary opened the book to the index in back and found the page for Ostovia.

"Three hundred sixty-nine," she said under her breath, leafing through the volume's tissuey pages. The article on the

Principality of Ostovia took up the bottom third of the page and provided information on the Ostovian economy, which was devoted largely to timber, farming, vineyards, and banking. "No photographs, blast it," she swore under her breath. Then she thought to turn the page.

And there they were. Father and son. In a news photograph of some kind, standing on the steps of a church or a public building. From better days in the old country.

Prince Anton was in some kind of Ostovian folk costume, and was smiling and waving his ornamental cap to the unseen crowd behind the photographer. Nicolae, who looked about nine or ten years old, was in a miniature version of his father's garb. He wore a big grin, lopsided to his left, with a pronounced dimple. He seemed a very happy lad. He could not have known the horrors that lay ahead.

Mary opened her bag and pulled out the snapshot of Beansie and his friends. She blinked, and looked back and forth between the two photographs.

"Detective Sauer has got to see this," she muttered. She went back to the librarian, who was reshelving some books. "Excuse me, but might I check this volume out?"

The woman pursed her lips. "Reference books are not allowed to leave the building. You may, of course, come visit and use it any time."

Mary, agitated and panting, rushed into the office with a brown paper bag under her arm. Jeanette was typing an address on a Twentieth Century Club envelope in her Remington. A box next to her was half full of finished envelopes.

"Heavens," she said, looking up. "Where's the fire?"

Mary threw herself on one of the chairs in front of

Jeanette's desk and tossed the bag next to the Remington typewriter. It landed with a resonant *thud*. "No fire. But I've had quite a jolt."

"What is it?" Jeanette sounded suddenly concerned. "What happened? Are you all right?"

"I *really* want to tell you, Jeanette. I really, really do. But not yet. I need to talk to Detective Sauer first. But if I'm correct, I think I've stumbled onto a huge scandal."

Jeanette couldn't hide her curiosity. "Is it something to do with one of our cases?"

"Let's just say if what I've uncovered is what I think it is, Moody Investigations could be on front pages all over the world."

Jeanette's expression soured. "It's that business having to do with the poor dead Ostovian king."

Mary glowered at her. "It's poor dead *prince*. Ostovia's a principality, not a kingdom. And for the moment, I don't care to talk about it. Now did anything happen while I was out?"

Jeanette handed her a blue envelope. "Your dispatch from Miss Borrell just arrived."

Mary grabbed the letter and the paper bag, and went into her office. Sitting down at her desk, she tore open the blue envelope and pulled out two folded pieces of stationery. Josie's account of Ranko Kovac didn't so much provide new information, as amplify what had been in her earlier telegrams. The man operated on the margins of Manhattan's music world, feeding comely young things into vaudeville and off-Broadway shows. Instead of the singing ingénue roles they expected—on their ostensible way to the Metropolitan Opera House—most ended up in choruses and dance lines. Some, understanding their predicament, fled home. But others became companions to older, well-off men who had no intention of doing the honorable thing. Not a few girls' lives had been ruined. None of that was illegal, of course, let alone criminal. Kovac knew how to skirt the law.

It would give Mary the greatest satisfaction if, somehow, she could help put that vile man out of business. But it was this morning's epiphany that she ruminated about, until Jeanette interrupted her train of thought.

"Mary," her associate said, standing in the inner office doorway, "there's a young man here to see you. Says he needs to speak to you personally."

Mary hopped up. "Well, let's see who we have." She marched out past Jeanette to see a dark-haired, olive-skinned fellow standing there, with a shoebox under his left arm. For a few seconds, she couldn't place him. Then she remembered.

"Ah, Mr. Gino Rossi, the pawnbroker's grandson," she said. "Welcome to Moody Investigations." She shook his hand. "Did you happen to recall something about the boy who sold you the watch?"

"I did, Miss MacDougall," he said. "I came downtown to get some new shoes and thought I'd stop by." He grinned and lifted up his left foot, displaying a glinting black patent leather Oxford. "You like 'em?"

"Very handsome, Mr. Rossi. Now why don't you come into my office and tell me what you remembered."

A little after two o'clock, Mary heard the outer door of the office click open. She jumped up from her desk and went out to find Detective Sauer. He and Jeanette were exchanging smiles, which disappeared the very instant they saw her. *That dinner on Saturday must have been rather pleasant*, Mary mused. But she had no time to speculate on their evolving relationship.

"Good afternoon, ladies," the detective said. "I have the pleasure of informing you that my old chum in Cleveland, Inspector Finnegan, has identified Ranko Kovac. The name, as you rightly suspected, Miss MacDougall, is an alias. His real name is David Brankovich. As a younger fellow, he ran confidence schemes around Ohio and Indiana. He had apparently been something of a musical prodigy as a lad, till he went bad. Finnegan's sending me the most recent warrant on him. If we nab him, we'll extradite him to Cleveland."

Jeanette actually applauded. "Bravo, Detective Sauer."

To Mary's surprise, he smiled and took a little bow—a very un-Sauer-like gesture from the sober detective.

"Just doing what they pay me for," he said with a shrug. "I spoke with Mrs. Timmons this morning and she expects him in town on Thursday to sign the contract and collect her share of the daughter's tuition. And that's when we'll spring our trap."

"Isn't it wonderful, Mary?" beamed Jeanette, though her comment seemed more addressed to the policeman than her cousin.

"Mrs. Timmons agreed to my notion that I pose as the brother that she doesn't actually have," the detective said. "And I was wondering, Mrs. Harrison, if you would pretend to be her fictional sister-in-law." He glanced over at Mary. "I'm afraid you're rather too young for the role."

Jeanette's smile grew even wider. "Yes, of course, I'd be happy to play-act for such a good cause."

"Excellent," Mary said. Her cousin seemed to have overcome her antipathy to sleuthing, so long as a certain policeman was involved. "It sounds like you two have things well in hand. Now, Detective Sauer, could you come into my office? I need to speak with you about an urgent matter."

Mary noticed that Jeanette looked a bit miffed to be excluded. It seemed risky to involve her cousin in the affair—

given the potential for danger and scandal. Still, Jeanette deserved to know what the theft of Jiggs's watch had possibly uncovered. It was time to brief her on the remarkable affair that was unfolding.

"Jeanette, would you mind coming in, too? You may want to take notes."

Her face showing both curiosity and concern, Jeanette entered the inner office, notepad in hand. She and the policeman sat down facing Mary.

Detective Sauer eyed her warily. "You're not still gnawing on that Ostovian bone, are you?"

"Afraid so. And we're just about to get to the marrow." Mary opened the brown paper bag and extracted a blue book with gold letters on the spine and cover. "I have here *The American Almanac Cyclopedia and Atlas.* The edition of 1900, from the second-hand bookstore on Fourth Avenue East." She opened it to page 370, twisted it around, and pushed it toward him. "Note the photograph. Prince Anton and his son, Duke Nicolae—before the boy became Prince Nicolae."

The detective leaned over and examined it very closely. "Yes, it looks much like our drowning victim, allowing for the passage of several years."

Mary nodded. "I think so, too. I saw a picture of the boy lying in the casket, you know."

Her visitor looked equally startled and irritated. "How in the world did you manage that?"

Jeanette's expression indicated she wondered the same thing. But it seemed she was going to let Detective Sauer administer the dressing-down, if it came to that.

"It's not important. What *is* important is this." Mary opened the bottom right drawer of her desk, pulled out her bag, and extracted the snapshot that Mrs. Purcell had loaned her. She laid it in front of him. "The boy on the right is Tavish

Angus MacKenzie, known to one and all as Beansie."

Detective Sauer bent over the photo, squinting down at it. "Well, well… They could be brothers, couldn't they? Practically twins." He rubbed his temples, as if he were developing a headache. "You think we've got the wrong boy in the coffin, don't you?"

"I think it's very likely," Mary answered, trying to control her excitement. "Beansie's been missing for weeks now. What if someone murdered him, drowned him in the bay, and planted the Ostovian prince's signet ring on him?

"Oh, my word!" Jeanette gasped.

"The killers hoped," Mary continued, "that everyone would draw the conclusion that the prince had died accidentally or was murdered. It doesn't matter which. So long as he's thought dead. As a result, Nicolae's uncle—who is said to have agents after the boy—will give up the hunt. The real prince escapes, to fight another day."

Detective Sauer leaned back in his chair, knitting his fingers behind his head. "As theories go, that's pretty remarkable. But it's only a theory. And we have contrary testimony. Father Petrescu identified the dead boy as Nicolae. Two other Ostovians who had seen him in the old country agreed. An official from the Ostovian mission in Washington, who came with a man from the State Department, identified him. And, more important to me, Chief Troyer—my boss—is quite adamant. The body belongs to the prince and the case is closed."

"But what if it is Beansie? Will there be no accounting for his murder?" Mary paused dramatically. "Are relations with a small eastern European principality more important than truth and justice?"

"Don't be naïve, Miss MacDougall," the detective said tiredly. "Of course they are. Especially relations with a country holding a billion in currency in its banks."

Mary groaned with frustration. "Well, that just *stinks*. Beansie was an American citizen who deserved the full protection of his government."

The detective gave a bitter laugh. "He was a ragamuffin who lived on the streets. People like him don't count for much in our America."

"At least let me bring Mrs. Purcell to see the body," Mary pleaded. "She knew Beansie better than any other adult. I wouldn't ask his chums. They don't deserve to remember him that way."

Detective Sauer shook his head. "That's impossible. The body's already been buried in the cemetery in West Duluth. His uncle didn't want to inter a martyr in the family crypt back in Ostovia. Might be a focal point for protest."

"Well then, dig him up!" Mary spat, outraged that some despot thousands of miles away was perverting the course of American justice.

"That is *not* going to happen, Miss MacDougall. I'm very much afraid that you've lost this particular battle."

Mary felt angry enough to throw the blasted almanac at him. But she took a long, deep breath and tamped down her indignation.

"Couldn't you at least let Mrs. Purcell see the autopsy photographs of him?"

Detective Sauer stood, clearly indicating that their little conference was at an end. "You know it won't make a drop of difference. The case is closed. But if it makes you feel better, I'll arrange to show a few pictures to Mrs. Purcell."

After the detective left, Mary regarded Jeanette. "Do your worst. I dabbled in dark international affairs and Emma will have to know about it, then father, and I'll be shipped off to live in a tower like Rapunzel, letting my hair grow to ridiculous lengths."

Jeanette crossed her arms and, to Mary's surprise, it didn't seem she was angry. "Yes, well, dabbling in international affairs involving conspiracies of assassination and murder does seem rather dangerous—beyond even your audacity. But, so far as I can tell, you're being honest about it. That counts for something. And barring any more Ostovian unpleasantness, I'm inclined to keep quiet. Since you're still in one piece and you're not on the front pages, I'll consider it a decent outcome. Besides, I'm not your chaperone anymore."

Mary almost leapt across the desk to hug Jeanette, but restrained herself. "Thank you, I'm very grateful."

"Don't thank *me*," Jeanette answered. "I'm withdrawing out of pure self-defense. What concerns me more is what do we tell Jiggs and the boys?"

Mary had asked herself the same bleak question. "I don't know. I really don't know."

"At least our part of this awful business is at an end," Jeanette said. "What more can you possibly do?"

Mary suspected, though, that the affair of Beansie and Nicolae was not quite done with her yet. And, if nothing else, Mary MacDougall was no quitter.

Chapter XXI

"This feels *so* wrong," Jeanette whispered to Mary, as the two women walked down Wallace Avenue the next afternoon. "As though we're breaking into the man's house, and taking advantage of that dear old lady. What if he's at home? What then?"

"You don't need to whisper," Mary laughed. "No one can hear us. It's the middle of a workday. Mr. Pettyjohn should be hard at it keeping his books at the Imperial Flour Mill. If for some reason he's at home, we'll simply ask him a few innocuous questions and be on our way. But I'm betting the coast is clear, apart from Mrs. Pettyjohn, who'll happily invite us in. So no question of anything illegal, like housebreaking. There, does that make you feel better?"

"Not really," Jeanette grumbled.

And, indeed, within three minutes they found themselves sitting pretty in Quentin Pettyjohn's living room, amidst much Egyptian bric-a-brac, while his mother fixed them up some cups of tea. She brought the first one out somewhat precariously in her tremulous hands, once again quite giddy to have callers. As a safety precaution, Jeanette went into the kitchen with her to get the other two cups.

"It's so good to see you again," Mary said, blowing on her hot, over-steeped tea. "We enjoyed our first visit so much, didn't we, Jeanette?"

Jeanette nodded vigorously. "Oh yes," she gushed. "Very much so."

The tentative look on Mrs. Pettyjohn's face hinted that she didn't quite remember that first visit, let alone who they were, but she seemed determined to hide the fact and be a charming hostess.

"I'm so sorry, but my husband and my son are off at work, of course, this being Thursday."

The poor old dear, Mary thought. Not only did she not know what day it was, she couldn't remember her husband was gone. But perhaps it was kinder that way, thinking your beloved might walk through the door at any moment. Better than pondering the grim old reaper's nasty truth.

"Well, of course they'd be at work," Mary said. "But as long as we're here, we might as well enjoy a nice chat."

"Oh, yes, let's," Mrs. Pettyjohn agreed with a sweet smile.

And chat they did, for a good fifteen minutes. About the weather. About Quentin's very important position at Imperial Flour. About Mary's exciting weekend in the Twin Cities. Then it was time for Mary to make her move.

"I was wondering," she said, "if I might use your powder room."

"Yes, of course, my dear," Mrs. Pettyjohn said. "It's upstairs and on the left."

As Mary climbed the stairs, clutching her bag, she could hear Jeanette asking about the house and how long the Pettyjohns had lived there. Her job was to keep the old dear occupied while Mary snooped around.

The bathroom was, as promised, just on the left at the top of the stairs. The door was open, but Mary shut it as loudly as possible. The door opposite was open and it looked like the old lady's room, full of lace and doilies and whatnot. A lavender scent wafted out of it. Then she tiptoed down the hallway, to the rooms whose windows she had spied with her father's field glasses. The door on the left gaped open, revealing a bedroom that clearly belonged to Mr. Pettyjohn—its walls hung with many a papyrus scroll.

The door opposite was locked. Mary began to work the keyhole with one of her picks. Almost instantly, she could hear the meowing of felines, responding to the sound of the metal scraping on metal. After half a minute, the latch clicked open and Mary slipped into what could only be called a temple.

The walls were painted with a gold-like pigment. More papyrus scrolls, depicting ancient Egyptian figures, hung all around. The curtains were cracked open enough to illuminate the room, but in a shadowy way. A number of unlit candles and incense burners covered an altar ornately carved out of rosewood. And in the center of the altar stood the colorful statue of a woman wearing ancient Egyptian garb—normal in figure, but with the head of a cat.

Mary had seen her before, in books. "Bastet," she said under her breath. "The cat goddess. Well, Mr. Pettyjohn has certainly afforded you a place of honor."

Suddenly, she was aware of something—several some-things, in fact—rubbing up against her ankles, meowing amiably. She knelt down and started patting pretty, furry little heads.

"You must be Mrs. Fesler's Princess," she said to the black-and-ginger tabby. "And this pretty girl must be Pixie." Mrs. Sternberg's white and cinnamon moggie tried to push Princess out of the way. And against Mary's left thigh, rubbing harder than either of the ladies, and purring like a motor engine, it was Romeo, Miss Campbell's Russian blue. Having gained her attention, he promptly rolled over on his back, as if to command: *Rub tummy! Now!*

Meanwhile, nibbling away at one of the several food

bowls beneath the curtained window, the Egyptian Mau was quite indifferent to Mary's presence. That cat, undoubtedly Mr. Pettyjohn's Bastet, took a single look at her, then went back to her food. But what a beautiful animal! Almost like a miniature leopard. It wasn't unreasonable to think that a goddess might embody herself in such a creature.

Of course, where there were cats and food and water, additional accommodations needed to be made available. And several little sandboxes were tucked up against an inside wall.

Though the cats kept demanding Mary's continued attention, time was a-wasting. Mary hopped up and wrote a brief note on the back of a Moody Investigations business card.

Please come visit me at my office at your earliest convenience, she scribbled with her pencil. *The cats must be returned. Your servant, Miss Mary MacDougall.*

She left the card on the altar.

As she turned to leave, she nearly jumped out of her skin. For it brief instant, it seemed like a man had suddenly appeared in the room with her, out of nowhere. But it was only a cream-tinted robe, linen probably, covered with colorful embroidered Egyptian motifs, resting on a department store mannequin whose painted eyes stared senselessly ahead. Mr. Pettyjohn's vestment, no doubt, for when he held "services" in the worship of Bastet.

Taking care not to let any of her new feline friends escape, Mary slipped out into the hallway, quietly shutting the door behind her.

❦ ❦ ❦

Laid out on Mary's oak desktop, the autopsy images were colder and more brutal by far than the shot of Beansie resting in his coffin. The undertaker's art hadn't yet cleaned and buffed and sanitized him. His face was just a blotchy, dead thing speckled with dirt, hollow and empty, his hair a tangled mess. The heavily lashed eyes were two narrow slits. The lips were slightly parted, showing crooked teeth. He had a concave, hairless chest with scrawny arms lying next to him. He looked as insubstantial as a ghost.

Ever since she first heard of him, Beansie had been alive to Mary. Now, seeing the photos of him, his skinny figure laid out on the coroner's table, it felt like a violent blow to the pit of her stomach. She hadn't had to look death in the face since her mother left, and she had forgotten the dreadful, dark immensity of it.

"I'm not used to this," she said, looking up at Detective Sauer. Feeling a slight dampness in the corners of her eyes, she knuckled at them, to make it go away.

The detective showed no signs of sympathy, his face hard as granite. "Yet you insist on pursuing a career in this game," he said grimly. "Well, what you see here is one of the everyday realities of police and detective work."

The comment was perfectly reasonable, and Mary knew she needed to buck up. Drawing a deep breath, she fanned the three photos out on her desk. "I see no signs of trauma. No bruising about the neck or arms." She tried to keep her voice steady and sound coolly professional.

"As if he simply drowned," the detective said. "Even if it is your Tavish MacKenzie, it could well be an accidental death. It was bay water in his lungs, after all, not something out of a bath tub."

"Seriously, Detective? With the Ostovian signet ring sewn into his jacket?"

He sighed. "Yes, there is that, isn't there?"

Mary and the policeman sat silently for a few minutes, until they heard the hallway door click open. It was Jeanette and Mrs. Purcell. Mary quickly introduced the soup-kitchen proprietor to the policeman in the front office, out of view of the photos. The detective complimented the woman on her charitable work, then got down to brass tacks.

"Before we show you these photographs, I must ask you to promise something, Mrs. Purcell."

She looked a bit overwhelmed. "I suppose. If it's in my power."

"Oh, it is," he said. "I need you to never tell a soul what you've seen here. It could get me fired. I'm only doing this as a favor to Miss MacDougall. Can I rely on your complete discretion?"

Mrs. Purcell squared her shoulders and nodded. "Of course, Mr. Sauer. My lips are sealed."

"I would add, Mrs. Purcell," the detective said, "that these photographs are not pleasant to look at."

She took a deep breath. "I understand."

Mary ushered Mrs. Purcell into the inner office. She spied the three photos arrayed on the desk, and stepped forward for a closer look.

Her reaction was instantaneous and heart-wrenching.

"*Oh, no*! The poor lamb!"

Mary had the good sense to say nothing, but it tore at her to see the woman's distress. If this were a regular part of sleuthing, it could give her serious reservations about her cho-sen vocation. While it might be amusing to read about murder in a detective story, it wasn't much fun being close to one.

Tears running down her cheeks, Mrs. Purcell turned to Detective Sauer. "How did this happen? How did Tavish die?"

"So you're sure it's him?" the detective asked.

She nodded, picking up the photo that showed the lad's face in detail. "Poor lamb," she repeated under her breath.

"Please explain how you're so certain."

"Well, I *know* it's him, to begin with," she answered with a little snap of impatience. She picked up the picture showing the boy's bare torso, arms, and hands. "I'm quite certain. But if you need specific evidence, look at the left index finger." She tapped the spot with her own index finger. "The tip is cut off, halfway down the nail. Tavish did that working in our kitchen last winter, cutting stew meat. He was joking and chattering, like he always did, not paying attention, and the knife slipped. We had no idea he knew so many cuss words. He swore off cookery after that."

Detective Sauer grabbed the picture from her and examined it closely. "Well, I'll be... All right then, we have a positive, unique identification. Now as to what happened, ma'am, he drowned. Out in the bay. Found on the shore near the new sawmill. You know the one."

Mrs. Purcell nodded. "I do. But it doesn't make any sense. No sense at all. Tavish swore he wouldn't go out in a boat if you paid him. Almost drowned when he was little. Deadly afraid of the water. Wouldn't go near it." She gave a bitter laugh. "Didn't even care much for a bathtub. He might have died accidentally any which way, but not by drowning." She knitted her brows together. "Why would he be out there, near the water? No, it doesn't make any sense at all."

Chapter XXII

Seated alone at a table in the new library's main reading room the next day, Mary glanced down at her timepiece. Edmond was late. *Again.* She fidgeted impatiently but reminded herself that he had a job, too. And the note she had left him at Herr Neumann's studio, inviting him to lunch at Giovanni's, might not have reached him soon enough.

Drumming her fingers on the light-stained oak, she looked up at the window in front of her and admired the handsome Tiffany stained glass that adorned it. The piece depicted Minnehaha, standing close by the waterfall that bore her name. On the left side of the tall, rectangular glass were the words: "He named her Minnehaha, Laughing Water." Mary could vividly remember reciting from Longfellow's epic poem in front of her tenth grade English class—a triumph, if she did say so.

As she looked back toward the top of the main staircase, Edmond appeared from below and scanned the big reading room. He spotted her quickly, grinned, and came striding over.

Mary supposed that it wore off, the longer a couple was together—that thrill when you catch sight of each other. But that would be a long time in the future for them. Seeing Edmond now, the whole of him, certainly gave her a flush of excitement. The thick black hair. The piercing dark eyes. The animal magnetism of his every movement. He was quite easily one of the most attractive men she had ever known. That he had a quick wit, undeniable talent, and an effortless charm made him all the more delicious.

"Sorry I'm late," he said, sliding into the chair opposite her. "Neumann needed to talk to me about some Oddfellow who's in the mural. He wants his face changed—says he looks too genial. Wants more gravitas, evidently."

"Not to worry." Mary spoke quietly, so as not to bother—or inform—any nearby patrons. "We still have plenty of time for lunch. But before we leave, I just wanted to have a little chat."

Edmond's smile deflated. "Oh dear, have I done something?"

"I've been thinking about California."

His eyes widened. "You have? You'll come?"

Mary knew the look on her face gave him his answer.

"I don't think I'm going to like what you're about to say," he said.

"This just seems like the wrong time. For the both of us." Mary took his hand. "I understand how enticing it may sound—the adventure of it and all. I do. But I'm quite certain that you should, for a year or two, stay in Minnesota. Establish your reputation. Build up your bank balance. And then, to paraphrase Greeley, go west to that artists' colony in Monterey, young man."

She smiled at her turn of phrase, but she could tell that Edmond was unamused and unpersuaded.

"The teaching job in Minneapolis that you mentioned sounds splendid," she continued, liking the idea of Edmond being a short train ride away, rather than half a continent. "It would give you plenty of free time to do your own work and take some commissions, as well. In fact, I have a project in mind that will pay you quite handsomely."

Edmond's expression was a mixture of curiosity and wariness. "Do tell."

After Sunday's upbraiding by Jeanette, Mary had resolved to be more above-board about matters involving Edmond—such as not hiding him from her father. And this process had to start somewhere. Now was as good a time as any to spring her idea.

"I'd like you to do a full-length portrait of Father," she said.

The strangled gasp Edmond gave out almost made her giggle.

"I'm not sure that's a good idea," he said with a grimace. "Walking into the lion's den, you know."

"It's a *splendid* idea, Edmond, a fine project. And it will give you a chance to get to know Father, and him you. I'm convinced that if you two could just have a few decent conversations, you'd get along like old chums. It would take a number of sittings, wouldn't it?"

Edmond looked uncomfortable. "Don't get me wrong. I know he's a good man. And I'm sure he adores you. But Paul wrote me about meeting him. Your father was a bit exasperated about the marriage. Said there'd be hell to pay if Paul didn't treat your aunt perfectly. Paul's a stouter fellow than I am, and if *he* found your father intimidating, I'd probably be reduced to a quivering lump."

"Oh, don't be silly," Mary sniffed. "Father's bark is much worse than his bite."

"So you're saying he bites?"

Mary wrinkled her nose at him.

"But what would we talk about?" he continued. "I'd imagine he'd have no truck with my views on economics and politics. I mean, I am a socialist, for heaven's sake. And what does he know about the arts? Could we talk about music?

Painting? Literature?"

Mary didn't have an answer for his objections, so they sat silently for a moment as Edmond peered up over his shoulder at Minnehaha. "That stained glass. Very handsome. Who made it?"

"It's Tiffany, by a craftswoman named Anne Weston. She lives in Duluth."

"Well, maybe you could get Miss Weston to do a portrait of your father. In stained glass."

"Very funny," Mary said, getting to her feet. "This discussion isn't over. Not by a long shot. But I think we both could use a bit of sustenance." As Edmond came around the table, she linked her arm through his and they headed for the staircase. "You'll love Giovanni's. The lemon scaloppini is divine."

They descended the library's staircase and emerged out into the bright October sun. Clearly, Edmond's reaction did not bode well. Mary was used to getting her way and thought he was just being foolish, not seeing the sense in what she proposed. She had to convince him that staying in Duluth—or perhaps teaching in Minneapolis—would be much more lucrative and helpful to his career than some silly adventure in California.

But what if he's absolutely determined to go? said a nagging voice in her head. *What then, Mary MacDougall?* She didn't know the answer, and now wasn't the time to decide.

"Have you been following the Ostovian story?" she asked as they strolled eastward.

"Well, it's rotten that the poor kid happened to drown," Edmond said. "But I don't know why his death is more important than any other child's, just because he's a prince."

Mary nodded. "Exactly as I feel." She wasn't about to tell him how deeply she was embroiled in the matter. The men in her life tended to be overprotective.

"I'd love to know how he ended up in Duluth, though," he said. "A bit off the beaten track for nobility, wouldn't you say?"

"He was trying to escape his evil uncle and keep his cause alive, apparently. Why else?"

Edmond shook his head. "All of eastern Europe is in turmoil. The Russian czar freed the serfs, setting them at liberty from their masters, basically, to go eat grass. They're worse off now than they ever were before. The Austro-Hungarian empire's vassal states are chafing under the saddle. There's a big head of steam getting set to blow. It'll only take a few bullets to set the thing off like a powder keg. There'll be hell to pay, mark my words."

Mary sighed. "Seems like there's so much bad news these days. Let's talk about something more pleasant."

"That reminds me," Edmond said. "I got a letter this morning from Rosie Lehmann. You remember her, don't you?"

This was *not* the pleasant news Mary wanted to hear. "Of course I remember her," she said sweetly. She could hardly forget the woman, having seen every inch of her in an artistic nude photograph by Paul Forbes. "I remember her well." Mary recalled how the divorcée fluttered around Edmond at that party in Ishpeming and helped him finish his bank mural—after Mary, indirectly, caused him to break his arm.

"Thing is, she's gone back to Chicago for the winter to do some modeling, teach a bit, and take a portrait commission. Her first, actually. And she's invited me down for a visit this winter. Thought I might enjoy a few days in the Windy City. She's offered me her sofa."

"Well," Mary said through gritted teeth, "doesn't that sound like fun."

Chapter XXIII

Jeanette dug her gold wedding band out of her bag and slipped it onto her ring finger. The very feel of it brought a rush of vivid memories.

What a fine team she and Daniel had made—best friends, lovers, confidantes, partners in every aspect of life. She would have given a million dollars to simply stand at the sink one more time and hand him the rinsed dishes to dry, as they did every evening for five years. Even now, in the depths of the night, she would sometimes ache to again have him next to her in bed, to hear the rhythm of his breathing, to feel the warmth he gave off.

It still shocked her how something so extraordinary had ended in just a matter of days.

But now was not the time to go all weepy over that little paradise they had made together. Today the widowed Mrs. Harrison was transforming herself into Mrs. Elwood Walsh, the fictional wife of Mrs. Timmons's fictional brother—to be portrayed by Detective Robert Sauer.

They were to be present at the Timmons house when Ranko Kovac came to collect his ill-gotten gains and shanghai young Miss Timmons off to a life of depravity in New York City. With any good luck, Mr. Kovac would have no idea of the surprise that awaited him.

"Jeanette!" came Mary's voice from the inner office.

"What time is it?"

Jeanette grumbled a little under her breath and replied, "I thought you carried a watch."

"I do, but our railroad clock keeps better time."

Jeanette twisted around and peered at the big wall clock. "Exactly a quarter to eleven."

There was the sound of a chair rolling on wood and Mary came out of her office. "He should be here by now."

Jeanette rolled her eyes. "Yes, I understand. You're just dying to know how the police chief reacted to Mrs. Purcell's revelation. You've said as much half a dozen times this morning. I'm curious, too, but first things first. Mr. Kovac needs to be dispensed with. Detective Sauer made it very clear he'd be here in plenty of time for us to get to Mrs. Timmons's place before the fun begins."

Mary ignored her. "The detective has had a whole day to let the chief know what I've uncovered," she said. "The new evidence requires a fresh police investigation."

Jeanette had been dubious about participating in detective work from the start. Lately, though, she had to admit that it was becoming more appealing. Certainly, today's encounter with Ranko Kovac might actually be exciting. But Mary involving herself in a matter of princes and assassins and international intrigue was a march too far. She wished her cousin would let the matter drop.

"Don't forget, Mary, that Mr. Pettyjohn rang up about stopping by after work. You'll have to be here." The message Mary had left him on her business card had apparently produced the desired effect. It was time for the cat-napper to make an accounting of his misdeeds.

"Yes, I know, I know," the young detective snapped, pacing anxiously.

"I have an idea," Jeanette said to her cousin. "Why don't

you go have a walk? Burn off some energy?"

Mary shrugged. "I don't want to be out when Detective Sauer shows up."

And finally he did, a few minutes later. He was barely through the door when Mary rushed up to him.

"What did the chief have to say about Beansie?" she asked impatiently.

The detective looked over at Jeanette, raising his eyebrows, then back at Mary. "You won't like it."

Mary frowned. "You mean he isn't going to follow up on my lead?"

"The case is closed. The body is officially that of Nicolae Floria, former Prince of Ostovia. That's what the chief says. That's what the State Department says. Mrs. Purcell's statement won't change a thing."

Fury flared on Mary's face. "But that's wrong. It's stupid. It's unjust. They murdered him. *They murdered Beansie!*"

The detective looked no happier than she. "Miss MacDougall, you're the daughter of a millionaire, a man accustomed to power. It surprises me that you, of all people, haven't learned yet that power and money generally do trump justice. Happens all the time. The prince's uncle, the banks in Ostovia, their allies on Wall Street and in Washington, D.C.— all want Nicolae dead, out of the picture. They like this news and my chief has felt the pressure to make sure the story stays this way. Doesn't matter if the real prince is actually alive somewhere. His absence, even for a few years, allows the bloodsuckers time to do their work."

Mary plopped down in the client chair by Jeanette's desk. "But it's just *awful*."

"I *am* sorry," Detective Sauer said. Then his expression hardened. "But I would warn you against doing anything foolish, like talking to a reporter. It would go very badly for you and your father if you did. And please leave the Ostovians alone." He turned his gaze to Jeanette. "Now, Mrs. Harrison, I think it's about time you and I got over to Mrs. Timmons's."

Before she walked out with the detective, Jeanette stopped in front of Mary, still slumping and pouting, arms crossed, in that straight-backed chair. She put a hand on her cousin's shoulder. "You're right, Mary, it *is* awful. But Detective Sauer is correct. Let sleeping dogs lie. For heaven's sake, don't do anything impulsive. Now why don't you go out for that walk."

Mrs. Timmons was waiting on the front porch of her house on East Fourth Street, looking very nervous. And Jeanette didn't blame the woman in the least. It was exhilarating, if a bit nerve-racking, helping the police capture a criminal.

"Have you had any further word from Mr. Kovac?" Detective Sauer asked her.

"No, only that he would be here sometime after noon. I do hope he shows up."

"I have a feeling he'll want his four hundred dollars and a pretty young soprano to bring back to New York with him. Don't worry, it'll go smooth as silk."

Mrs. Timmons didn't look reassured. She drew in a deep breath. "Well, come into my parlor, said the spider to the confidence trickster."

"That's it, ma'am, keeping your jocularity about the situation," the detective said.

Jeanette smiled, not at Mrs. Timmons's little joke, but at Robert Sauer's somber response. He came across as such a serious and staid fellow—until you got to know his dry sense of humor.

He focused on Jeanette as the two of them sat on the sofa

in Mrs. Timmons's living room. The lady of the house stood to their side, crossing and uncrossing her arms nervously, knitting and unknitting her hands.

"Keep in mind, Mrs. Harrison," the detective said, "that you're now Mrs. Walsh, the sister-in-law. And I'm your husband Elwood, the lady's brother."

"And how long have we been married, Elwood?"

"Oh, let's say ten years, Gertrude."

Jeanette laughed. It was as good a name as any. "And how many children do we have?"

His face showed a hint of a grin. "How many can you stand?"

Jeanette had actually considered that, back when she had a real husband. "Three, I think. Two boys and a girl."

The detective nodded. "Sounds about right. The boys'll have to play ball, and hunt and fish."

"Of course. But the girl can come, if she wants."

Just then there came a sharp rapping on the front door.

Jeanette stiffened. "Oh, dear," she muttered.

Detective Sauer patted her hand. "Don't worry, you'll do fine. And I have men outside, just in case."

Mrs. Timmons took a deep breath, walked over, and swung the door open. "Come in, Mr. Kovac," she bubbled, neatly hiding her earlier discomfiture. "So fine to see you again."

"And you, as well, Mrs. Timmons," he replied, with some sort of eastern European accent. He seemed perfectly self-confident and genial, dapper and slender in his crisply tailored suit. His beard and moustache were impeccably trimmed and his shoes glinted. In his left hand he carried a thin briefcase of fine alligator, in his right an elegant gray fedora. "An exciting day for all of us, particularly for Miss Lorna." He peered around as he came into the living room. "Is she not with us this afternoon?"

"School, I'm afraid," Mrs. Timmons said. "Saying good-bye to her classmates."

For a few seconds, Jeanette tried to recall who the man reminded her of, at least in his manner. Then, with a twist of nausea, the name and face came flooding back to her. Kurt von Wassenburg. The scoundrel who, with his "mother," had relieved Jeanette of every penny she possessed. Confidence tricksters, she had learned, are consummately adept at building trust with their victims. Kovac had that air about him.

"Ah, well," he said, "we can finalize her plans in the morning. I have her ticket to Chicago for one o'clock tomorrow, and, of course, I will accompany her." He turned his magnetic gaze to Jeanette and Detective Sauer, clicked his heels, and made a quick little bow. "Good afternoon. I am Ranko Kovac. And whom do I have the pleasure of addressing?"

"Where are my manners?" Mrs. Timmons said, doing a good imitation of being flustered. "This is my brother, Mr. Elwood Walsh, and his lovely wife, Mrs. Walsh. Since I am a widow, with no man about the house, as you know, I wanted Elwood to meet you."

Detective Sauer stood. "You understand, I'm sure, Mr. Kovac. One can't be too careful these days, can one? I mean, deciding to ship my sweet young niece off to New York City requires some sober deliberation."

The two men gripped each other's hands and Kovac said, "Of course, of course. There are some bad sorts out there all too ready to take advantage of good folk. Shameful, just shameful." He made a fierce frown and shook his head.

Jeanette wasn't sure what it was, but some little wave of electricity seemed to go back and forth between Kovac and the detective as their hands touched—Kovac's lively eyes showing a glimmer of *something*.

Recognition?

The comprehension of an animal about to put its foot into a trap?

He suddenly looked distracted and held up a single finger, as in *hold on*. He opened his alligator briefcase, quickly glancing inside. "Would you believe it? How forgetful of me. I have left the contract at the hotel. Please do forgive me, but I must dash back and get it. I'm sure I can return within the hour." He began to back toward the door.

With an expression as blank as a sheet of paper, Detective Sauer stepped toward the man and firmly grabbed his left arm. "David Brankovich, I'm..."

The blow to his face came so quickly—seemingly out of thin air—that it amazed Jeanette the detective managed to remain on his feet. His own counterstrike caught the confidence man in the gut and lifted him in the air, sending the briefcase flying. In a few winks, the two men were brawling on Mrs. Timmons's living room floor, grunting and growling, punches flying. Jeanette looked around for something to bean Brankovich with, but she was afraid she might just as easily hit Detective Sauer.

All of a sudden, Brankovich clambered to his feet. He kicked the detective viciously in the ribs and managed to bolt out of the house.

Rushing to the open door, Jeanette screamed, "*Help! Police!*" She got onto the porch just in time to see a very large man in a brown suit, out on the public sidewalk, throw himself on Kovac, knock him flat, and pummel him with a pair of ham-sized fists.

"You busted my arm, you bloody bastard!" Brankovich howled, in a distinctly American accent. He was rewarded with a blow to the face, and he went silent.

Jeanette and Mrs. Timmons regarded the remarkable scene with open mouths. Detective Sauer staggered out, wincing and holding his ribs. Blood was seeping from his nose.

"Perhaps this wasn't the best plan after all," he groaned. "I am sorry, ladies, that you had to see it. My fault. Didn't think he'd do a runner."

Mrs. Timmons turned to him. "He knew something was wrong. But how?"

"Once in a while," the detective said with a grimace, "they can just smell a copper." Then probing his side, he winced.

Jeanette wanted to hug the poor man, she was so worried about him. But if a rib happened to be broken? *Not* a good idea. She pulled her hankie out of her bag and daubed at his bloody nose. "Are you all right, Robert? Did he hurt you?"

He looked surprised at her concern, but not displeased. "A little bit, I suppose. But it was worth it. Anyways, I'd wager Officer Horvat there hurt him worse."

Chapter XXIV

As his cobblers hammered away back in the workroom, Father Petrescu fixed Mary with an icy stare. It was the expression of a man angered by the temerity of a mere female to contradict him. Mary had seen it a few times, and it angered *her*.

"So you do not believe me, Miss MacDougall? You do not believe I could tell it was Prince Nicolae in that coffin? I, who saw him in the old country? Who has seen many photographs of him? You think it was some ragged boy from the street with a Scottish name?" He snorted in disgust. "Well, it seems then that the great John MacDougall has a fool for a daughter."

Mrs. Petrescu frowned at her husband. "Marius, please! She is a customer."

"Shut up, Larisa," he snapped.

The woman flinched and bit her lower lip.

Mary could sense her cheeks flushing. She could feel her forced, narrow smile freeze on her face. She didn't enjoy being called a fool by anyone, let alone a tradesman. But she understood she shouldn't react harshly. She needed to keep her equanimity. If she lashed out, she lost.

She knew one thing for sure—something more was going on here than an Ostovian priest losing his temper over an uppity young woman. If only she could figure out what.

"But shouldn't you be glad to know that it wasn't Prince Nicolae they found in the bay?" she countered. "If there is any doubt about the boy's identity, wouldn't you want to know if your prince was still alive?"

"The prince is perfectly fine where he is." Father Petrescu continued to glare at her, before looking upward, in the manner of some religious painting. "Nicolae sits in glory in heaven, among ancestors and the saints. He is in a better place." He leaned toward Mary, his dark eyes burning. "People who spread wicked falsehoods come to no good end." He stabbed his right index finger in her direction, almost touching her clavicle. "You need to stop telling these tales *immediately*."

Mary almost gasped. Had the man just threatened her? A priest, no less? Before she could sputter a reply, he turned on his heel and stomped back into his workshop, muttering what sounded like Romanian imprecations.

Mrs. Petrescu regarded Mary with a look of dismay. "I apologize for my husband, Miss MacDougall. This whole affair of Prince Nicolae has affected him greatly." She went over to her little desk and sat, giving out a deep, pained sigh. "Sometimes it seems too great a burden for any of us to bear."

Mary decided to drop the topic. It wouldn't do to press the woman further. Then she noticed the fancy cardboard box sitting at the corner of Mrs. Petrescu's desk—the box of hand-kerchiefs she had left with the woman for monogramming.

"I won't keep you any longer, Mrs. Petrescu. By the way, if you've finished with the hankies, I can pay and take them with me."

Mrs. Petrescu stared at the box, as if she couldn't remem-ber what was in it. "Oh, I'm so sorry," she finally said. "I am afraid I have more work left to do. I will have them delivered to your house tomorrow or the day after." She gave Mary a remorseful look. "Will you still want your new shoes, Miss

MacDougall? After... After my husband's outburst?"

"Absolutely. I'm really looking forward to hiking the woods in a good pair of boots. It'll be splendid to have them, despite a little argument with their maker." She smiled at Mrs. Petrescu. "Before I go, a question."

"Of course," the woman nodded.

"If your husband ministers to the Ostovian community, don't they support him? Financially, I mean?"

"You are wondering why he has a cobbler's shop?"

Mary nodded.

"Our congregants do provide us with support. But when we first arrived, there was no help at all. My husband needed a way to care for his family and his ministry. Since he had been a shoemaker before he became a priest..." She made a sweeping gesture around the storefront. "This shop sustains us. And we have earned enough to buy another building, the one next door. We started the bakery last year."

"So Mrs. Luca works for you?"

Mrs. Petrescu nodded. "A wonderful baker, is she not? By and by, our son will run the cobbler's shop on his own."

"Not all alone, I hope. I assume the other boy's a good, hard worker, too."

"Radu? Yes, Radu would be a fine employee, if he and his Uncle Teodor, who helps Mrs. Luca, choose to stay in Duluth. We can only pray that they remain."

Mary said goodbye and went out the door. She had left her office about an hour ago, waiting until Jeanette and Detective Sauer had departed for Mrs. Timmons's place—she didn't want the detective to suspect she was heading straight back to the Ostovians.

By now the wind had picked up and the sky had darkened. A few drops of rain were beginning to plop down on the wooden sidewalk. Mary's stomach reminded her it was lunchtime, and there was Mrs. Luca's bakery and café, right in front of her. Why not stay dry for a while and have a bite to eat?

As before, the baker was on duty behind her counter, next to the cash register, her nose in a new book.

"Hello again, Mrs. Luca," Mary said. "And what are we reading today?"

The woman looked up, her face brightening with a smile. "Ah, hello, Miss MacDougall, good to see you again." She held up a gray volume with red-colored printing on the cover.

"Oh, I love *Last of the Mohicans*," Mary said. "Chingachgook and Natty Bumpo and the fiendish Magua. A splendid adventure. Have you read the other books in the saga?"

Mrs. Luca indicated she had not and eagerly wrote down the titles as Mary dictated them.

"Now, I'm positively *starving*," Mary said. "May I have another one of those fine ham paste sandwiches and a cup of your excellent hot cocoa?"

"Just give me a few moments, please."

Mrs. Luca limped through the door behind the counter as Mary sat at a tiny table by the window. The gloomy, damp October afternoon reflected her mood perfectly. The encounter with Father Petrescu had unsettled her. Why had he reacted so vehemently to Mary's new information?

A few minutes later Mrs. Luca returned carrying a tray arrayed with sandwich, cocoa, and a bowl of something steaming and delicious-looking.

"You must try my new vegetable soup," she said. "No extra charge, of course."

"Why, thanks so much. It smells scrumptious."

The soup was, in fact, superb, packed with lots of vegetables—from turnips and potatoes to tomatoes and white beans—in a rich beef broth.

Mary nibbled and slurped away for a good twenty minutes, peering out the window onto Third Street. Mrs. Luca's cocoa was, as usual, delicious. A light drizzle was coming down now, causing people to scurry along at double speed. Mary hoped she could get back to the office without getting soaked. Stupid of her, not bringing an umbrella.

She wondered if the rain was as cold and penetrating out in Monterey, where Edmond wanted to go. The area never had proper winters, that much she knew. So she supposed a rainy day in California might, at least, be pleasantly warm. In principle, spending some indolent time out there had a certain appeal. There would be sightseeing and hiking and lively meals with Edmond and his friends. Not to mention the pleasure of the gentleman's company. But to her it sounded like a holiday, not a months-long residency.

Mary could practically feel her little business getting a purchase on some real success. People who might have once looked at her askance—a young lady gone *sleuthing*?— now might regard her with a certain respect. That was even more valuable to her than making money.

Would she throw that away so soon for a man? Even a man as appealing as Edmond? Most women would, she supposed. But Mary MacDougall wasn't most women.

"Miss MacDougall?"

Mary turned and looked up. "Yes, Mrs. Luca?"

"How did you like the soup?"

"It's first-rate. Just the thing for a cold, wet day."

"Would you like some dessert?"

Mary made a comically pronounced pout. "Oh, I was afraid you'd ask that. Your chocolate tart looks quite tempting, but I think I'll stick with one of those wonderful sweet cheese pastries, if you please."

When Mrs. Luca came back with the pastry, Mary asked her to sit down. "I'm curious about something," she said. "When you lived in Ostovia, did you ever have an opportunity to see Prince Anton and his son?"

"Oh, yes, I did. Duke Anton... He was a duke then, his father being the prince. Well, he and little Nicolae were as far away from me as you are now. The Imperial Russian Ballet had come to Ostovia and we were in the theater lobby during the interval. I asked Nicolae if he liked the ballet. He looked up at me and said it was wonderful and he wanted to be a dancer when he grew up. His father laughed and said the good Lord had other plans for Nicolae Floria."

Suddenly, the woman was weeping. "I am so sorry, but it pains me to think what the future held for that little boy. Nicolae would have been so just and kind to his people. It breaks my heart to think of him, cast out of his country, drowned in the cold, dark water."

Mary reached over and patted her hand. "Oh, dear, I didn't mean to upset you." Without even thinking about it, she whispered, "He may still be alive, you know."

Still snuffling, Mrs. Luca stared at her with wide eyes. "What? What do you mean?"

"I'm quite sure Nicolae didn't die here," Mary said. "It was another boy who drowned in the bay, a local lad who looked very much like him. It was his body in the coffin. And I have evidence he may have been murdered."

Mrs. Luca wiped her eyes with a plain white hankie that she pulled from her pocket. "Explain, please."

"The dead boy was named Beansie MacKenzie, and he went missing several weeks ago. Someone who knew him insists he couldn't have drowned accidentally, because he would never go near the water. He was terrifically scared of it."

Mary would have thought Mrs. Luca would be giddy with

relief, but she just looked baffled.

"I'm determined to find out who killed this poor boy," Mary said. "But you can take comfort in knowing that Nicolae may still be among the living."

It seemed Mrs. Luca finally comprehended what Mary had said. "Thank you, thank you, thank you." She put her hands together. "I will pray that you are right."

Outside, a light pebbly rain was coming down. Mary started off toward the streetcar stop, when she ran into Dorin Petrescu, the priest's son, who was heading back to the shop.

"Hello, Miss MacDougall," he said with a shy smile, looking like he was summoning up his courage to say something. He didn't seem to notice the many beads of rain collecting in his hair.

"How are you, Dorin?" Mary said, resisting the urge to wipe a dark smudge of shoe polish off his left cheek. They nipped back under the shoe shop awning to get out of the drizzle.

"Very well, thank you. I am hoping that you might introduce me to your father. It would be a great honor to meet him. And I believe I would be well qualified to work as a translator. In addition to English and Romanian, I speak German and Russian. But, of course, I am happy to do anything at all at your father's firm."

It certainly didn't sound as if Dorin was interested in pursuing a vocation in shoemaking, as his mother seemed to assume and his father was likely counting on.

"When my father gets back from his trip," she said, "I'll talk to him about you. But I can't promise that he'll see you. He's a very busy man."

"Thank you so very much, Miss MacDougall," he said. "That would be excellent."

Suddenly, the shop door swung open and out came the

other apprentice, Radu. He wore a dirty canvas apron and was wiping his hands on an equally soiled towel.

"Dorin," he said, "stop bothering the lady." He shot Mary a teasing, lopsided smile. "Your father wants you, *right now*."

Dorin quickly said goodbye and the two boys went inside, while Mary stood there under the awning.

That smile.

Lopsided, with a striking dimple.

Very much like the smile and dimple Mary had recently seen in the 1900 edition of *The American Almanac*.

She stood there, stunned, hardly daring to believe it.

Surely, she thought, heart racing, *it couldn't be* Nicolae? *The rightful Prince of Ostovia? Working in a shoemaker's shop in the West End?*

Chapter XXV

Arriving back at the office a bit after two, Mary took off her soaked coat and hat. Even though she had practically gotten drenched during her sprint from the streetcar to the 335 building, she had barely noticed. She was beside herself with excitement.

She *had* seen him, she was certain—Prince Nicolae Floria of Ostovia. He had been hiding in plain sight all along. Well, perhaps the workroom of a cobbler's shop couldn't be called "plain sight." Still, if Mary hadn't bothered to check the almanac for his photo, she likely never would have recognized him.

She had almost been tempted to follow him back into the shop, but thought better of it. Father Petrescu would have been especially displeased to realize she knew that he was the protector of the hale and hearty Nicolae Floria. It grieved her to suspect it, but now she had to wonder if the priest had something to do with Beansie MacKenzie's horrific fate. Even Mrs. Petrescu might be involved. And now *they* knew that *she* knew.

Of course, blundering in with accusations and anger wouldn't do. She needed time to plan her next, vitally important move. It had to be subtle, it had to be smart.

Back at her desk, she pulled out the almanac and stared at

the photograph of Prince Anton and then-Duke Nicolae, feeling ever surer of her conclusion. That smile was so unique, so vivid. What were the chances that Radu Bogdan *wasn't* the deposed prince? It was certainly the same boy, just a few years older, taller and more mature.

Mary understood why the prince's supporters would want to keep his presence in Duluth a secret—secret, perhaps, even from much of the Ostovian community. After all, Prince Vladislav could well have sympathizers in Ostovian outposts across the country who might inform on Nicolae.

But Mary couldn't get past what to her was the central concern: *How had poor Beansie MacKenzie ended up in a coffin, passed off as the Prince of Ostovia? Who put him there? Who murdered him? Had the Petrescus used him to foil Vladislav's assassins?*

Whatever she uncovered, it was essential that there be an accounting for what happened to Beansie.

Mary did not give one single fig what the State Department and the Ostovian mission in Washington preferred. And all those bankers who wanted to exploit Ostovia could go to hell. If she had to trek all the way to President Roosevelt's office to get a hearing, by God she would do it.

But for the time being, she was stuck in the office waiting for news of Jeanette and Detective Sauer. She certainly was curious to know how the counterfeit couple fared at Mrs. Timmons's house. And then there was Quentin Pettyjohn, who had promised to visit later in the afternoon. Mary had yet to decide how she was going to deal with him—much of that depended on his contrition or lack thereof.

Truth be told, the cat case now seemed particularly silly, paling in comparison to an international conspiracy. The matter of Prince Nicolae was the kind of investigation Mary MacDougall dreamed of—unmasking a terrible crime to the world, not to mention gaining a little bit of glory for Mary MacDougall.

The rain was not letting up, and the wind was whooshing and roaring. She could well imagine towering waves out on the big lake, which was known to get dangerously violent in a heavy storm.

To warm up and calm down, she made a cup of tea and settled in at her desk. She thought about tomorrow night. Edmond had invited her to the party at Herr Neumann's house, honoring one of his old students visiting from Bavaria. He was touring the middle west on a painting trip. She hoped the damp weather would have retreated by then.

Of course, Mary's interest was far less in the visiting painter than in the painter whom she knew so well. Under different circumstances, she would have looked forward to a long, pleasant evening in Edmond's company. But more and more, his presumption that she would lark off to California with him—leaving behind everything she'd worked for—had annoyed her. It was coming up to the moment when she would have to say what needed saying.

Putting that unpleasant thought aside, she started a volume by Eugène François Vidocq, the great French detective. It was called *The Thieves,* and it recounted some of his adventures. Supposedly, he had inspired Poe to create C. Auguste Dupin, the first detective in the history of fiction. A remarkable man, Vidocq—a reformed criminal himself. She had read his memoirs just a year ago.

Even with the tempest outside, the Vidocq book was engrossing—enough so that she didn't notice the time passing.

Nor the stranger who had slipped into the office, unannounced. Until she looked up and saw him, standing before her in the doorway to her inner office.

"Heavens!" she exclaimed. "You startled me. I didn't hear

you come in."

The man was clearly a laborer. He had on well-worn dungarees, a brown canvas jacket dampened with rain, and a soaked brown golf cap pulled down over his ears. A bushy dark mustache decorated his upper lip. He looked strong, sinewy—standing with his hands clasped behind his back, in the European manner.

"You are Miss MacDougall?" he said in a thick accent.

"Yes, how can I help you?"

"Perhaps it is I who can help *you*," he said. "What do you know of Prince Nicolae?"

Mary's heart began to race. *Did he have information for her?*

"I know a little," she said, rising from her chair. "And what, may I ask, is your name?"

"My name does not matter," the man said in a flat, quiet tone. He stood motionless.

A warning bell went off in Mary's head. The fellow didn't act like he was there for a nice chat. And it was distressingly clear that—friend or foe—he had her boxed in.

"Do you think the prince is still alive?" he asked.

Mary didn't reply. Outside, more thunder rumbled and lightning flashed. There was a steady, heavy splatter of rain on the window—the perfect setting for a deadly encounter.

The man seemed to interpret her silence as a yes. "So you do think he is alive. Who else have you told?"

Mary hadn't, in fact, had a chance yet to tell anyone about her encounter with Nicolae. "No one. I've told no one." Wondering if that was the best thing to say, she gave a nervous laugh. "Who would believe it anyway?"

Where were Jeanette and Detective Sauer, she thought anxiously. *They ought to be here by now.*

"I am glad to hear it, Miss MacDougall. And I am sure you

can understand that it is in Ostovia's best interest that no one else believes the prince is alive."

Mary suddenly remembered the angry look on Father Petrescu's face when she revealed her knowledge of the dead boy's actual identity. Had *he* sent this man? Had he decided that Mary needed to be silenced—one way or another? Worse yet, was the man here on Mrs. Petrescu's orders?

As the awful peril of her situation sank in, Mary felt an odd emotion. Not fear. Not regret. But rage.

"Ostovia's best interest?" she snarled. "How dare you come to this country, this city, and act like barbarians. You've no right to kill anyone in Duluth—prince or orphan boy. Do you actually think the police will let you get away with threatening John MacDougall's daughter? They'll hunt you down like a dog." She stopped to catch her breath. She was so angry she was shaking. "Now get out of my office! Right now!"

The man looked surprised—and mildly amused—by her outburst. "Miss MacDougall, if we can elude Vladislav's assassins for this many months, I think we can elude the police of this backwater town. The unsolved murder of a socially prominent young lady? So sad."

With an apologetic shrug, he brought both hands from behind his back. That's when Mary saw the blade of an automatic knife click open. He held the weapon in his right hand, in an easy, practiced grip. "Do not worry, there will be no pain," he said, stepping to his left around the desk. "I will make it quick."

Mary shuffled in the other direction, mashing down the panic. She had no weapon. Only Fujian White Crane technique. Parry the knife attack, as Mrs. Chin taught her. Then, a disabling blow. Nose. Adam's apple. Groin.

She rolled her chair in front of her, as a makeshift barrier between her and the assailant—drawing him around the desk, so she could get into the outer office and flee.

He actually laughed. "So you mean to stop me with a chair? You are a brave girl, but I am afraid you must die."

The man still had a slight smirk on his face when, out of nowhere, Jeanette's Remington typewriter came flying through the air, slamming into the back of his head. As it hit with a meaty *thunk*, a loud *diiing* nonsensically echoed through the office.

The would-be ripper crumpled to the floor, dazed and groaning, as the typewriter landed with a crash.

Around the corner of the doorframe, like some improbable guardian angel, Mr. Quentin Pettyjohn peered at the man, then at Mary, his eyes and mouth wide open.

"Miss MacDougall! Are you all right?"

Mary scampered around her desk, plucked up the knife, and then stepped over the supine assassin, who was still moaning piteously.

"Quick, Mr. Pettyjohn," she panted, grabbing his arm, "we've got to get out of here and get help."

They rushed into the hallway, heading to the clock repair shop next door. Mary found the door locked, then pounded on it. No one answered, so they headed to the dental office toward the back.

"Look there! He's getting away," Mr. Pettyjohn shouted.

Mary twirled around and saw her would-be killer stagger toward the stairs at the front of the building, rubbing his head and muttering darkly in Romanian. Mr. Pettyjohn started after him.

"No, let him go. It's too dangerous."

They went back into Mary's office and she locked the door, in case the villain returned. As she flicked the knife blade shut, Mr. Pettyjohn went into her inner office and re-trieved the mangled typewriter. He placed it gently back on

Jeanette's desk. "I'm afraid it'll need some repairs." Then he suddenly went all white and swayed a bit on his feet. "Goodness, I do believe I might faint."

Mary rushed over to him and eased him into one of Jeanette's client chairs. Then she darted into her office and tossed the knife in a drawer. If Jeanette should see the nasty little thing, she'd want to know how Mary came to have such a weapon.

Coming back out of her office, she saw that her rescuer seemed to be reviving, the color coming back into his cheeks.

"Oh, Mr. Pettyjohn," she said, perching in front of him on the corner of Jeanette's desk, "you've been through so much and I must apologize. But I have to ask you for a very, *very* big favor."

"Of course," he nodded, straightening up in the chair.

"Please keep secret what you saw here and what you just did. It will be not only to my advantage, but to yours. Do I have your word?"

"But the police should know. That man was threatening you. With a knife!"

"Please, Mr. Pettyjohn, promise me you won't tell a soul."

He looked quite baffled. "I don't understand, but I promise."

Mary impulsively leaned over and gave him a quick hug.

"Thank you, Mr. Pettyjohn. You saved my life."

Only a few seconds after she released the startled bookkeeper, she heard a key unlocking the hallway door. She turned to see Jeanette step in, looking quite surprised.

"Mary," she exclaimed. "Mr. Pettyjohn. What are you two doing? *Why* did you have the door locked?" Her eyes shifted to her desk and a look of horror came over her face. "And what in the world happened to my Remington?"

Chapter XXVI

Jeanette almost cried when she saw the condition of her fine new typewriter—sitting forlornly askew on her desk, with the platen knob and carriage return lever both bent out of shape, and the metal frame by the keyboard noticeably warped. She went over and petted it, almost as if it were a living thing. She turned back to Mary and Mr. Pettyjohn.

"Who did this?" she demanded.

Mr. Pettyjohn stared at her, looking a little shell-shocked. Mary, for her part, seemed suspiciously, well, *perky*.

"It all happened so quickly," she said, "it's hard to explain."

"Well, try," Jeanette growled.

"I can tell you," Mr. Pettyjohn piped up, suddenly coming to life. "I came, of course, at Miss MacDougall's request and—"

"No, Mr. Pettyjohn, let me tell the tale," Mary interrupted, shooting the man a meaningful look. "You see, Jeanette, I took your advice and had myself a nice long walk after you and the detective left. By the way, how did the Timmons affair go? I'm just dying to know."

Something smelled pretty fishy and Jeanette was not about to let Mary change the subject. "There's time for that later. Tell me about my Remington."

Mary sighed. "Well, I was killing time reading the Vidocq memoir I told you about. Waiting, you know, for someone to show up. You, Mr. Pettyjohn, *anyone*. At all events, I was reading my book. Gripping stuff, I can tell you. I was quite lost in it. And suddenly I heard men's voices in the front office. I jumped up and ran out here. And what should I see but Mr. Pettyjohn threatening a shady-looking fellow with his umbrella. The sneak thief had hold of your Remington. Aimed to filch it, evidently. And he would have, if our friend here hadn't come along."

Jeanette noted that Mr. Pettyjohn seemed as riveted by this account of his heroism as she was. He started to say something but Mary hushed him.

"I don't doubt that Mr. Pettyjohn would have whacked the fellow a good one, but the culprit kept backing away, toward my office door. Unfortunately for him, he was holding onto the machine with both arms—the thing's heavy, after all—and he couldn't really defend himself. He kept cursing Mr. Pettyjohn in the most offensive way, until he finally knew he was cornered. He dumped the Remington on the floor. You can see the mark right over there."

Mary pointed at the floor just outside her door. And indeed, there was a noticeable gouge in the wood. Just to Jeanette's right lay a rolled-up umbrella, still soaked with rain, with a heavy, burly wooden handle. Mr. Pettyjohn's, no doubt.

"He bolted right by Mr. Pettyjohn, but not without getting a good whack to the backside. *Right, Mr. Pettyjohn*?"

Smiling nervously, the cat-napper nodded. Jeanette had a sneaking suspicion all was not as it seemed. "You've called the police then?"

Mary shook her head. "No, I'd rather not. I don't want to be any more of a nuisance to them than I already am. No one was hurt, other than the Remington." She turned to their guest.

"You're all right, aren't you, Mr. Pettyjohn?"

"Oh, yes indeed," he said nervously. "Fit as a fiddle."

More suspicious yet, thought Jeanette. But she was in no mood to joust with Mary. "It doesn't look repairable," she said, shaking her head. "How am I supposed to get any work done without it?"

"Don't worry, we'll get you a new one," Mary reassured her. "Now, though, we need to clear the air with Mr. Pettyjohn about his, umm, little guests."

Jeanette suddenly remembered what had been at the top of her mind, just before she'd walked into the office. "I have a cabbie waiting downstairs. I thought there might be a chance you had talked to Mr. Pettyjohn already, and we could head home without needing to take the streetcar in the rain."

Mary turned to Mr. Pettyjohn. "Why don't we all take the cab home and we'll talk along the way. We can drop you off on Wallace Avenue."

Five minutes later they were trundling east on Second Street, crowded three abreast in the cab—the rain plopping loudly away on the cover above them.

"I have an idea why you took Pixie and Princess and Romeo," Mary said, from the center seat. "But I'd like to hear what you have to say for yourself."

The bookkeeper frowned and looked up at the carriage cover. "Oh, dear. How to explain to someone who may not understand a matter of faith."

Mary narrowed her eyes. "Please do your best."

He took a deep breath. "I have been a student of ancient Egypt since I was a young man. I read books voraciously. As you've seen, I collect Egyptian art and artifacts. And I have been a cat lover all my life. What I'm about to tell you may sound peculiar, I suppose. But it's the truth. Well, at least the truth as I experienced it."

"We're all ears," Mary said. "Aren't we, Jeanette?"

"Indeed," Jeanette said. "All ears." After the day she'd had, she didn't think *anything* could sound peculiar.

"Last year I was suffering from terrible insomnia," Mr. Pettyjohn said. "Barely caught a wink for weeks on end. Don't know what the problem was. One night I finally fell into a deep slumber. I was transported to a temple in a lush, beautiful desert oasis. Possibly outside Thebes, around the reign of Senuseret the First is my best guess. And there I met Bastet."

Well, I was wrong about "peculiar," thought Jeanette. *Delusional was more like it.*

"The cat goddess," said Mary.

Mr. Pettyjohn's face was practically glowing with the recollection. "Actually, the goddess of cats and many other things. I cannot begin to tell you how lovely she was. She spoke to me, telling me that she required a priest to worship her—so many having fallen away over the centuries. That I was to build her a temple and, when the time was right, collect felines that embodied her."

Pure lunacy, thought Jeanette. What the poor man needed was an alienist.

"So you erected your temple in a spare bedroom and abducted your trusting friends' little kitties," Mary summed up.

Her accusation caused him to squirm. "But I only chose the cats in whom I could perceive the goddess. They deserve more than tins of tuna fish and scratches behind the ears. They deserve to be worshipped."

"Well," Mary said firmly, "the three that aren't yours are all going home, back to their rightful owners. *Tomorrow, if possible.*"

He cringed, looking equally contrite and miserable. "But Mrs. Fesler and the others will be rather angry, I should think. They would be well within their rights to report me to the police."

"That they would," Mary agreed. "And more likely than not, Bastet will not rescue you. I suggest that we first tell Mrs. Fesler who the culprit is."

Mr. Pettyjohn groaned. "Must you? Couldn't we just return the cats anonymously?"

"No, Mrs. Fesler is my client and I represent her interests. I expect you to be at home tomorrow at noon. Mrs. Harrison and I will collect the animals and deliver them to Mrs. Fesler. Then it's up to her and the others to decide your fate. Now do you promise to make no fuss? Abide by their decision?"

Looking thoroughly remorseful, he nodded.

"I'll try to persuade Mrs. Fesler to forgive and forget. But you have to promise me you'll *never* do such an irresponsible thing ever again."

Mr. Pettyjohn held up his right hand, like a witness taking the oath. "I swear, on the sacred heart of Bastet herself."

As soon as the chastened gentleman stepped out of the cab, dashing up his sidewalk in the rain, Mary turned to Jeanette.

"Now tell me everything that happened with Ranko Kovac."

Jeanette did just that. It gratified her when Mary winced, upon hearing that Detective Sauer may have sustained a broken rib or two, and a bloody nose. The girl actually seemed fond of him and concerned about any injury. No doubt about it, Robert Sauer was a fine fellow. Jeanette looked forward to working with him again soon.

"Sounds like you two did a splendid job for the Timmonses," Mary said, as they pulled up the MacDougall driveway. "Another scoundrel off the street and an innocent young lady saved from a dreadful misadventure."

Jeanette gave her a sideways glance. "Yes, apparently *two* young ladies dodged the bullet today. But I think, in your case, there's more to the story than you're letting on."

Mary gave her a sweet, guileless smile. "I wonder, Jeanette, when this damnable rain will stop. I'm starting to feel like a duck in a downpour." And she hopped out of the cab and darted inside.

"*Quentin Pettyjohn* took our cats?"

Mrs. Fesler stood there in her parlor early the next afternoon, pondering Mary's amazing revelation. It was beautiful and sunny outside, a nice change from Thursday's damp and cold.

"Really? Mr. Pettyjohn? I can't imagine him having the gumption to do such a thing."

As the conversation ensued, Pixie and Romeo were having a fine old time exploring Mrs. Fesler's parlor. Princess seemed glad to be home, hovering close to her mistress's ankles. Meanwhile, one of the woman's other resident felines, Blackie, had perched himself on the back of the sofa, observing the proceedings with some interest.

"Well, he said he didn't do it on his own," Mary said. "He acted on orders from a higher authority."

"Higher authority?"

Jeanette almost laughed at Mrs. Fesler's befuddlement. The whole motive for the cat-napping affair seemed positively preposterous.

"Mr. Pettyjohn has an affinity for all things Egyptian," Mary explained, "including its ancient religion. In fact, he is a worshipper of the old cat goddess Bastet."

Mrs. Fesler frowned. "And I thought he was a Methodist."

"So when the goddess and he had a little rendezvous off in dreamland," Mary continued, "she commanded him to gather up felines that manifested her own divinity, so to speak. He saw that sacred spark in Princess, Pixie, and Romeo, in addition to his own cat."

"But, but…" Mrs. Fesler said, struggling to take it in. "That's just silly."

"No argument here," Mary agreed.

"I think the world of Princess, but she's no goddess, I can tell you. Sometimes a *very* naughty little girl." Mrs. Fesler bent over and scratched Princess behind the ears, provoking a low, vibrating *purrrr*. "If you ask me, poor Mr. Pettyjohn needs a stint with a brain doctor. Deities don't go around Duluth willy-nilly, you know, commanding people to kidnap other people's cats."

"I should hope not," Mary said. "But in spite of everything, please consider forgiving him. Mr. Pettyjohn is at your mercy. He swore on the sacred heart of Bastet herself that he'd never do anything like this again. He knows he's made a terrible mess of things and regrets it deeply."

Jeanette could tell that Mrs. Fesler—having digested the notion that the man believed he was able to consort with a goddess—was feeling not a little bit peeved. One couldn't blame her, but Jeanette found herself agreeing with Mary's notion of clemency for Mr. Pettyjohn.

"He's really very sorry, you know," she put in, "and all he wants is to remain a member of your club."

"I have to confess, I'm not sure what to do about our Mr. Pettyjohn. I'm not sure at all," Mrs. Fesler said. "But please, Miss MacDougall, do tell me what I owe you and I'll settle my account."

Mary turned to Jeanette. "Do you know off the top of your head?"

"Afraid not," Jeanette answered. "The rate is five dollars a day. So no more than twenty-five or thirty dollars, for five or six days. I need to consult our logs."

Mrs. Fesler grimaced. "That's a lot of money." She bent over and snatched up Princess, cuddling the animal. "I hope you're grateful for all the trouble I've gone through to get you back, you little imp." She winked at Mary. "She isn't, you know. Grateful, that is."

"Of course she isn't," Jeanette laughed. "She's a cat."

Chapter XXVII

As they rode away from Mrs. Fesler's house, Mary was determined to enjoy the rest of the day and not ruminate about poor Beansie and would-be rippers and whatnot. But she couldn't help seeing, in her mind's eye, the blade of that automatic knife flick out. She shuddered inside. What was to stop the man from making another run at her? The only thing for it was to be on constant guard and pack a revolver in her bag.

Thankfully, yesterday's dismal dampness had fled in the night like a thief, and good riddance. The afternoon was simply too glorious for anything but sheer pleasure—sunny, warmish, and brimming with autumnal color everywhere. A rare outburst of summer in mid-October.

And she'd be with Edmond that evening at Herr Neumann's dinner party. Normally, that would have brightened her mood even more. Normally, she loved a nice party. But she had a premonition that tonight they'd be settling the matter of Monterey. And Mary knew that neither of them would be happy with the outcome.

"Do you think she'll let Mr. Pettyjohn off?" Jeanette asked, as Bill whistled a jaunty tune up in the driver's seat.

"I do hope so," Mary answered. "I believe he's learned his lesson, don't you?"

"Well, I think he knows not to snatch cats from people's houses any more. As you suggested to him, he ought to take in animals that manifest the goddess *and* need a home. Everyone benefits."

"Indeed. Our furry friends need roofs over their heads."

"I'll send Mrs. Fesler's bill out as soon as I have my new typewriter. Another Remington will do fine."

Mary smiled. She had been waiting for Jeanette to bring up the matter of the trashed typewriter. Her cousin seemed inordinately fond of the machine, which Mary found amusing. After all, wasn't it just a collection of metallic bits and pieces? Nothing of great value, really.

"Order a new one whenever you want," she said. "Are you certain you don't want to go to the dinner party tonight? It would take your mind off your poor, dead Remington. And Edmond specifically told me you're more than welcome. Frau Neumann has been marinating the sauerbraten for a whole week. It sounds absolutely delicious, don't you think?"

"It does. But thank you, no. I have a stack of letters to reply to. And Detective Sauer loaned me a new book he just finished. By a young writer named Joe... John... No." Jeanette paused to summon up the name. "*Jack.* London. His first novel, apparently. About a headstrong young woman who goes to the Yukon against her family's wishes."

"Well, headstrong young women certainly can make life interesting for their families, don't you think?"

Jeanette raised one eyebrow. "Yes, they certainly can. By the way, thank you for informing me that you're seeing Edmond. I'm glad our little talk made an impression. And I'll be quite relieved when you tell your father that Edmond is in town. Full disclosure, don't they call it?"

When they arrived home, Mary found three items waiting for her in the front hallway. A letter from Father, a letter from Tena, and the expected box of hankies from Mrs. Petrescu. She grabbed them all and headed upstairs, ripping open the note from Tena as she went.

Mary's aunt wrote that their intimate nuptials would be held in Tena's own parlor the week after Christmas—presided over by an Allegheny County judge whose wife was a friend of hers. Then, after New Year's, the newlyweds were heading off to Egypt for their honeymoon. Tena said they intended to make a trip to Duluth in the springtime, and she hoped that Mary would be there. Paul had told her that Edmond was going to California in the spring, and that he hoped to bring Mary with him. Did she really intend to accompany him? Very bold, indeed. Had she broached the subject with her father?

Mary was instantly incensed. What was Edmond thinking, putting that notion in Paul's head? Yet more reason to make her position clear and final, *this evening*!

Next, she scanned Father's dispatch. Much of it had to do with boring details of a deal he had made to become a partner in a Maine timber venture. He said he should be home on or about the twenty-fourth.

Truth be told, Mary would be happy to see the old grouch. The house always seemed a bit empty when he wasn't around. She did need to figure out a way to tell him about Edmond being in town, but she had another week to ponder that.

She set the two letters on her dresser next to the hankie box that Mrs. Petrescu had sent. When she finished dressing, she pulled out her small beaded handbag and put her Smith & Wesson .38 into it. Too bulky, she decided. And what if someone caught a glimpse of it? Then she pulled out her new .32, another Smith & Wesson. It nestled quite demurely in the handbag. After her encounter with that Ostovian thug, she had no intention of sallying forth unarmed in coming days. She would not be caught out helpless again.

The Neumann house was about eight blocks up the hill. It was nondescript on the outside but bursting with art and music inside. While Fraulein Neumann played Grieg on the baby grand—quite handsomely, in fact—her father showed Mary around the place. Many of his own pieces graced the walls, along with works by friends and students. He introduced her to the guest of honor, his former student, now a successful landscapist living in Munich. Mary recognized several local artists in attendance, along with a couple of well-heeled collectors. The German wine seemed to have put everyone in a convivial mood.

It amused Mary to find Edmond hard at work in the kitchen, his sleeves rolled up, peeling potatoes for Frau Neumann. "Usually all thumbs at this sort of thing," he laughed, "but no serious wounds so far. Go wait for me out on the back porch. I'll bring some wine. If you're hungry, there are pears on the table."

"But take care," Frau Neumann put in with a grin, "to leave plenty of room for sauerbraten."

Mary made her way to the rear of the house, greeting people as she went. She stepped outside into a lovely space that glowed with autumnal colors in the early evening's light. In the crisp air, she caught a smoky whiff of leaves being burned somewhere nearby. She sat at the table and picked up one of the pears—enjoying the spot and relishing the beauty of the moment. A few minutes later, Edmond joined her, bearing two goblets of white wine.

"Isn't it pleasant?" he said, sitting down and handing her the wine.

"Delightful." Mary put aside the uneaten pear and took the glass. "I could stay out here forever."

"You wouldn't rather be chasing some bank robber?"

"No," she said adamantly. "Tonight I'd let him steal all the gold in the vault."

"Well then, I hope you don't mind if I steal one of these." He leaned over and gently kissed her.

"Very nice," she said, savoring the unexpectedness of it. "As kissing bandits go, you're a wily one. Hope you've no plans to do it professionally."

"No, strictly an amateur when it comes to smooching." He leaned back in his chair, grinning. "But competent, I hope."

"Oh, yes indeed," Mary nodded with a coy smile.

"Speaking of my profession, the art school in Minneapolis does want me to teach again. The scandal of last year has been forgiven." He took a sip of his wine. "I told them I could fill in over the winter, but I'm off to California in April." His eyes met Mary's and his expression turned serious. "Say you'll come with me. *You must!*"

Despite the calming effects of the wine, Mary felt her frustration flaring. "We *do* need to talk about that, Edmond. Apparently Paul and Tena are under the impression that I've already agreed to head west with you."

A look of dismay came over his face. "Sorry. I shouldn't have mentioned it when I wrote Paul. I hope I didn't get you in hot water."

Mary shook her head. "No, no, it's not that. But you still don't seem to understand. I have a career. I can't just go running off to Monterey like some flibbertigibbet."

"And *I* don't understand why you wouldn't jump at the chance." Edmond sounded equally frustrated. "Duluth is fine, I suppose. So is Minneapolis. But I'm craving something fresh—new scenery, new people, new outlook." He gave her a vexed look. "Why *wouldn't* you want go somewhere totally different, totally fresh? Be someone other than the great John MacDougall's daughter? Nobody in Monterey will know who you are, and if they do, they won't care. Now be honest—

doesn't that sound more stimulating than doing the same old thing day after day in the same old Duluth? "

Mary sniffed. "I rather like being the 'same old' Mary. I guess I don't view my life here as dismally as you seem to."

"Now don't go twisting my words around. I just think you'd benefit from something new and exciting."

"You want excitement, Edmond?" Mary said. "I'll give you excitement. I just saved a young woman from putting herself in the clutches of a confidence trickster who might have ruined her. I recovered three beloved pet cats abducted by an adherent of an Egyptian religious cult." She thought that sounded more dramatic than a trio of kitties being stolen by an eccentric bookkeeper. "I tracked down a pocket watch that contained a young man's only photograph of his dear, deceased mother. And I believe I've uncovered the murder of an innocent young man by European assassins."

Instead of looking impressed, Edmond looked appalled. "*Assassins*? I suppose it involves that Ostovian prince, doesn't it?"

"Well, as a matter of fact, it does. But I can't tell you anything more."

He groaned. "Why do you find that sort of business appealing? It's dangerous. It's ugly. It's awful. It absolutely baffles me."

"And I don't see why you find moving to the wild west so appealing."

"Hardly the wild west," Edmond muttered. "You're just a day away from San Francisco. Besides, it's not as though you couldn't come back here in six months or a year and start up your business again. It's not like you have clients lined up out the door."

"But how can I build a business if I disappear for months on end?" She felt they were talking in circles. "I thought this

223

was working so well, having you here in Duluth. I know I can find more commissions for you, even if you don't want to paint Father. Meanwhile, I can continue my detecting, and we can get together whenever the fancy strikes."

Edmond took another slow sip. "That's all well and good. But there is the matter of your father. I know perfectly well that if you and I are to go forward, I have to face him and we have to find some accommodation. Truth be told, I haven't minded you keeping me secreted away. But it just postpones facing up to him."

"You're quite right," she said. "I'm done with deceit and dissembling. I'm going to tell him you've been here for weeks now and I want him to get to know you."

Edmond looked uncomfortable. "May I tell you the truth?"

Mary thought that sounded rather ominous. "All right."

"You're the first rich person I've ever known who I've genuinely liked."

Mary almost argued that she wasn't all that rich, but knew that was disingenuous. "That's painting a lot of well-off people with a very broad brush, isn't it?"

"A few I've met were pleasant enough. Some were arrogant. Some were outright bastards, in the way they treated people. And however cordial some of them might seem, most of them could not give the slightest damn about folks below them on the social ladder. That's why I find being in their world so unsettling, Mary. It's not a place where I belong, even with you in it."

Alarm bells rang in her head. Mary had a sudden fear that she might lose Edmond to this ridiculous notion that well-to-do people were all callous and indifferent to the human condition. Granted, he wasn't entirely wrong. Mary knew of wealthy individuals who could give Ebenezer Scrooge and King Midas runs for their money. But she had to prove to him that John

MacDougall wasn't one of them.

"You're not being fair, Edmond," she said. "You have to give Father a chance. You have to spend some time with him, just talking. I know you'll end up liking him and he you."

Edmond tilted his head. "I'll do it on one condition."

Mary brightened. "What?"

He leaned across the table and took her hands. "Say you'll come to California with me. You don't have to promise to stay. Just come and give it a month or two. Just think of it as a holiday."

She pulled her hands back, feeling her whole body tense. "Edmond, *I have a career.* I can't walk away from it, just as I'm getting started."

"More a whim than a career," he huffed.

Mary's anger flared.

"Whim? *Whim?*"

Glaring at him, she bolted to her feet. "If you don't mind, Mr. Roy, I think I'll go mingle." And she tramped back inside the house, fuming.

"Mary," came his voice, as she went into the house, "I'm sorry."

She managed to avoid sitting next to Edmond at the dinner table. In fact, she managed to avoid saying another word to him all evening. She stayed for a half hour after the meal concluded, before saying her thank yous to the Neumanns and slipping out the door.

The night was clear, and Mary could see a canopy of twinkling stars in the crystalline sky. She headed downhill toward Superior Street, trudging from one puddle of gaslight to the next as she mulled over her argument with Edmond.

"Whim," she muttered darkly. "*Whim indeed.* And after I saved his neck. He thinks my career is a *whim?*" She wondered if he had ever taken her seriously, ever really respected her.

While Mary didn't consider herself a trained business-woman, she had enough of John MacDougall in her to know that you don't get anywhere chasing butterflies. Edmond's California adventure seemed just that. Exciting and stimulating, perhaps. But a business proposition? Probably not. Yet he dared to mock her for focusing on her dream. How could the man be so pig-headed? Why wouldn't he listen to reason?

She was walking down a block where no houses had been built yet, full of dense brush and scrubby trees, when the pattering of footsteps behind her caught her attention. Her breath quickened. She twirled around to see a man coming in her direction, silhouetted in the gaslight. She couldn't make out his face, but his manner and his ragged cap seemed sickeningly familiar.

She snapped open her purse and firmly gripped the metallic object inside. And not a moment too soon, as the fellow revealed a long knife in his right hand.

Mary quickly drew the Smith & Wesson out of her bag and cocked it, her hand quaking.

The Ostovian stopped in his tracks, about ten feet away, as he heard the click.

"Come to try again?" Mary said, painfully aware of the flutter in her voice.

He stood there, knife balanced lightly in his hand. "You are... What is the word?" He peered at her with a certain malevolent amusement. "Resourceful? You would think killing a young woman would not be so difficult."

Mary drew a deep breath. "It's pointless, eliminating me. Other people know about the prince. It won't make any difference."

"Even if you put a bullet in me," the man said, sounding a little uncertain, "I will still get to you with my knife. A little gun like that could not kill me quick enough."

"Tell that to William McKinley," Mary said. "A little gun like this killed *him*." She purposely neglected to mention that it had taken the president a few days to die.

"You say others know?"

Mary nodded. "The police have been told the murdered boy was a look-alike. I've seen the real prince myself, though I'd expect he's a long way from Duluth by now."

The man made a crooked little smile. "Killing the orphan boy, it was nothing personal."

Her anger erupted. "Well, it was damned personal for Beansie! He had as much right to a future, to happiness, as any prince."

"You are very naïve if you think that, Miss MacDougall." The man slipped the knife back into the sheath on his hip. With a tip of his cap, he darted into the brush, vanishing instantly.

Her heart pounding like a bass drum, Mary wobbled and very nearly tipped over. She sat down on the curb, panting and trying to collect herself. When she got up a moment later, she slipped the revolver into her coat pocket and continued on downhill. Who had sent this slasher? It had to be Father Petrescu. To think of it! A so-called "man of God" who murdered children and dispatched assassins.

"Mary, wait!"

Mary glanced back, as Edmond came trotting up to her, breathing hard and looking decidedly upset.

"I didn't know you'd gone off in the dark all alone." He took a couple of deep breaths. "I wish you'd've let me come with you. Argument or not, it's not safe."

She wasn't about to dispute the point. And truth be told, she was terrifically relieved to see him. Her encounter with the Ostovian had drained the anger right out of her.

"I'm sorry about our kerfuffle," he said. "I didn't mean to

belittle your work. I shouldn't have said it. It just popped out. I was hoping we could see eye to eye on this whole California business."

"I'm sorry, too. Seems like we both got a little wound up." She put her arm through his. "Come along, now, Mr. Roy. I could use a nice cup of something warm and I expect you could, too."

She sent Edmond out the kitchen door at about ten-thirty, after hot cider and mostly innocuous conversation. But at the end of their chat, she reiterated—as gently as possible—that she could not go to Monterey. And, as she anticipated, neither of them was happy with the outcome, despite their long parting embrace.

As Mary headed up to her bedroom, she turned her thoughts away from Edmond to something else. Tomorrow she would have to confront Father Petrescu. Spying the brown paper-wrapped box up on her dresser, she wondered again if Mrs. Petrescu had been part of the conspiracy. She earnestly hoped not.

She grabbed the scissors from her dressing table, snipped the string, ripped the brown paper open, and lifted the box top. The first handkerchief showed her monogram in lovely blue silk script. She held it up for a closer look.

"Handsome work," she muttered. "Most handsome."

Then she noticed a folded piece of white paper that had been hidden beneath the first hankie.

She unfolded it and read aloud what was written on it in a spidery hand.

"A cup of cocoa put him to sleep, easing him to his rest."

She pondered the words for a few long seconds, before

they sank in.

"Oh my goodness," she gasped. "*Oh my goodness*!"

Chapter XXVIII

As she rode the streetcar west that Saturday morning, Mary had no idea what might happen. She was heading for terra incognita. If she were being perfectly honest, she would have to admit that the undertaking challenged the very limits of her courage. What she intended to do could be dangerous— more dangerous, perhaps, even than her encounters with the Ostovian thug. If it went badly, it could go very badly indeed.

Truth be told, Mary wouldn't have minded having Detective Sauer with her. But greater powers had declared the matter off limits, tying the detective's hands.

It was up to Mary and Mary alone to face the murderer. This time, though, she brought the .38 in her bag—a more serious sort of caliber, a caliber that left no doubt.

The streetcar rattled through a bustling downtown and made its way into the West End. On Third Street Mary hopped off and crossed over to the other side. Half a block down, she paused in front of the Petrescus' shop. Peering through the window, she caught the eye of Mrs. Petrescu, who was tidying up a display table full of embroidered items. The woman's eyes widened and she stared back. Mary gave her a curt nod.

Mrs. Petrescu was complicit in the murder, on some level. *She had to be.* But at least she had decided to come clean. Unless, of course, the whole thing was a trap.

Mary took two deep breaths and marched into the bakery.

Two women were waiting in front of the counter, with no one in sight behind it. But a moment later, Mrs. Luca came limping out of the back room with two loaves of dark brown bread. It wasn't until she handed them to the taller woman and took several coins in payment that she noticed Mary standing there. She gave her a friendly nod, then turned to the second customer.

"I am happy to see you again, Miss MacDougall," she said when they were finally alone.

"You may not be, when you hear what I have to say," Mary replied evenly. "I know what you did and why you did it. And before I leave, I expect to have your written confession."

The baker's face underwent a transformation, turning from welcoming to wary. "I do not know what you mean." She came around the counter toward Mary.

"No. No closer, ma'am," Mary said, pulling her gun out of her bag.

The older woman gasped at the sight of it. "Have you gone mad?"

Mary made a pointing gesture with the gun. "I suggest we go somewhere out of sight, perhaps back in your kitchen."

Mrs. Luca stared at the Smith & Wesson, then gave a shrug. "As you wish. Am I allowed to close up the shop?"

Mary kept the gun pointed at Mrs. Luca as she walked over to the front door, pulled down the shade, and clicked the lock shut. Mary followed her into the back room, past the shelves and worktables full of battered pans and trays and bowls, past two ovens and stacked bags of flour. The room smelled like the MacDougall kitchen after the morning's bread was baked—warm and welcoming. But Mary could think only of the atrocity that had been committed there.

A door in the back opened into a vestibule, which gave access to an alleyway and a narrow staircase. Mrs. Luca stopped

231

and regarded Mary with a tight smile. Her face was a mask now, hiding whatever gears were turning in her head. She looked tired, but Mary knew there had to be plenty of strength left in those arms and hands. Arms and hands that hefted heavy bags of flour. Arms and hands that kneaded dough. Arms and hands that had killed.

"What is it you think I have done?" Mrs. Luca asked in a dead monotone.

"You killed Beansie MacKenzie," Mary replied, her heart pounding. "To protect Nicolae Floria. I want you to tell me the whole story."

Mrs. Luca tut-tutted. "Perhaps someone is feeding you lies, Miss MacDougall."

"Don't insult my intelligence," Mary spat. "I know you drugged Beansie's cocoa. I know you threw him in the bay."

In fact, Mary didn't know any of this to a certainty. She was bluffing. But Mrs. Petrescu's message, "A cup of cocoa put him to sleep, easing him to his rest," pointed her in the logical direction. Who else was famous in the West End for her cocoa? Hadn't Mrs. Luca herself said that? "I use only Van Houten's finest powder," Mary recalled her saying.

After Mary had read Mrs. Petrescu's note, she started piecing things together. Jiggs said Beansie liked to find odd jobs in restaurants, where he might be able to cadge free meals. Why couldn't he have come into Mrs. Luca's bakery looking for work?

Detective Sauer had left no doubt that Beansie had drowned, there being bay water in his lungs. Mrs. Purcell had recalled that the boy was deathly afraid of the water and wouldn't have willingly gone near it. There were no marks or signs of a struggle on his body. Someone had to have slipped him a narcotic.

And then there was Mrs. Luca herself. Mary had enjoyed

talking to the woman, who seemed quite literate and cultured. She had mentioned attending the same ballet as Nicolae and his father—an elevated interest for a mere baker, if, indeed, that was what she had been. Heaven only knew that immigrants often needed to do work below their former stations in the old country. But Mrs. Luca clearly was something more than an ordinary working woman.

"Let us go upstairs to my room," Mrs. Luca said. "We can talk there. I am quite worn out and my leg aches. I want to sit in my chair."

Mary worried that Mrs. Luca's knife man might be waiting upstairs. But she had her revolver firmly gripped in her hand and she was confident she couldn't miss in such close quarters. And the woman did indeed look exhausted.

"Just go up the stairs," Mrs. Luca instructed. "I will be right behind you."

"I don't think so. After you. I insist."

"As you wish."

Mrs. Luca led the way up the narrow, shadowy steps slowly, favoring her gammy left leg, with Mary a safe distance behind. The dingy hallway they came into—illuminated by a dim, gas-lit sconce—had four doors. Mrs. Luca went down and unlocked the second one on the right. Mary followed her in, eyeing the other three doors for any sign of movement.

Mrs. Luca headed toward a battered dresser. With a sharp intake of breath, Mary spied a pistol sitting on top of it.

"Stop right there!" she barked. "Touch that gun and I'll shoot."

Giving an exaggerated sigh, Mrs. Luca backed away from the dresser. "The gun is unloaded. Have a look."

Mary stepped over and confirmed it. All five chambers were empty.

"I merely wanted to get my heroin tablets, for my pain.

They are in the top drawer. Would you mind?"

Opening the drawer, Mary found a cardboard pillbox labeled Bayer Heroin, nestled among some socks. She handed it to Mrs. Luca, who took a white tablet from the box and quickly gulped it down.

Mary scanned the small room, with its spartan furnishings. A narrow, swayback bed in the corner. A washstand under a mirror on the wall. A faded chair next to a small table with a lamp. The flowered wallpaper was darkened and stained. A single dusty window overlooked Third Street. The only sign of indulgence was the bookshelf displaying twenty or so volumes. *The Last of the Mohicans* was lying on the table.

Mrs. Luca hobbled over to her chair and collapsed into it. She gave Mary a dismal look of resignation. "After your encounter last night with Teodor, I knew it was hopeless. We could not control the situation. If others knew about the details of our actions, as you told him, it was pointless to kill you." There was no apology in her voice, only regret.

Mary, feeling safer, put the revolver back in her purse. "What do you mean?"

Mrs. Luca's eyes went to the window. "Adrian Dimitriu and Teodor Bogdan—the man I sent to deal with you—have left Duluth with Nicolae."

"Where are they going?"

"I have no idea. Vladislav employs torturers, you know. It is best that I have nothing to reveal."

"But why didn't you go with them?"

Mrs. Luca shut her eyes and sighed. "Because I can go no farther. I am old and tired and sick. I would only slow them down. Nicolae begged for me to come. But no, not this time."

Mary felt a momentary flash of sympathy for the woman. She was in a horrible, horrible pickle—but very much of her own making.

"You know, Mrs. Luca, that the truth has to come out. People have to learn that Beansie MacKenzie—"

"Please call him by his proper name. Tavish. Let us afford him some dignity."

Mary nodded. Quite right. All that was left now for the poor youngster was dignity. *And justice.* "People have to know that he didn't wander near the bay and accidentally drown. They have to know that he became an unwitting pawn in a deadly gambit to protect your prince. They have to know that he was murdered. That's what I've promised myself. That's what I owe him."

Then she remembered Father Petrescu's overwrought anger—threats, even—when she probed him about the prince's supposed death. His reaction had seemed out of proportion, for someone who was uninvolved. "Did Father Petrescu help you?"

The woman looked dismayed. "Good heavens, no. Father Petrescu is no murderer. He is sometimes gruff, but he is a good man. He and Larisa were very angry with me, when they found out. But fortunately they kept quiet and played their roles."

"Did Nicolae know what you were planning?"

"There was no reason to tell him." She gestured toward the bed. "Please do sit down. And thank you for putting away your gun."

Mary perched on the edge of the mattress, which squeaked painfully as it sagged.

"You should know that I took no pleasure in what I had to do. In fact, I liked Tavish. He was a funny boy."

Mary wasn't about to give the woman any satisfaction on that count, and kept silent.

"Let me explain how it happened."

Mary nodded.

"At the time when Nicolae, Prince Anton's son, was born, I worked as a governess in Paris. You see, I was an Ostovian girl who loved to dance, and I became quite good at it. After much hard work, I won a place in the corps de ballet of the Paris Opera. I was one of *les petits rats*. The little rats, they called us. It was glamorous, sometimes. But many suffered at the hands of wicked men. I was lucky. I was not among the pretty ones. So I just danced and danced and danced." Her voice faded and she took on the far-away look of someone remembering a magical past. Then she sighed, returning to grim reality. "But that ended when a carriage accident ruined my left leg. I became a maid, then a governess for well-to-do families in Paris. The prince heard about me and asked me to come home to care for Nicolae. I could not refuse my prince."

From the drawer in the table next to her chair, she pulled out a photograph of a plump, adorable infant in a gilded frame and showed it to Mary. "I fell in love with the little boy. He was such a good child. So when it became clear that Vladislav had poisoned Anton, and became regent to the young prince, we knew something terrible was fated for my precious Nikkie. We could not allow that, we loyalists."

"And you went on the run."

Tears glistened in Mrs. Luca's eyes. "Vienna. Zurich. Marseilles. Lisbon. With Vladislav's agents pursuing us every inch of the way. The killers very nearly got to Nikkie in New York City. Teodor's brother held them off, giving us time to escape, but sacrificed his life. Then to Buffalo and Cleveland and finally here. Father Petrescu was certain he could conceal us, at least for a time. He had me run his bakery and gave Nicolae the disguise of a cobbler's apprentice. We have been here over a year now."

"But you knew Vladislav's assassins were still hunting you," Mary said. "And suddenly, like a gift from heaven, a look-alike appears in your shop."

Mrs. Luca squared her shoulders. "We had to try," she huffed. "Vladislav has not seen his nephew for over two years, and boys grow and change so quickly at that age. Even though Tavish was about the same age, he was smaller than my Nikkie."

"Of course he was," Mary snapped. "He didn't grow up in a palace. A child can't thrive without enough food, without a good home."

Mrs. Luca looked irritated at being interrupted. "As I was saying, if you had not seen Nikkie in two years, you might well think that Tavish was him. Perhaps if Vladislav believed his nephew was truly dead, he would call off his hounds."

"And you sacrificed Nicolae's signet ring to make the ruse seem more real."

"A pity to lose it, but it *is* just a piece of jewelry."

Mary steeled herself to ask the next question, dreading the answer. "How did you kill Tavish?"

"I asked him to help clean up the bakery," Mrs. Luca answered in a flat tone, avoiding Mary's eyes. "He would work for a few hours, and I would give him a quarter and a meal with my hot cocoa. I told him not to tell anyone—I said I did not want other boys pestering me. I was kindly to him. I made him feel special."

"But you killed him nonetheless."

Mrs. Luca nodded in a hang-dog sort of way. "In the end he felt no pain. He did not suffer."

Mary suddenly felt flushed and breathless, as if the full weight of the crime had come down on her shoulders. This had been a real boy who had lived a hard life. This had been a real boy who would never have the chance to grow and make a success of himself, who would never fall in love. It broke Mary's heart to think of him being snuffed out for the sake of another boy who had no more right to live than he did.

She needed some air. She stood and went over to the window, pulling up the sash. Turning back to Mrs. Luca, she said, "The details, please."

"He came six or seven times. I wanted to be sure no one would miss him, no one would bother to look for him. I had to wait for the right moment. The last time, I drugged the cocoa and he fell into a deep, peaceful sleep. That boy, he had such a fondness for my cocoa. I really think that is why he kept returning—for the cocoa, not for the money."

For a few savage seconds Mary wanted to pull the gun out again and shoot the woman where she sat. *A monster.* She was a monster.

"But that's not how you killed him."

Mrs. Luca shook her head. "I sewed the ring into his jacket, then we took him to the bay. Poor Teodor, he could not do it, could not drown the boy. So I did what had to be done."

The woman clasped those murdering hands, as if in prayer. It revolted Mary.

"Please do not let Tavish's death be in vain. Please keep the secret, Miss MacDougall. I know I may burn in hell, but it was all for the good of Ostovia. I had to try to keep my Nikkie safe." She looked at Mary with a pleading expression.

Mary stared at the woman for a few long, terrible seconds. "There has to be an accounting in this world, too, Mrs. Luca. There has to be justice for Tavish MacKenzie. *Someone has to pay.* Until that happens, I won't rest." She reached into her purse, and pulled out two folded sheets of stationery and a fountain pen.

"Now, if you please, write down what you've just told me, and sign and date it. Then I'll be on my way."

She stepped over, laying the paper and pen on top of *The Last of the Mohicans*.

Mrs. Luca shook her head. "Let me rest, please. Come back in a couple of hours."

Mary wished it was that simple, but she didn't trust the woman. She might not write down anything or she might report Mary to the police for holding her at gunpoint. There was no telling what she was capable of. No, Mary had to have the confession in hand when she walked out of this room.

"I'll wait, then, while you catch a few winks. Then the written confession."

Mrs. Luca laughed. "You can shoot me, if you wish, Miss MacDougall. But do you really think I would endanger my Nikkie's life by giving you a written confession? How long would it take before it ends up in the hands of some newspaper reporter and the whole world knows that he is still alive?"

So, thought Mary, *we're at loggerheads*. She could pull out the pistol again, but clearly it wouldn't make any difference. She couldn't force the woman to do anything. She was stymied and needed to regroup.

"I'm not done with you, Mrs. Luca," she vowed. "Not by a long shot."

"Goodbye, Miss MacDougall," the murderer said, shutting her eyes.

Mary turned and left the room. She went slowly down the dingy, dim stairs, through the bakery, and out onto the street. Mrs. Petrescu, who was standing in front of her shop, arms tightly crossed, eyed her, as if to ask *what happened?*

All Mary knew was that this affair, as she told Mrs. Luca, was not over. Justice would be served, one way or another.

Then, from the window up above the bakery—the window that Mary had just opened—there came the single, sharp **BANG** of a pistol shot.

Chapter XXIX

Jeanette was sitting in the kitchen, sipping tea and chatting with Mrs. Erdahl, the cook, when she heard the ring of the telephone echoing from the front of the house. A moment later, Emma Beach appeared.

"A gentleman's on the phone wanting to talk to Mary. But when I told him she wasn't here, he asked for you."

"Who is it?"

"Sorry, he declined to say. But he did say it was urgent."

Jeanette did a quickstep to the oak pedestal near the front vestibule, where the house's sole candlestick phone stood. She lifted the transmitter to her mouth and put the receiver next to her ear.

"Hullo," she said, enunciating clearly, "Mrs. Harrison here. To whom am I speaking?"

"It's Detective Sauer. Do you know where Mary is?"

Jeanette thought he sounded on edge. "Why no, I don't. She left about an hour and a half ago to run errands."

"Do you think she's at her office?"

"Unlikely, on a Saturday. I'm pretty sure, though, she's not with Mr. Roy. Seems they had a bit of a tiff last night. They were at a party at Herr Neumann's and…"

"Mrs. Harrison," the detective snapped, cutting her off, "did she give you any notion of where she might have gone this morning?"

"Well, she was going on again about that dreadful business with Beansie and the Ostovian prince and how your chief of police is a nincompoop and how justice ought to be served."

There was a deep groan from the other end of the line.

"I was afraid of that," the detective said. "I just received word that there's been a shooting out in the West End, very near the Petrescus' cobbler's shop. And given your cousin's obsession with the Ostovian matter..."

As his words trailed off, Jeanette almost felt sick to her stomach. "Good lord! You don't think she's gone and done anything rash, do you? Put herself in danger?"

"I certainly hope not. But in case... Well, I thought it might be a good idea if you came along with me. I can pick you up in ten minutes."

As they rattled west on Third Street in the detective's carriage, Jeanette spotted a milling clump of people on the south side of the road, in front of a shoemaker's shop. And among them appeared to be at least two uniformed police officers, trying to impose some order. Detective Sauer slowed the carriage, tugged on the reins, and made a neat U-turn right into a spot in front of the crowd.

"Detective Sauer!" a burley policeman boomed, striding toward them, as the detective helped Jeanette down from the carriage.

"Sergeant O'Gara," the detective said. "What happened here?"

"We have a woman upstairs there." The officer pointed to an open second-storey window. "Dead of a gunshot wound to the head."

Jeanette felt her knees begin to buckle. "Oh no!" she

moaned. "Not Mary!"

The officer gazed at her with concern. "Did this Mary run this here bakery? Gray-haired? About fifty or sixty?"

A wave of relief came over Jeanette. "Oh, thank goodness!" She almost laughed with relief. "No, my cousin does not run a bakery. And she's only about twenty."

"The young lady we're concerned about," the detective said, "is Miss MacDougall."

"Aaah," Sergeant O'Gara said. "There's a Miss MacDougall in the shoe shop. She was standing out here with Father Petrescu's wife when the shot rang out. She'd been up there with the Luca woman a few minutes before, but she said she wouldn't say anything more until you arrived, Detective Sauer."

"I think I'd best have a look upstairs first," the detective said. "Mrs. Harrison, perhaps you could have a word with our young friend and see how she's doing. Gently, now. Don't push her too much."

Jeanette watched him worm his way through the crowd with Sergeant O'Gara. Setting her jaw and straightening her shoulders, she headed into the cobbler's shop. She found Mary sitting ramrod straight in a plain chair by a table full of fancy embroidered items. She had a teacup in her hand, though she seemed to have no interest in sipping from it. The girl had the startled, tremulous look of someone who had just seen a ghost. Her eyes widened when she spied Jeanette.

"What in the world are *you* doing here?"

"I might ask you the same thing," Jeanette grumbled, standing before her cousin with hands on hips. "When Detective Sauer heard about the shooting, so close to the Petrescus' place, he called me, wondering where you were. We were both scared to death you'd gone and gotten yourself killed."

"So he's here then?"

"Upstairs next door, doing whatever unpleasant things he needs to do. Now I have a simple question for you: *Are you quite mad?*" Not exactly the gentleness the detective had suggested, but Jeanette was not the least bit inclined to go easy on her cousin.

"I sometimes wonder," Mary lamented.

The door in back opened and a small, auburn-haired woman emerged, carrying a shawl. She came over and placed it on Mary's shoulders, her fierce, dark eyes giving Jeanette the once-over.

"Jeanette," Mary said, "this is Mrs. Petrescu, who embroidered my hankies and did the lace for my new gown. Mrs. Petrescu, my cousin Mrs. Harrison."

Jeanette was in no mood for small talk and neither, it seemed, was Mrs. Petrescu, who spoke up immediately in her thick Ostovian accent.

"I am sorry for the danger in which I put Miss MacDougall. But a horrible crime was done in the name of the prince. I knew of it and held my tongue far too long, to my shame. It seemed the police would do nothing. This young lady, foolish or not, has great courage. She was the only one who seemed willing to take action, the only one I could turn to."

"To get at the truth about what happened to the MacKenzie boy?" Jeanette asked.

"Yes, that is right."

"And what does the dead woman upstairs have to do with all this?"

"She killed him, Jeanette," said Mary. "She took him to the bay and drowned him. With her own hands."

The shop door swung open and Detective Sauer came in, doffing his hat before the three women. His expression was particularly grim. Jeanette could only imagine the terrible scene he had just witnessed.

"Clearly a suicide," the detective said. "Open and shut. An officer's searching the room for a note or any other evidence. Not much more to do up there. Now, Miss MacDougall, were you in that apartment before the gunshot?"

"I was," Mary acknowledged.

"How did you come to be there and what happened? Every detail, please."

As the detective scribbled in his notebook, Mary described the brief missive she had received from Mrs. Petrescu, who looked relieved to finally have the truth coming out. Then, in as much detail as she could recall, Mary told Mrs. Luca's story. Of how she became the boy's governess and protector. Of engineering his escape from Ostovia. Of outrunning assassins across two continents and an ocean.

"And they go to ground in Duluth, Minnesota," the detective said.

"Right. But Mrs. Luca knew they weren't safe, even here," Mary continued. "So when Tavish walked into the bakery one day, with a face very much like the prince's, the scheme bubbled up in her mind."

The detective nodded. "Present the world with a dead prince and the assassins might be called off. At least for a while."

"Exactly," Mary said. "Mrs. Luca paid the boy to clean up, and plied him with hot meals and cocoa. He came back time and again. She said he was very fond of her wonderful cocoa. Couldn't get enough of it. A fatal fondness, you might say— the last time he came, she laced the cocoa with a narcotic. Then she and one of the men took him to the bay."

"And from the water in his lungs," the detective said, "we know he was alive when he went into the water."

Mary nodded. "The man refused to kill the boy, so Mrs. Luca did it herself."

Jeanette couldn't help shuddering. "Ghastly woman!"

"My husband and I had no idea she would do such a thing," Mrs. Petrescu put in with a tone of mortification. "No idea at all. My husband is a man of God. He would not have allowed it."

"But you two covered it up, just the same," the detective growled. "Until you found your spine, ma'am."

Jeanette had never seen anyone look as rueful as the Ostovian woman did at that moment. There could be no reasonable response and she gave none, staring down at her feet.

Detective Sauer took a deep breath. "Is Prince Nicolae still here?"

Mrs. Petrescu, still looking down, shook her head. "No. He and the two men... They have left."

"Where to?"

She looked up and shrugged. "They knew well enough not to say."

"Why do you suppose Mrs. Luca didn't go with them?" Jeanette asked.

"I think she felt too exhausted to keep running," Mary said. "Too worn out."

"Well," Jeanette said, "I feel no pity for that woman. She took the coward's path, killing herself like that."

"I'm afraid I may have forced her hand," Mary said.

"What do you mean?" Detective Sauer asked.

Mary sighed. "I made it rather clear that there had to be some kind of justice for Tavish. I made it quite plain that I wasn't about to let the matter drop."

Jeanette could tell the experience had shaken her cousin to the core, had taken her down a few pegs. That typical Mary cockiness had evaporated—an unusual circumstance.

"I think, though," Mary continued, her voice shaky, "that Mrs. Luca decided to be her own judge, her own jury, her own executioner. To give me what I asked for. To pay for her terrible crime."

"No, you *did not* make her shoot herself," Mrs. Petrescu insisted. "It is much simpler. She had cancer in her stomach. She knew she did not have long. She could go no farther with Nicolae. She hoped, perhaps, to satisfy you, Miss MacDougall. But no, you did not make her shoot herself. Her work was done. She wanted to rest."

Mary looked as though she wanted desperately to believe that, and so did Jeanette.

"Still, it didn't end the way I intended. I wanted her arrested and tried and convicted. I wanted the world to know *everything*. And now it will just be covered up—and Tavish's death will go for naught."

As Mary spoke, Jeanette finally understood that inside this ambitious, confident young lady—still a teenager—there beat a heart fiercely determined to do good, to reveal truth. Would anyone, even John MacDougall, be able to stop Mary from following her maverick path?

"It was undoubtedly very plucky of you to browbeat a murderer," Detective Sauer said, glaring at Mary. "But did you realize she had a gun within reach? What was to stop her from plugging you in the heart?"

"It was unloaded and on the dresser, Detective. Clearly, she put a bullet in the chamber the instant I left. I was a little bit afraid, I'll admit. But once I saw her and heard her, I knew she'd given up. Anyhow, I had my own pistol at the ready."

"You have a gun?" Jeanette squeaked.

"Well, two actually," Mary shrugged, eliciting a groan from the detective. "And I've only shot one bullet in anger."

"Reporters will be coming, so it's best you two leave

now," he sighed. "I don't know how this'll play out with the chief. I'll get one of the men to drive you home. In the meantime, I would suggest you remain mum about the whole business."

They were a few blocks shy of the MacDougall house on Superior Street, when Jeanette turned to Mary and said, "I don't think I'm going to tell your father about this…this incident. It's painfully obvious that you will do what you will do, and no one can stop you. But please, Mary, do consider this—a dead detective can't solve any cases."

Chapter XXX

"Miss MacDougall," Jiggs said, doffing his cap, "the boys an' me really want to thank you for what you done for Beansie. There I was figgerin' he stole my watch, when all the time he was lyin' in a hospital, no one knowin' his name. And you managed to get him planted here in a proper grave, in a nice boneyard, to boot." He shook his head. "But poor, poor ol' Beansie. He dint deserve this."

Mary and Jeanette were standing together with the three boys there in Shady Oak Cemetery. At their feet was a fresh grave and a simple granite headstone—with a name, two dates, and two brief lines of text, all engraved in classic Roman type. Up above, slate-tinted clouds scudded along and a bitter wind threatened to cut through Mary's overcoat—a reminder that November wasn't far off, then the plunge into winter. It was a grim day for a grim task, but it couldn't be put off.

"Thank you, miss," said Gordo. "It's a real Christian thing you done."

"Thanks an awful lot," Bert added, with quivering chin. "You found a real pretty place for Beansie."

"You're all quite welcome, gentlemen," Mary replied, touched by the boys' gratitude.

Beansie's three chums were all in what she supposed were their best duds—clean, pressed knee pants and fairly tidy looking worsted jackets. It appeared they had even purchased new neckties for the occasion. The trio had on the same ragged caps they all wore the first time she set eyes on them.

It had been quite a job, arranging for this little memorial. It took an ample donation to the cemetery's general fund to obtain a grave that no body would occupy. The managing secretary nervously agreed to keep Mary's scheme a secret, so long as her sincere intention was to some day transfer the deceased individual to the plot. Getting the headstone done and planted in such short order also required financial incentives.

While Mary felt guilty about misleading the boys, the secret of Tavish and Nicolae had to be held close, until she could decide what to do. And, moreover, she felt somehow protective of Jiggs and his friends. She wanted to keep them away from the awful truth that Tavish had been murdered with cold, cruel calculation. She was bound and determined that some day—when the truth came out—Tavish *would* end up here, in this handsome spot, beneath an old, spreading oak tree.

After a few long moments of silence, Jiggs turned around and blinked at Mary. "The headstone's perfect, miss. Couldn't be nicer."

"And the verse is so pretty," Bert added. "Read the words out loud, Jiggsie."

Jiggs looked back to the slab of gray granite, straightened his back, and spoke: "Tavish 'Beansie' MacKenzie. 1889 to 1902. Good night, sweet prince. And flights of angels sing thee to thy rest!"

"Didja get that verse from the Bible, Miss MacDougall?" asked Bert.

Mary shook her head. "No, it's from an old, old story about a sad young prince."

"Well, Beansie wasn't no prince," observed Gordo. "But who'll know the difference up in heaven, huh?"

Jeanette cleared her throat. "Before we go, I think a prayer may be in order."

"Quite so," agreed Mary, realizing the need to give Beansie the proper benediction that he deserved.

"Let me say it," said Bert. "I know a good one."

And he recited the Lord's Prayer, getting it word perfect. Not for the first time in this affair, Mary wanted to weep. But she somehow stanched her tears.

After another moment of silence, she put her arm over Gordo's shoulder. "Now I was wondering if you gentlemen," she said, "would be interested in taking lunch with Mrs. Harrison and me at Gustafsson's Café. As my guests, of course."

All three boys lit up like light bulbs.

"Gustafsson's!" Bert exclaimed.

"Would we ever!" Jiggs said

The two of them went off with Jeanette, heading down the gentle slope of grass toward the lane, where Bill and the surrey awaited. But Mary held back Gordo and said, "Before we go, I need to have a private word with you."

"Yes, miss?" The boy looked a bit wary.

"Did you know that I figured out who stole Jiggs's timepiece?"

His eyes widening, he shook his head. "No, miss."

"Take off your cap."

"What? Why?"

"Just take it off."

Looking suddenly nervous, he did what she ordered.

"The pawnbroker told me the thief's a young fellow," Mary said, "with a cowlick just like this." Quick as a wink, she yanked lightly on Gordo's lively sprig of hair and he shrank back out of her grip. "And if I should ever hear of him hurting his friends again or thieving, there'll be hell to pay. Does he understand?"

Gordo lowered his eyes, clearly ashamed. "Yes, ma'am," he said with distinct contrition. "You betcha he understands."

As Mary waited for the check after lunch, she asked Jiggs if he would mind walking back to the office with Jeanette and her. The three of them said goodbye to Bert and Gordo outside the restaurant and proceeded west on Second Street.

"What's it you need, miss?" Jiggs asked.

"It seems like a thousand years ago," Mary said, "but we talked about you doing some work for me. Picking things up, dropping things off, and so forth. Being my jack-of-all-trades. Do you remember?"

"Sure I do, Miss MacDougall. I didn't say nothin' more, but I was hopin' you still want me to help. You just call me at the stable, and I'll be there like a shot. Or I can come into your office a couple times a day to check in."

"And once in a while, Jiggs, during an investigation, we could use an extra pair of eyes. No one would suspect a young fellow like you of being an operative. Would you be interested?"

"Would I!?" His grin was prodigious. "Me? A detective? Sign me right up."

When they arrived at the 335 West building, Jiggs tipped his cap. "So long, ladies, it's been a pleasure." He sauntered off, practically walking on air.

Up in the office Jeanette took off her coat and sat down at her desk. "Such a fine machine," she said, regarding her new Remington. "It's too bad the other one got smashed up, but it's nice to have an employer with a bottomless bank account."

Mary laughed as she riffled through the several letters that had arrived in the morning post. "Look," she said, holding up one of the envelopes. "Mrs. Fesler's payment." She ripped it open and extracted a check, as well as a sheet of stationery, which she unfolded.

"Dear Miss MacDougall and Mrs. Harrison," she read aloud. "Thank you again for your assistance. Mr. Pettyjohn remains full of remorse and promises to reimburse me fully for the cost of your services. The other members of the cat fanciers club have, for now, forgiven him, and he will continue as a member of the club—provided he does no more illicit work on behalf of a certain Egyptian deity. Sincerely yours, Mrs. Alfred Fesler."

"I'm glad he got off lightly," Jeanette said, feeding a Moody Investigations letterhead into the Remington.

"Me too," Mary said, making for her own desk as Jeanette began *rat-tat-tatting* merrily away. Quentin Pettyjohn, after all, had saved a certain headstrong damsel in distress and deserved a bit of compassion.

About an hour later, Aksel Adamsen popped in to invite both Mary and Jeanette to the Halloween party he was hosting. "If you're inspired to wear a costume," he enthused, "that would be just grand. I'm dressing up as the Tin Man from Oz and Miss Kozlow is coming as Dorothy."

Jeanette's eyebrows went up. "Oh, I didn't know you were acquainted with Miss Kozlow."

"I wasn't," Aksel said, "until Mary introduced us at the piano recital. I think Eliza's just swell, don't you?"

"Oh, yes, just swell," Jeanette agreed.

"Yes, indeed, swell," Mary said, trying not to sound too excited about the successful outcome of her underhanded matchmaking.

Just then the office door swung open yet again and in strode Edmond Roy.

"Edmond, hello," Mary beamed. "What a pleasant surprise." She slipped over and took his arm. "Edmond, I'd like you to meet my old friend Aksel Adamsen. Aksel, this is Edmond Roy, an artist who's helping with the Oddfellows mural."

"Pleased to meet you, Mr. Roy," Aksel said, shaking Edmond's hand. "Say, you wouldn't happen to enjoy costume parties, would you?"

"Yes," Jeanette teased, "we're in need of a cowardly lion."

"Well then, I'm your man... I mean lion," Edmond grinned. "I have the unruly mane for the job." He ran his fingers through his thick, dark hair. "And I'm so timid, you'd hardly believe it."

"And I'll be Aunt Em," Jeanette said, "being, most likely, the oldest person at the festivities. Mary, what do you think of Glinda, the Good Witch of the South?"

"Witch of the South?" Mary wrinkled her nose. "Hardly the role for a girl from the frozen north. No, I have another character in mind." She smiled coyly. "I've always wanted to be an immortal with vast powers to influence puny humans. I think I'll go as Bastet, the Epyptian cat goddess. Edmond, could you fashion me a feline mask? Papier-mâché perhaps? Pretty please?"

Aksel seemed delighted to have recruited more partygoers, but, looking at his watch, excused himself. "Sorry, must run. Meeting with a client and his banker."

The instant Aksel disappeared, Edmond turned to Mary. "Could I speak with you? Privately?"

Mary looked at Jeanette, who made a gesture of dismissal with her right hand. "I told you, I'm out of the chaperone business. Go on, have your little private conference."

Mary ushered Edmond into her office and shut the door. They stood facing each other, and Mary reached for his hand. It was big and warm and strong and a little rough—from all that turpentine, no doubt.

"I suppose it's too much to think that you've come to your senses and decided to stay in Duluth," she said.

When Edmond's shoulders slumped, Mary knew that nothing had changed.

"Sorry, Mary. California's something I have to do. But I'm not planning to leave until the spring. You'll have four or five months to change your mind."

She shook her head. "That's not going to happen."

"So, it's a stalemate."

"I'm afraid so."

For now, Mary thought. *A stalemate for now.* She wasn't done with Edmond yet. She would not let him get away. Of that she was certain.

"Well, there is one thing I'm game for trying," Edmond said, brushing a stray hair from her forehead.

Mary raised her eyebrows. "What?"

"I'd like to properly get to know your father, over coffee or dinner. Or perhaps we could watch the stock ticker together."

Mary burst out laughing.

"In the worst of cases," Edmond continued, "we'd only end up in a fistfight."

"That can be arranged. Dinner, that is, not a fistfight. In fact, I'm confident you two will get on splendidly."

"Well, he and I do have one important thing in common."

"What's that?"

He grabbed her gently by the waist and drew her close.

"We both care deeply for a wild, vexing, impetuous, brilliant young lady named Mary MacDougall."

Chapter XXXI

Although her father occasionally conducted business meetings in his walnut-lined home office, Mary never had. Because, of course, she had never had any business to conduct, until now. So she was feeling understandably nervous when Detective Sauer appeared at her front door with the two gentlemen who had asked to see her. He intimated that her complete cooperation would be required.

As Emma Beach looked on in the foyer, with an air of bemusement, Mary ushered the three gentlemen into the office. She sat herself in her father's rolling leather chair behind his desk, feeling slightly above her station there. Detective Sauer sat on the other side of the desk, to her left. On the right was Chauncey Troyer, the chief of police. And in the center sat Mr. Rufus Wells of the State Department—a pale, blond wisp of a man in a gray suit, so slender he might have disappeared, if viewed from the side. For her part, Jeanette perched on the edge of the window seat in the full wash of the afternoon sun. Mary had insisted she be present, for moral support.

"As we all know," Mr. Wells began, "Miss MacDougall has ascertained that Prince Nicolae of Ostovia did not drown in St. Louis Bay. But for now and for the foreseeable future, it remains in everyone's interest to proceed as if he did. The prince and his supporters have bought time for him to stay safe and gather his strength. He may yet grow into a man and attempt to reclaim the principality that was taken from him.

"We suspect his uncle realizes that the drowned boy was a ruse, and may continue hunting for him. Vlad the Vicious, as we call him in the office, is far too canny not to take that possibility into account. But with Nicolae supposedly out of the picture, he can claim complete control—a situation that pleases the great Ostovian banks. And if the Ostovian banks are pleased, so too are the banks of Wall Street. And if the banks of Wall Street are pleased…"

"…the present administration in Washington is pleased," Mary grumbled. "I know. *I know.* But a blameless boy named Tavish MacKenzie got entangled in the plot and was murdered. And how can that go unpunished?"

Mr. Wells tented his fingers in front of him. "Your passion for justice is exemplary, Miss MacDougall. And the skillful manner in which you acquitted yourself is remarkable—for someone so young and inexperienced. You are quite the unlikeliest operative I've ever laid eyes on."

Mary shot the man a hard, sham smile. His flattery seemed condescending, to say the least. He was merely buttering her up.

"But, you see," he continued, tipping his head slightly to the side, "I did not come to negotiate. I came to deliver an ultimatum."

Jeanette's face went pale, but Mary was determined to show no sign of being intimidated. She crossed her arms and stared at him.

"You and Mrs. Harrison are to tell no one of this. If you do, costs will be exacted from your father and his businesses. *Substantial* costs. And criminal charges may quite possibly be levied against you, Miss MacDougall, *personally*. Correct, Chief Troyer?"

The chief, a bulldog of a man, nodded slowly. "Afraid so.

Sorry, Miss MacDougall, but best you toe the line this time."

Mary glanced at Detective Sauer, who looked back help-lessly. She knew he was on her side, but he couldn't do a thing. The whole situation was abominable. She felt as if she were going to explode.

Mr. Wells's voice took on a conciliatory tone. "If you agree to stay mum, I promise that sometime next summer the coffin interred in West Duluth—thought to contain the remains of Prince Nicolae of Ostovia—will be quietly transposed to the plot you purchased at Shady Oak Cemetery. Master MacKenzie will end up where he belongs."

Mary was a bit surprised. How had Mr. Wells even learned of her little deception? Clearly, someone in the government had been keeping tabs on her—which chilled her as much as it flattered her

Mr. Wells rose. "I think that concludes our official busi-ness. Gentlemen, Mrs. Harrison, if you wouldn't mind, I'd like a private word with Miss MacDougall."

The chief looked a little miffed at not being included. But he and the other two filed dutifully out of the library, Jeanette shutting the door behind them.

Mary had to admit she was intrigued. "What did you want to talk about, Mr. Wells?" she asked, standing and coming around the desk.

He looked her up and down, as if appraising her. "Do you happen to have any immediate plans to travel in Germany or the Austro-Hungarian Empire?"

Mary's eyes widened. "Why in the world do you ask?"

"A young lady of means, such as yourself, would have lit-tle or no trouble roving freely about Europe. No one would suspect her of anything other than enjoying the sights and the culture of the old continent. And as she did, she might visit and observe certain areas of interest, ask seemingly innocent questions that might uncover useful information about our German-speaking friends."

Good Lord, Mary thought. *He wants me to be a spy!*

"You needn't decide right now, Miss MacDougall. But if you should happen to undertake a European tour, or would be open to an itinerary of our devising—well, your country would be most grateful for your help." He reached into his inner coat pocket and pulled out a calling card showing only his name and an address in Washington, D.C.

"If you want to talk about it, simply send me a telegram with some innocuous greeting," he said, handing her the card. "Someone will be in touch. Needless to say, your discretion is required. In other words, our private chat just now did not take place."

From the front porch, Mary and Jeanette watched the three men make their way down the walk and steps to Superior Street, where Chief Troyer's carriage was waiting for them. They stood for a moment on the sidewalk—Mr. Wells and the chief talking, while Detective Sauer slouched dispiritedly off to the side, silent. Then they climbed up into the carriage and drove away toward downtown.

Almost simultaneously, a cab coming from the direction of downtown swung around and parked in front of the house.

Up on the porch, Mary gasped. "Oh dear, it's Father!"

"Oh, dear, indeed!" Jeanette echoed. "Do you think he saw…?"

John MacDougall alit from the cab and huffed up the first set of steps—the cabbie right behind him with his valises. The business mogul shot his daughter a quizzical look, furrowing his brow.

"Did I just see Chief Troyer and Detective Sauer and some other fellow driving away from *my* house, Mary?"

She took a deep breath. "You did."

"They were visiting *you*?"

"Well, yes."

"Why?" The query came out as a low rumble. "What have you done *now*?"

If I explained it, your hair would turn white, Mary thought. "I wish I could tell you, Father. But I'm sworn to secrecy."

The peeved patriarch turned to Jeanette, who grimaced. "I'm sorry, John. I'm not allowed to say, either."

He focused his narrowed eyes back on his daughter. "You *will* tell me what's going on," he demanded.

Mary went up on her tiptoes, and kissed him on his bearded cheek. "Welcome home, Father. Your timing's perfect. We're having a guest for dinner tonight and it will be *so* good to have you here."

"Who?" he asked, not looking the least bit placated. "Who's coming?"

Mary smiled sweetly. "My friend, Mr. Roy. He's expressed a great interest in getting to know you. Isn't that wonderful?"

John MacDougall groaned and turned toward the open front door. "Emma!" he bellowed.

As if by magic, the housekeeper appeared on the porch almost instantaneously.

"Emma, would you please get me a nice, big whiskey."

~ *The End* ~

Acknowledgements

This book isn't just the product of the author sitting at the keyboard sweating out 70,000 words. No, indeed. Without my editors, beta readers, and proofreaders, it wouldn't be nearly the book that it is. One more time—and hopefully not the last time—I want to thank Marlo Garnsworthy, Kate Collins, Jeri Smith, Marie Joseph, Julie King, and Sue Wichmann for all their contributions to *A Fatal Fondness*. Ladies, I owe you!

About the Author

Richard Audry is the pen name of D. R. Martin. As Richard Audry, he is the author of four Mary MacDougall historical mysteries and three King Harald Canine Cozy mysteries. Under his own name, he has written the rip-roaring Johnny Graphic ghost adventure trilogy. He's also the author of the hardboiled PI mystery *Smoking Ruin* and two books of literary commentary: *Travis McGee & Me* and *Four Science Fiction Masters*. You can follow D. R. at drmartinbooks.com and www.facebook.com/richardaudryauthor/.

If you enjoyed *A Fatal Fondness*, be sure to read these other enthralling tales of mystery by Richard Audry...

A Mary MacDougall Mystery Duet

The year is 1901 and young Mary MacDougall has a rather improbable ambition—to become a consulting detective. *A Mary MacDougall Mystery Duet* features the two cases that establish her as a force to be reckoned with. In the first novella, *A Pretty Little Plot*, Mary's painting instructor is charged with kidnapping two of his students. And it's up to Mary to save him or condemn him. The second novella, *The Stolen Star*, follows Mary as she unpeels layers of deceit and duplicity during a snowy Christmas season, in the hunt for a purloined and very valuable sapphire. *In addition to the paperback and Kindle edition of* Duet, *the novellas* A Pretty Little Plot *and* The Stolen Star *are available separately as e-books.*

A Daughter's Doubt

Mary MacDougall's first case of 1902 seems simple enough. Did Agnes Olcott really die of cholera off in Dillmont, Michigan? Or were there darker doings at the Westerholm Institution for Women, as the woman's daughter suspects? With the reluctant help of her aunt and her dear friend Edmond Roy, the young detective struggles to reveal the true fate of Mrs. Olcott. As she digs ever deeper, the enemy Mary provokes could spell disaster for her and the people she loves.

The Karma of King Harald

When springtime arrives in picturesque New Bergen, so too do the tourists and antiquers. This year, though, there are some unwelcome visitors. Extortion. Arson. And murder. Join Andy Skyberg and his crime-sniffing mutt King Harald as they embark on their very first mystery adventure.

King Harald's Heist

As the leaves begin to change color in New Bergen, Andy Skyberg wants to turn his full attention to his sister's new restaurant—and to the beautiful Finnish architect who's managing the project. But Andy's big ol' mutt King Harald has a kennel full of trouble in store for him, beginning with a pilfered thousand-dollar bill and a naughty garden gnome. Before long, the crime-sniffing pooch finds even more deep doo-doo to toss his boss into.

King Harald's Snow Job

Christmastime is fast approaching and Andy Skyberg is itching to blow town for a weekend of holiday cheer with old friends. But first, his Aunt Bev needs a teensy bit of help. She's managing the Girls' Weekend Out event at the Beaver Tail Resort and summons Andy. He figures he can spare a few hours before hitting the road. But a giant blizzard socks them all in. And before you know it, Andy and his jumbo mutt King Harald are up to their noses in another case. It's a winter wonderland of fast-paced fun and merry madness.